A BAD CONNECTION

"Why don't you tell me what it's all about?" I said quickly. "We always welcome listener opinions, good or bad."

"Like I said in the note, the end is coming quicker than you think. Much quicker. It will end with a bang, not a whimper. It's the end for you and for those godless Sanjay-ites."

I took a deep breath, my mind skidding over my options. Was it best to keep this person talking? Or break off the connection? I sat there, fraught with indecision; then I noticed Vera tapping on the window, pointing frantically to one of her famous hand-lettered signs. This was a new one. She pointed to the note in her hand and then to her sign. She'd written BOMB with a bright blue Magic Marker. BOMB. I squinted, trying to figure out Vera Mae's latest acronym.

Bomb. *Bomb!* Ohmigod. We'd just gotten a bomb threat.

Thoughts scurried through my head like manic squirrels as I tried to deal with the reality of the threat. Was it a joke? Was it serious? And if there really was a bomb, where was it?

DEAD AIR

A Talk Radio Mystery

Mary Kennedy

AN OBSIDIAN MYSTERY

OBSIDIAN

Published by New American Library, a division of
Penguin Group (USA) Inc., 375 Hudson Street,
New York, New York 10014, USA
Penguin Group (Canada), 90 Eglinton Avenue East, Suite 700, Toronto,
Ontario M4P 2Y3, Canada (a division of Pearson Penguin Canada Inc.)
Penguin Books Ltd., 80 Strand, London WC2R 0RL, England
Penguin Ireland, 25 St. Stephen's Green, Dublin 2,
Ireland (a division of Penguin Books Ltd.)
Penguin Group (Australia), 250 Camberwell Road, Camberwell, Victoria 3124,
Australia (a division of Pearson Australia Group Pty. Ltd.)
Penguin Books India Pvt. Ltd., 11 Community Centre, Panchsheel Park,
New Delhi - 110 017, India
Penguin Group (NZ), 67 Apollo Drive, Rosedale, North Shore 0632,
New Zealand (a division of Pearson New Zealand Ltd.)
Penguin Books (South Africa) (Pty.) Ltd., 24 Sturdee Avenue,
Rosebank, Johannesburg 2196, South Africa

Penguin Books Ltd., Registered Offices:
80 Strand, London WC2R 0RL, England

First published by Obsidian, an imprint of New American Library,
a division of Penguin Group (USA) Inc.

First Printing, January 2010
10 9 8 7 6 5 4 3 2 1

To Holly Root, who made it all happen

Chapter 1

I think it was the call from the furrie that put me over the top.

I'd just started my afternoon show at WYME Radio when Vera Mae Atkins, my producer, scrawled the word "furvert" on a piece of paper and waved it at me from the production room.

Furvert?

Once she had my attention, she flashed me a pussycat smile. "You have a call from Seymour on line one, Dr. Maggie. He says he's a furrie." Then her lips gave a telltale quiver and I spotted the wicked gleam in her eye, a seismic shaking in her narrow shoulders. I expected her to break into the happy dance at any moment.

Enjoy! She mouthed the word through the large glass window that separates the production area from the cramped recording booth where I sit for two hours every weekday. She circled her index finger next to her ear in a Looney Tunes gesture and tossed me a broad wink.

Okay, the truth finally hit me. I had a furvert on the line.

"Furvert," in case you're wondering, is a derogatory term— a mixture of the words "furrie" and "pervert." What's a fur-

rie (sometimes called a plushie by those in the know)?
Here's an *Idiot's Guide* explanation. If you enjoy dressing
up like a chipmunk and having sex with someone wearing a
raccoon costume, you would call yourself a furrie. Or maybe
you're a snow leopard who likes to do the horizontal mambo
with a giraffe. Or you could be a brown bear with a yen for a
wildebeest—well, I'm sure you get the idea.

If that's what floats your boat, then Vera Mae—and
others—would call you a furvert.

Most days, my training as a clinical psychologist leads me
to be less judgmental, more accepting of all alternative life-
styles, including furries and their bizarre couplings. At least
that's what a psychoanalytic approach would endorse. Two
consenting adults dressing up as animals and having sex—
no harm, no foul.

But here's the thing (as Dr. Phil would say)—I just wasn't
in the mood to be PC today.

I bit back a sigh. As the host of *On the Couch with
Maggie Walsh*, I've had my share of unhappy callers—bored
housewives, bitter employees, frazzled parents, desperate sin-
gles, and out-and-out crazies. In my quiet moments, I com-
pare myself to Dr. Phil, or, as Vera Mae likes to say, "Dr.
Phil without the money, fame, or glory."

Gee, thanks for reminding me, Vera.

I punched line one. "Hello! You're on the couch with
Maggie—"

Before I could belt out the rest of my signature welcome,
a male voice slammed over the line, practically hyperventi-
lating with rage.

"So you think we're a bunch of weirdos, is that it? A
bunch of crazy kooks?"

Uh-oh. This was going to be worse than I'd thought. I
glanced up to see Vera Mae grinning from ear to ear, her

towering beehive bouncing from side to side like a dashboard bobblehead. Vera Mae, who hails from southern Georgia, believes that "the higher the hairdo, the closer to God." Her carrot-colored tresses could give Marge Simpson a run for her money.

She held up a sign with YES! on it, followed by another that read DAMN STRAIGHT!

I should explain that Vera Mae has an infinite number of these hand-lettered signs, and she delights in holding them up at strategic moments during my call-in show.

I like to think of her as a Dixie version of a Greek chorus.

"Really, sir, I have no idea—"

"Your coverage of our annual furrie convention in Cypress Grove left a lot to be desired, young lady," the voice went on in a harsh rasp. A smoker's voice, I decided. One of those gravelly whines that made you think he'd inhaled an entire truckload of Camels and was threatening to hack up a lung any minute. "I'd expected that at the very least you'd invite our esteemed president, Clarence Whittaker, on your show as a featured guest . . . but no, you walked right by him at the Furrie Awards without even a hello."

I frowned, trying to remember. The Furrie Awards. Oh, yeah. I'd done a live remote broadcast outside the Cypress Grove Convention Center last week, covering the Annual East Coast Furrie Convention, but it was all a blur.

Which one was Clarence Whittaker, anyway? Was he the guy in the Smokey the bear getup? Or the portly skunk with the swishy tail? Or maybe the gray fox who'd patted my behind with his mangy paw? There must have been two hundred people milling around the square, all dressed as their favorite animal, paws entwined, drinking champagne and dancing in a conga line.

Is it any wonder I'd blocked the whole scene from my

memory? As Freud would say, there are no accidents. I wanted to forget, so my mind was a blank.

"It's discrimination; that's what it is! I'm sure my congressman would like to hear about this. It's un-American." His voice quivered with self-righteousness.

"Hmm. Well, I certainly apologize if I overlooked your esteemed . . . uh . . . leader, but—"

"But nothing! Did you know that over half of our furrie members are in a committed relationship with another furrie? And that most of us are college-educated and upstanding members of the community? We're doctors, lawyers, and teachers. We even have a few preachers in our midst . . ."

This call was going nowhere. I looked up at the window. Vera Mae was pretending to slit her throat.

"No, I didn't know that, but I'll make a note of it. And the next time you come to town, I'll be sure—"

"Well, listen, girlie, the next time we come to town, you be sure to give us the attention we deserve. And don't forget the furrie slogan." He had another coughing fit as I leaned toward the board to cut him off.

"I'll certainly do that. And thank you for calling WYME."

I punched a button and disconnected him. "Well, Vera Mae, I guess now we'll never know what the furrie slogan is, will we? What a loss."

"Oh, I can think of a good slogan for that group," she purred. "How's this?" She leaned forward so her mouth was almost touching her microphone. "Once you try yak . . . you never go back!"

Ouch. "My producer thinks she's a comedian," I said quickly. I could just picture the phones ringing off the hook at her yak comment. "Who do we have next, Vera?" I struggled to put a note of professionalism into my voice.

After all, I am a licensed PhD psychologist, although my grad school adviser would probably burst an aneurysm at the career path I've taken. The truth is, I'd gotten sick of New York winters and rising real estate prices. When I spotted an ad for a radio psychologist in sunny Florida, I auditioned for the job and grabbed it.

I'm thirty-two and single and I figured this was the time to do something a little reckless in my life. So I closed my private practice in Manhattan, sold my IKEA furniture, and moved into a two-story mock-hacienda-style town house in a tiny town called Cypress Grove, Florida. It's north of Boca, not too far from Palm Beach, a pleasant drive to Fort Lauderdale.

As the chamber of commerce says, "Cypress Grove—it's near everyplace else you'd rather be!"

That was three months ago, and I've never looked back. Well, not too often, anyway.

Vera Mae stopped snapping her gum and sprang to attention. "We have Sharlene on line two." Meaningful pause. "Again."

Could this day get any worse? Sharlene calls my show like clockwork, three times a week, always ready to complain about Walter, her supercontrolling husband. She's a classic codependent, never ready to take responsibility for herself or change her life, and her voice grates on my nerves like teeth on tinfoil. Even over the phone line, she manages to suck the energy out of me.

I leaned forward to hit line two but spotted Vera Mae waving at me frantically.

"Is there a problem, Vera Mae?"

"Oh, wait a minute. Dang it, I goofed. Sharlene will have to wait a darned minute. Because now it's time for a word from our new sponsor, the Last Call Funeral Home."

Vera Mae jammed a cassette in the machine, but nothing happened.

Dead silence. I made a "what gives?" signal with my hands in the air.

"Oops, sorry, Dr. Maggie, but someone filed a blank cassette by mistake. You'll have to read the ad copy live; it's sitting right there by the mike."

Ah, the joys of small-town radio.

Reading the occasional commercial, or "spot," as they're called, is part of my job description. So I sat up straight, adjusted my headphones, and crossed my legs. No time for a bathroom break when there was a sixty-second spot to read.

Since our last copywriter quit two weeks ago, Irina, the Swedish receptionist, is the new WYME scribe. Irina is doing her best to learn English, but puns, humor, and slang expressions go whizzing over her beautiful blond head. This has led to some embarrassing double entendres that I know will be the highlight of the blooper reel trotted out at the next WYME office party.

But how can Irina think straight with our studly sports announcer, Big Jim Wilcox, breathing down her neck? Or worse yet, staring down her impressive cleavage.

I put on my best talk radio voice, oozing warmth and sincerity, like a QVC host.

"So just call on the friendly folk at the Last Call Funeral Home in your hour of needs." *Needs?* "Er, need," I said hastily. *Couldn't someone at least proofread Irina's work?* "We have many ways of helping your dead ones." *Dead ones?* Vera Mae snickered, and I glared at her. "Um, that should be loved ones, folks. Sorry about that. Yes, it definitely should be loved ones."

Finally I got to the Last Call slogan: "Remember, at the

Last Call Funeral Home, we leave no stone unturned in our quest to help you."

No stone unturned? I bet Jim Wilcox helped her with this one. It was just the sort of sophomoric humor that would appeal to the middle-aged sports jock.

"Ready to take a call? Sharlene is still on the line," Vera Mae said in a sugary voice.

"Bring it on!" I was gritting my teeth so hard, I knew I'd need a bite plate before the day was out.

"Line two!"

"Hello, Sharlene, you're on the couch . . ."

"Oh, Dr. Maggie, you've just got to help me," Sharlene wailed. "I don't think I can take another minute of this. It's just not fair!" She began sobbing and snuffling, a walking ad for divorce court.

"Now, Sharlene, try to calm down and tell me what's going on. I'm sure I can help you." Actually, I was pretty sure a good lawyer could help Sharlene a lot more than I could, but for the moment, she was my problem. More muffled sobs. "Is it your husband? Is that what's troubling you today?"

This provoked an even bigger wail from Sharlene. "He's ruining my life. My mama warned me not to marry him. I always thought I could change him."

"Sharlene, you know we've talked about this issue before. When a woman marries a man hoping to change him . . ." I allowed myself a small, knowing chuckle. "Changing a man is as likely as—"

"As teaching a pig to fly!" Vera Mae's voice boomed into the booth. I think I liked it better when Vera Mae confined herself to holding up signs. Her homespun wisdom can be a bit unnerving on live radio, but she has a heart as big as an IMAX screen.

"Thank you for that gem of wisdom, Vera Mae."

I could hear muffled sobs from Sharlene. "Sharlene, do you remember some of the options we discussed the last time you called? We talked about various strategies you could use in dealing with Walter."

Vera reached for one of her favorite signs and held it up.

KHATTC.

Translation: Kick his ass to the curb. This is Vera Mae's surefire solution for an errant husband or boyfriend.

Don't ask; don't reason; don't plead. Just KHATTC.

"Well, I appreciate your help, Dr. Maggie, but somehow I just can't get up the energy to do anything. And you know, Walter can be real mean when's he's been drinking, and he seems to have a sixth sense or something, just like Patricia Arquette on *Medium*." I gave an involuntary little shudder. There was something creepy and predatory about Walter, and I hoped he never discovered my home address or phone number. I do my best to protect my privacy, but there's always an element of risk when you do a live radio show five days a week. ZabaSearch will get you every time.

You can't hide in a tiny market like Cypress Grove. You never know when a disgruntled listener might take offense to your advice and then track you down to even the score.

"Let's try to stick to the issue of you and Walter, Sharlene. Can you pinpoint a time when things started to go wrong between you?"

"Well," she said hesitantly, "things have never been the same since he threw me through the plate-glass window last Christmas."

Hmm. This poor girl needed more help than I could give her on a radio show.

"Oh, no!" Sharlene's voice rose to a terrified squeak. "I hear him coming, Dr. Maggie. I've got to hang up right now.

Lord knows what he'll do if he finds me talking to you. He's been making some threats and—"

"Sharlene!" A male voice boomed in the background, and suddenly the phone went dead. For a moment, I just stared at the microphone. Poor Sharlene. Would anyone be able to help her? Would she ever find the strength to leave Walter?

Finally, Vera Mae broke the silence. "Are you ready for another call?" She sounded shaken, and for once, she wasn't making any smart-ass jokes. "I'm leaving a line open for you, Sharlene," she added softly.

The next couple of calls were routine, and as we slipped into a commercial, Vera darted around the partition and stuck her head in the studio. "Maggie, there's some nut on line four. He's got his panties in a twist. I think it's about that Sanjay fellow we've scheduled for later today. He's making threats. Crazy threats."

Crazy threats? We came back from the break and Vera Mae said smoothly, "Take line four, Dr. Maggie. It's important."

"All our calls are important, Vera Mae," I said, confused. Who was on the line and what did he want? And why would he be upset about our upcoming featured guest, Guru Sanjay Gingii? Gingii was a popular radio and television personality. A little nutty, but harmless, in my professional opinion. New Age gurus aren't my cup of tea, but this guy has a huge following, a book deal, a movie deal, and a syndicated newspaper column.

"You're on the couch with Dr. Maggie," I said, swiveling back to the board.

"Your days are numbered," a muffled voice said. The voice was soft, insinuating, chilling. I swallowed hard, and my mouth suddenly went dry. I felt the skin prickle across my shoulders. "Did you read the note I sent you?"

"The note?"

"It's in a bright yellow envelope. It was hand delivered this morning."

I looked over at Vera, who was frantically flipping through the listener mail. She held up a canary yellow envelope with no stamp and waved it at me. Then she ripped it open, read the note inside, and blanched.

"Did you read the note?" the caller persisted.

"Why don't you tell me what it's all about?" I said quickly. "We always welcome listener opinions, good or bad."

A nasty chuckle from the mystery caller. "This one's bad," he rasped. "This is going to be the apocalypse."

"The apocalypse?"

"Like I said in the note, the end is coming quicker than you think. Much quicker. It will end with a bang, not a whimper. It's the end for you and for those godless Sanjay-ites."

Sanjay-ites? Oh, yeah, the people who dressed in white and were followers of Sanjay Gingii. There was something eerie about the whispery voice, and I felt little icy fingers tap-dance up and down my spine. I couldn't tell whether it was a man or a woman.

I took a deep breath, my mind skidding over my options. Was it best to keep this person talking? Or break off the connection?

I sat there, fraught with indecision as the caller rambled on. I noticed Vera tapping on the window, pointing frantic-ally to one of her famous hand-lettered signs.

This was a new one. She pointed to the note in her hand and then to her sign. She'd written BOMB with a bright blue Magic Marker.

BOMB. I squinted, trying to figure out Vera Mae's latest acronym.

BOMB. Better Oppose Mixed Beverages? I was stumped.

BOMB. Beer on My Breath?

More frantic pantomiming from Vera Mae. Her face was drained of color and she was sagging against the console, her features slack. I tried to ignore the hard lump that had suddenly formed in the pit of my stomach.

BOMB.

Bomb. *Bomb!* Ohmigod. We'd just gotten a bomb threat.

My thoughts scurried through my head like a manic squirrel as I tried to deal with the reality of the threat. Was it a joke? Was it serious? And if there was really a bomb, where was it?

Would there be time to evacuate the station? Should I dial 911 or alert the switchboard first? Or the station manager? Was there some procedure I was supposed to follow?

I looked over at Vera Mae, and now her eyes were ballooning, her mouth open, frozen in horror like the subject of one of those Edvard Munch paintings.

I thought about my mother and my friends and the fact that I was way too young to be blasted to kingdom come.

And then an explosion rocked WYME and suddenly I didn't have to think anymore.

Chapter 2

I sat perfectly still, trying to process what had happened. Either a meteorite had hit WYME or we'd been bombed. Okay, reality check. This wasn't the *Starship Enterprise*. It must have been a bomb.

The noise stopped, but I could still feel the vibration slicing through the soles of my feet and snaking its way up my body. An acrid smell filled the air, and my eyes burned as I scrambled out of my chair. The smoke alarms were blasting, filling the studio with a noise like a 747 getting ready for takeoff.

Then all hell broke loose in the studio. Vera Mae screamed and grabbed Tweetie Bird's cage, making tracks across the production studio with her precious cargo. Tweetie Bird is Vera Mae's aging pet parakeet, and she drags his heavy metal cage to the station with her every day.

"So it really was a bomb?" I said dazedly. "It must have been; I can smell smoke in the air." My mind felt as if it had slammed into a brick wall, but the crazy thing was, the smoke smelled familiar. An image of a movie theater flashed into my head for no reason at all.

"Hand me your sweater, Maggie!"

"You want me to take off my sweater?" My hand involuntarily went to the neckline of a short-sleeved raspberry sweater I had paired with some new Liz Claiborne slacks.

"Not the sweater you're wearing—the cardigan!" she snapped. "I have to put it over Tweetie's cage before he has a conniption." When I didn't react right away, she yanked the cardigan off the back of my chair. "C'mon, girl, time's a-wasting and you're standing there like Lot's wife. Let's blow this joint."

"Have you already called 911? And Donna at the switchboard? Shouldn't we notify the station manager?" I started shuffling through some papers, wondering how to shut down the audio board. What was the protocol at a time like this? We couldn't just run out the door, could we?

Apparently we could.

"Done and done and done. Now let's go!"

"Wait!" I opened the mike and slapped the first cassette I could find into the machine. The sounds of Celine Dion filled the air. I quickly turned down the volume and pushed away from the board. Music is good in an emergency, right? Didn't the orchestra play as the *Titanic* sank?

On second thought, maybe music wasn't the best choice in this situation. Too late now.

I could hear muffled shouts and running footsteps in the hallway outside the studio. Apparently everyone was evacuating, and through the tiny window in the door, I saw Big Jim Wilcox at the head of the pack. He elbowed the petite traffic secretary, Tammi Ngyuen, aside to bolt through the double glass doors. (Who says chivalry is dead?)

I grabbed my purse just as I heard sirens wailing outside. Police cars and, from the sounds of it, fire trucks. One of the advantages of living in a small town is that help is always close at hand. Both the police station and the fire station were within walking distance of the studio.

Vera Mae started to open the heavy door to the hallway, and I grabbed her. "Wait! You're supposed to put your hand on the door first to see if it's hot."

"That's plumb crazy. Anyone with a lick of sense can see that it's not hot. Didn't you see that movie *Backdraft*?"

"*Backdraft*. Is that the one where John Travolta played a fireman? I never thought that was one of his more convincing roles, did you? Of course, I never really believed he was an angel in *Michael*. Something about those grungy wings—"

"Sheesh, girl, quit your babbling and get out the door!" She gave me a vigorous one-handed push. "You shrinks are all alike. You talk too much, and you analyze everything to death."

I headed down the hallway, properly chastised, just in time to see the Cypress Grove FD burst into the reception area, dragging monster gray fire hoses behind them. Smoke alarms were shrieking in the background, an ear-piercing wail that didn't let up.

The leader, a tall, square-jawed guy who was a dead ringer for Kevin Costner, bellowed into a megaphone, "All personnel are ordered to evacuate the premises immediately. Repeat, immediately. Do not take any personal possessions. Stay close to the walls in a single file. Proceed in an orderly fashion out the front doors. Do not run; do not panic."

He glimpsed Vera Mae, trotting along with Tweetie in her cage, and reached out a gloved hand to bar her way. "Sorry, ma'am. You're not permitted to remove that cage from the building. Please put it down and proceed to the exit. "

"Look, sonny," Vera Mae said, drawing herself up to her full height of five feet two. "If that bird stays, then I stay."

"You need to vacate the building. That's an order," he barked. He'd moved ahead a few feet and started herding the secretarial staff along, when he glanced back and saw Vera Mae slip past the reception desk. Tweetie bird's cage was still thumping against her leg, and a frightened squawk emerged from under my sweater.

"Hey! I told you to drop it!" the firefighter protested.

"Oh, put a sock in it, Billie Dean Rochester. I knew your momma when she was teaching over at Cypress Grove Elementary, so don't even think of telling me what to do. Let's go, Maggie."

I followed Vera Mae outside, where the rest of the WYME staff had gathered in a tight little semicircle. We stood uncertainly in the hot Florida sunshine for about fifteen minutes, until I spotted a couple of firefighters making their way out of the building.

They'd taken off their helmets and were shrugging out of their heavy yellow coats. So there hadn't been a bomb after all? Was it just a false alarm? But what about the smoke and the noise of the explosion?

"That song's enough to drive anyone crazy," I heard one of the firefighters mutter.

I looked at Vera Mae. "I put on Celine Dion."

Vera Mae flushed. "That cassette was damaged. It only plays the first cut over and over."

"So my listeners are listening to 'My Heart Will Go On,' over and over?"

"Afraid so," Vera Mae said. "Wonder what this will do to the ratings?"

A good point. I made an executive decision. I decided to risk going back into the building. I had to change that cassette!

I skirted around the edge of the crowd, slipped by a

drop-dead-gorgeous guy mumbling into a walkie-talkie, and sneaked back into the station.

I was making my way down the hall, and I couldn't see any signs of fire or smoke damage. If it hadn't been for the firefighters and the boys in blue patrolling the corridors, you would have thought this were an ordinary day.

Luckily everyone was too busy rolling out equipment to notice me. Or were they packing up their equipment, getting ready to leave? I couldn't be sure.

One thing was certain. I wanted to get back into the booth and finish out my show.

And I would have, if it hadn't been for a six-foot male hunk blocking my path. It was the guy with the walkie-talkie I'd spotted outside. How had he managed to get ahead of me?

"Not so fast," he said, pulling my hand away from the door to the recording booth. "This area is off-limits, and you're supposed to be outside. All personnel are ordered to evacuate."

His grip was surprisingly strong, and I winced a little as I yanked my hand away. Who was he? He wasn't a cop and he wasn't a firefighter.

From the look on his face, I figured he wasn't a fan.

"I need to go inside to check on something."

"No."

I reached for the door again, and this time he grabbed my hand in midair. He had very nice hands, with strong fingers and warm skin. I'm embarrassed to admit that even in times of crisis, I pick up on things like this. I noticed that he also had broad shoulders, thick dark hair, and the sculpted features of a movie star.

How did I notice all this in a split second?

I admit it, I'm shallow.

"What part of 'no' don't you understand?"

Okay, he was hot looking, but he had the personality of a storm trooper. I breathed a sigh of relief. Cancel immediate sexual attraction; storm troopers are not my type.

Time for the famed Maggie Walsh feistiness to kick in.

"Nobody manhandles me, bozo. Do you know who I am?"

"I have absolutely no idea." A little smile played around the corners of his mouth, softening his chiseled features and adding to his attractiveness. Damn! I hate it when guys like this are good-looking. It makes it so much harder to keep an argument going.

"I'm Maggie Walsh." I waited for a look of recognition, a pleased smile, maybe even a request for an autograph. Which, of course, I would graciously grant.

Nothing. Nada.

"Maggie Walsh, host of WYME's *On the Couch with Maggie Walsh* show. I'm a . . . a radio personality." I stumbled a little over this last one because according to the latest Nielsen reports, the *Maggie Walsh* show was running neck and neck with *Bob Figgs and the Swine Report*. We were practically tied for last place.

Still, Bob Figgs called himself a radio personality, so why shouldn't I?

He raised one eyebrow. "Lady, I don't care if you're Rosie O'Donnell. You're going back outside, and that's an order." He frowned. "On the couch? That's the name of your show?"

"I'm a psychologist. A licensed psychologist," I said. "On the couch is a reference to Freud. He used to have his patients lie on a couch while he analyzed them. He thought it helped them free-associate as he delved into their unconscious. There isn't any sexual connotation to the term, if that's what you were thinking."

"I wasn't thinking that." He gave me the once-over, a look of cool appraisal in his smoky eyes. "In fact, that was the last thing on my mind." He had sexy eyes and a lazy, heart-thudding smile.

"It was?" Now I was getting annoyed. Not only did this guy have the personality of a Gestapo general, but he didn't even find me attractive. Clearly, my academic credentials didn't impress him, either.

Who was he, anyway? He couldn't be anyone official: He was wearing a pair of neatly pressed khakis, a white shirt and navy blazer, and boat shoes with no socks. Plus the annoying film-star good looks and the throaty voice.

I forced some iron into my voice and tried again. "And if you don't get out my way this very instant, I'm going to . . ."

I lost my train of thought just then because hunky guy stepped closer—so close I could see the golden flecks in his dark eyes and the sexy curve of his mouth.

"You're going to do what?" he murmured, making it sound like the sexiest thing anyone had ever said to me. His voice was low and husky, and I felt a funny little tingling at the base of my spine.

I paused for a second, ready to spring. "I'm going back in there, that's what!"

With a burst of adrenaline, I made a mad dash for the door once again, but something big and powerful stopped me. I slumped against the wall as if I had just run into a Subaru.

Hot guy let out a big sigh. "Okay, lady, we can do this the easy way or the hard way." He managed to slip one of my hands behind my back before I even realized what he was doing. "And I guess it has to be the hard way." Another quick move and the other hand followed it.

I felt something hard and metal fastening my hands behind my back.

"Maggie Walsh, I am putting you under arrest."

Oh, no! My hands were pinned behind me and hot guy
was perp-walking me down the hallway past the smoke-filled
reception area, toward the double glass doors that opened
onto the parking lot.

I gave myself a mental head slap. This was not going as
planned.

"You're a cop?" I gulped.

A low sexy chuckle. "Detective Rafe Martino. At your
service, ma'am."

"Look, they've arrested Maggie Walsh!"

Big Jim Wilcox couldn't keep the delight out of his
voice. "Why did you do it, Maggie? Do you have a statement for us? It will be a WYME exclusive. You'll be famous!" He fumbled around for a mike, realized he didn't
have one, and pulled out a pen and notebook from his back
pocket. "Let's hear your side of it, Maggie. Was it a love
affair gone bad, or did you finally snap?"

I gave him a withering look, and Vera Mae hurried over
along with Cyrus Still, the station manager.

"Good lord, Maggie. What in the world are you doing in
those handcuffs?" she demanded.

"Ask him!" It was impossible to gesture with my hands
shackled behind my back, so I had to nod my head up and
down like Mr. Ed.

"It's a case of false arrest—false imprisonment," I
squeaked. "This cop is taking me hostage. You'd better get
me a good lawyer, Vera Mae." I glared at Rafe, who was
standing next to me, a wide smile on his face. "Or maybe
get *him* one."

"Now, folks, let's just simmer down here. Nobody needs a lawyer." Cyrus gave me a speculative look and then turned his attention to Rafe. "Detective Martino, is there a problem here?"

He called him "Detective." So Cyrus knew this guy was a cop? Why am I always the last one to know these things?

"No problem," I muttered. "Just an innocent, private citizen getting strong-armed by one of Cypress Grove's finest."

"I didn't strong-arm you. You refused to obey me!" Rafe objected. "It's a crime to disobey an order from an officer of the law."

"I didn't know you were a cop," I said hotly. I gave him the once-over. He looked like a J.Crew refugee in those neatly pressed trousers and crisp cotton shirt. "Is that the new dress code for Cypress Grove's finest? You look like a preppie on spring break."

"I'm a detective," he said in an aggrieved tone. "We don't wear uniforms."

"I try to do my job and you arrest me? What happened to protect and serve?" I demanded.

Score one for Maggie.

"Detective Martino, did you identify yourself as a police officer?"

Score one for Cyrus.

"I didn't have a chance to flash my badge," he said. "I was too busy restraining her from entering the recording booth. She was going to put herself in harm's way."

"Now, Detective Martino, I'm sure Dr. Walsh didn't mean to make things difficult for you," Cyrus said in a softly wheedling way. "She's a very devoted employee; she was probably worried about her listeners."

"Yes, I was!" I thought about my poor listeners and could only hope their psyches were still intact.

I turned to my captor. "Have you ever listened to 'My Heart Will Go On' for twenty minutes straight? Wouldn't that count as cruel and unusual punishment? Like Chinese water torture? Or maybe bamboo shoots jammed under the fingernails?"

Rafe looked puzzled and started fumbling with the handcuffs. "I have no idea what you're talking about, but let's call a truce. No charges, no arrest."

I yanked my hands in front of me and rubbed my wrists. I gave him my best Maggie Walsh glare, the one that I used on psychotics and convicted felons. No reaction. This guy was good. Okay, I could play it cool, too.

"Have a nice day, Dr. Walsh."

I straightened my spine. Now was the time to deliver a snazzy zinger that he would never forget. A Maggie Walsh classic.

"Detective Martino?"

"Yes?" He turned back, his dark eyes questioning.

"Um, you have a nice day, too."

Talk about lame! One look into those sultry eyes and my best one-liner flew out of my head.

"So it wasn't really a bomb?" Jim Wilcox asked in his booming announcer's voice. I think he was secretly disappointed that I hadn't planned on blowing up the station. What a ratings booster that would have been!

I could just hear the teaser: "Local shrink goes berserk and blows up her own radio station. Get the full story tonight at six on WYME with Big Jim!" With a story like that, Jim might even be able to land a job at one of Miami's top stations doing the afternoon drive time. I bet it would go into his audition tape.

"The chief's gonna make a statement in a minute," one of

the firemen answered him. "Don't want to steal his thunder." He grinned at Jim, who was a local celebrity. He leaned close to whisper something in Jim's ear, and then Jim burst out laughing.

"You're putting me on!" Jim said, clapping him on the shoulder. "What was she thinking?"

"What's going on?" I asked.

"You'll know soon enough," Jim said, self-importantly. It was obvious the crisis, whatever it was, had been averted, but he wasn't going to let me in on the secret.

Just then, Fire Captain Chris Norton appeared on the grassy area in front of the station and removed his helmet. "We found the . . . uh . . . source of the explosion," he said. "Please step forward, Miss Yaslov."

Irina Yaslov, the station receptionist! She walked slowly out of the station, blinking in the bright Florida sunshine. "I made a big fault," she said tearfully. "I was making the popcorn," she said, wringing her hands and struggling with her imperfect English. "How was I to know there would be big boom? I make it many time before, and there is no boom. Just today."

"You were making popcorn? In the microwave?" So that's why I had flashed on a movie theater when I smelled something hot and buttery burning. And here I thought I was having an olfactory hallucination.

Poor Irina looked mortified, her eyes darting back and forth between Cyrus Stills and Jim Wilcox. "Yes," she said softly. "I used metal plate. Maybe not such a good idea. Microwave is—how you say?—history. Kaput."

"Well, sakes alive, girl. You should know better than to put a metal plate in a microwave. You scared us all half to death. You probably shortened Tweetie Bird's life." Vera Mae lifted a corner of my sweater to check on her bird, who was picking listlessly at a miniature corncob.

"It's okay," Big Jim said gallantly. "Irina here is from Iceland," he said helpfully to a female reporter I recognized from the *Cypress Grove Gazette*. "They probably cook things differently over there. They eat a lot of whale meat, you know."

"I am from Sweden, not Iceland!" Irina protested. "And no, I do not eat the whale meat." She shot an appealing look at Cyrus. "Really, I'm desolated this is happening, and I'm hoping not to be losing my job."

Cyrus ignored her and shook hands with the firefighters. "Sorry we dragged you out here for nothing, guys." Then he glared at Irina. "I'll see you in my office, missy. Someone's going to have to buy a new microwave and pay to have those scorch marks removed from the wall." He caught me staring at him. "What are you looking at? Don't you have a show running? And why is that song playing over and over?" he said irritably.

I glanced at my watch and scurried back into the building. Now that the fun was over, I had a show to do!

Chapter 3

When Guru Sanjay Gingii showed up for his three o'clock guest slot, I was still frazzled from Irina's popcorn misadventure. The mystery caller hadn't contacted us again, and I didn't have a clue about why he was so upset with the guru. A faint cloud of buttery smoke hung in the air, and Guru Sanjay wrinkled his nose when he walked into the booth.

Sanjay Gingii, a self-styled New Age "prophet" from South Beach, was in town for a conference at the Seabreeze Inn. My boss, Cyrus, is vice president of the Cypress Grove Chamber of Commerce, and he insisted that I invite the guru to be a guest on the show.

Guru Sanjay was tall and portly, dressed all in white, with a Nehru jacket pulled tight over his ballooning gut. He sported one of the worst comb-overs I've ever seen.

"I am sensing a dark presence in the air." He squinted his eyes and waved his hands in front of himself as if he were blindfolded. Finally he eased his bulky frame into the swivel chair next to me. After an uncomfortable silence, his eyes flew open and focused on me. "I am feeling a cloud of negativity, a miasma of despair."

His tone was low and mournful, a voice from another realm. Maybe even another planet.

His two assistants, bouncer types who looked like extras from *The Sopranos*, nodded solemnly, their arms crossed against their massive chests. They refused to sit down and remained standing on either side of the door.

"We had a little fire here today," I said chattily. "It's nothing, really, just some leftover smoke damage. By the way, I'm Maggie Walsh, host of *On the Couch*."

I stuck out my hand, but the guru didn't shake it. Instead he peered at it, then began rubbing his fat thumb over my palm in a creepy way, as if he were rolling a Cuban cigar.

"We go live in a couple of minutes." I forced myself to sound bubbly. "We've done lots of promo spots about you, and I bet the calls will come rolling in. So . . . uh . . . welcome to the show."

I felt a shiver slither down my spine. Talk about a dark presence—this guy was giving off serial-killer vibes with his loathsome touch. All my forensic training came front and center; I had a very bad feeling about the guru.

I suddenly knew, in a very visceral way, that he was a scam artist or a sociopath. How did I know this? Call it gut instinct, training, years of coming face-to-face with antisocials on a daily basis.

This guy was a fake, a grifter, a con man.

I just knew it in my bones.

"You are an old soul, Maggie," he said, his face very close to mine. "I can sense that you have lived many lifetimes because your chakras still seek harmony. Perhaps with my help, they can finally be realigned."

So he wants to realign my chakras? I just bet he does! Maybe he could rotate my tires at the same time, but I bet that wouldn't be nearly as much fun for him.

His stubby thumb left a greasy trail up my bare arm. I yanked my hand away just as Vera Mae slapped on her headphones and pointed at me.

"Line three, Dr. Maggie. Thelma has a question about . . . bioenergetic healing." Vera Mae permitted herself a small eye roll as Thelma's voice burst into the booth.

"Well, thank the Lord I finally got through! I've been calling for hours and all I got was Celine Dion and that dopey song—"

"Sorry about that, Thelma, but we're here now to help you." I plastered a grin on my face because someone once told me that smiling helps to inject warmth into your voice. "And your question is . . ."

"It's for your guest. Guru Sanjay, I just have to say, I've read all your books and I think you're just amazing. You're my hero!"

The guru gave a mock-humble bow. "I am but a channel, a funnel for all of life's mysteries, a river for spiritual healing. But if I have helped you in some small way, then I am gratified."

He glanced over at the two thugs at the door, and they nodded approvingly. I bet they had heard this all before.

"And your question is . . . ," I repeated, breaking up the lovefest.

"Well, I'm getting a lot of bad vibrations from my boss. I can see his aura, and let me tell you, it's mighty scary. I think he might be trying to control my mind."

"You were very wise to call me today, Thelma." The guru's voice was low and soothing. "Because I can feel some very negative energy emanating from the phone and disturbing the glowing white light at the center of your being. You are right to be alarmed." He paused. "Let me guess. Are you calling from work at this very moment?"

"Why, yes! Yes, I am calling from work." Thelma sounded awestruck. "That's incredible; you really are psychic!"

"When you are in tune with the universe, it cannot surprise you. I know all of its secrets. Now, how can I help you?"

"I guess I need some specific ways to deal with my boss," she said hesitantly. "I've read *Heal the Cosmos, Heal Yourself*, and I tried out some of the things you suggested."

"Ah, yes, *Heal the Cosmos*, my latest release. It's only $6.95 in paperback and just $12.95 for the audio version. Both are available on my Web site, GuruSanjay.com, and at fine bookstores everywhere."

Before Thelma could reply, Vera Mae piped up, "Say, Thelma, did you ever read a book called *Working with Jerks*? It's my bible. I bet it could give you some tips on how to deal with this guy."

"I've never heard of it, but I could look it up on Amazon—"

"Here is what you must do, Thelma," Guru Sanjay cut in swiftly. "You must stand firm as a spiritual seeker and not let any negativity influence your aura. You have within you the power to be a healer, a human energy force field, and you must emit only good energy." He paused dramatically. "Do you understand me? You have the power within you, Thelma. Never forget that."

I think he stole that line from Glinda, the Good Witch, in *The Wizard of Oz*, but I could tell Thelma was falling head over chakras for it. I hated to admit it, but put him in front of a mike and the guy had charisma. He had an uncanny way of tapping into people's thoughts and feelings and telling them what they wanted to hear. All good performers have this talent, and I reminded myself that sociopaths are experts at reading people and scoring on their hopes and dreams.

"Yes, I do have the power!" Thelma gushed. "You've helped me so much, Guru. I'll never be able to thank you!"

Again, the modest bow. Difficult to do sitting down, especially with an expanding gut in the way. Funny, but on television, he looked imposing, not fat, and I wondered whether he wore a corset for his public appearances.

"I am but an instrument. I am here today merely to explain the mysteries of the cosmos, through my understanding of kinetics and the human energy field."

That's all, just the mysteries of the cosmos? Maybe next week he can tackle global warming and the Middle East crisis. Oh, yeah, and the Riemann hypothesis; I've never been quite clear on how that works.

Out of the corner of my eye, I saw Vera fingering her selection of signs. I just knew she was itching to hold up the BS! one. I gave her a tired smile as we headed into a Sassy Snippers commercial.

Who knew I would actually welcome the chance to hear about Twyla Boyd's hair salon and her Thursday special on foils and perms?

Anything was better than the mystical mumbo jumbo coming from the guru!

"I can't believe you met him," Lark Merriweather said later that day. "If I could meet Guru Sanjay, even for five minutes, it would be the high point of my life." Lark is into all things New Age: pyramids, crystals, incense, tarot, *I Ching*, channeling, and chi.

She sat back with a little sigh, her cornflower blue eyes wistful. Lark is slim and petite with a choppy blond bob that suits her pixieish face. Physically, we're polar opposites. I tower over her at five-ten with straight auburn hair that can be sleek or frizzy depending on the famous Florida humidity.

"Really? I should have remembered you're into Eastern

mystics," I said ruefully. *Or pretend mystics*, I felt like saying. Deep in my bones, I knew that Guru Sanjay had as much in common with mysticism as I did with aboriginal tribes in New Guinea.

The sun was beginning to dip in the western sky, and the last traces of sunlight spilled onto the round oak dining table. I'd finished my shift at WYME a couple of hours earlier and we were sharing a veggie pizza in the kitchen of our town house. It's a cozy place with wide oak floors, exposed beams, and creamy walls dotted with colorful canvases that Lark picks up at local flea markets.

Lark and I have been roommates for the past three months and are on our way to becoming best friends. When I rented the three-bedroom condo on a quiet street lined with bright pink hibiscus bushes and flaming bougainvillea, Lark was the first person who asked to be my roommate.

Plus, she and Pugsley hit it off, and I knew it would be a good match. Pugsley is my three-year-old pug adopted from an animal shelter, and I've always subscribed to the adage "Love me, love my dog."

Lark is twenty-three but seems younger sometimes. Maybe it's because of her perpetually sunny personality. She has a kind of "life hasn't crushed me yet" optimism that's a nice balance to my Manhattan-style pessimism. Her favorite movie is *Forrest Gump*, and mine is anything by Woody Allen. That about sums it up.

Lark's studying to be a paralegal, and I had no idea she was a fan of the guru. I could have invited her to sit in on the broadcast today, even though we don't usually allow visitors in the booth.

"He's my idol. I can't believe I missed the show," she said plaintively. "Why didn't you let me know it was on today? I would have called in with a question. I've read all his books!"

I gave myself a mental head slap. "I'll bring you a tape of the show—how's that? And if you're really interested in going to one of his workshops, I can give you a couple of press passes he left at the station. He's doing a breakfast presentation in the morning, and there's a big awards ceremony tomorrow night. I have tickets for some of the events."

"Oh, I couldn't take your tickets!" Her eyes were shining with excitement. "How could you ever part with them?"

"I'm not going to use them. Really." I had to smile at her enthusiasm. "The dinner is right next door at the Seabreeze Inn, so the food should be good. The guru and his staff are staying there."

We live next to one of the town's nicest small hotels, and Ted Rollins, the manager, is a friend of mine. Sometimes I think he'd like to be more than friends, but somehow the chemistry just isn't there. Not for me, anyway.

"The Seabreeze, huh?" She shook her head in wonderment. "Just think. Guru Sanjay is only a few yards away from me, this very minute. I wonder what he's doing right now?" She peered out the window with her chin cupped in her hand, like Nicole Kidman staring out over the Paris rooftops in *Moulin Rouge*. "I bet he's meditating," she added in a dreamy voice.

"Ommmmmm."

"What?"

I grinned. "You said he was meditating."

"Oh, nobody says 'om' anymore. He's probably sitting in the lotus position, chanting his mantra." She sighed, as if the thrill of it all nearly sucked the air out of her chest.

Not a good image. A picture of a half-naked guru with his gut hanging over his yoga pants drifted into my mind, and I blinked quickly, willing it to disappear.

Lark continued to stare at the side entrance of the Seabreeze, as if willing Guru Sanjay to materialize like a genie out of a bottle. "I could practically reach out and touch him."

Ewww. Who would want to?

I nodded. "You'll have to catch him tomorrow if you really want to see him. He told me Team Sanjay is driving back to South Beach right after dinner. So this is his last night in town."

"Really!" Lark glanced at her watch and then scrambled to her feet, tugging her burgundy knit top down over her low-rise jeans. She gave a little hip twitch and adjusted her studded leather belt so it cinched her tiny waist more tightly. "You know, I just remembered I need to pick up a few things at the drugstore. Do you want anything?"

"No, I'm fine, but what about your pizza?" It was Lark's favorite, a mouth-watering concoction of goat cheese and fresh basil called Pizza Margarita, from Carlo's.

"What? Oh, the pizza . . . I'll take it with me." Lark popped into her bedroom for a moment and returned carrying her yellow leather faux-Coach bag. It was a knockoff but very realistic. I noticed she'd fluffed her hair and had dabbed on some new peach lip gloss. "I'll eat it in the car," she said, grabbing a generous slice and folding it over into a napkin, calzone style. "See you later!"

And with that, she was gone.

A minute later, I realized her car keys were still sitting on the counter.

"Can you cover the morning news? The eight o'clock drive time? Everyone's out on assignment this morning. Things are really hopping at the police station, and I think the mayor's gonna give a statement later today." Cyrus Still's voice boomed over the phone, crashing through my sleep-fogged brain with such force, it made my teeth hurt. Someone told me that Cyrus has permanent hearing loss from covering so many rock concerts in his younger days and that's why he always sounds like he's shouting into a hurricane.

"Wha—" I sat straight up in bed, winced, and glanced at the clock. Six a.m. I was barely conscious and my station manager wanted to discuss the news of the day. I didn't know which was more remarkable: the fact that Cyrus expected me to be coherent at the crack of dawn or the fact that I was working for someone who actually says things like "really hopping."

I desperately needed an infusion of caffeine, an adrenaline rush, and oh, yeah, a functioning brain. "I can be there in forty-five," I told him, running a brush through my hopelessly matted hair as I searched for my terry robe.

Thank god it's radio and not television, I thought, taking in my pale skin and sunken eyes in the wall mirror. A vision of loveliness. I'd fallen asleep watching Conan O'Brien and had barely woken up when Lark had tiptoed in, sometime after midnight.

Something niggled at the edges of my consciousness. News . . . the police station . . . the mayor. "Cyrus, what's going on?" I asked, padding along the terra-cotta tiled floor to the kitchen. No sign of Lark and no coffee brewing. Lark and I have an arrangement. Whoever wakes up first makes the coffee, and today that would be me. Lark's door was firmly shut.

"You mean you haven't heard the news?" Cyrus sounded incredulous.

I stifled a jaw-popping yawn. "Haven't a clue. Fill me in."

"The guru," he barked. "He's dead."

"Dead? Guru Sanjay is dead? Guru Sanjay the guy I interviewed?"

I couldn't get my mind around the fact. He'd seemed perfectly healthy yesterday, if a trifle overweight with a florid complexion that probably hinted at metabolic syndrome. But he couldn't really be dead, could he?

In *Heal the Cosmos*, Guru Sanjay insisted that death is just a state of mind, a transition of energy from one form to another. I wondered what this would do to his book sales.

"How many other gurus do you know?"

Ah, point taken. So Guru Sanjay was dead and was now part of that ultimate cosmic consciousness he always talked about. Now he was just a tiny (well, maybe not so tiny) blip of energy, flashing around the universe like a manic firefly. Ironic, isn't it?

But there was still Cyrus's nagging comment about cops and the mayor. I forced myself to focus. "Why are the police involved?"

I was cradling the phone on my shoulder so I could spoon half Dunkin' Donuts decaf and half French vanilla high voltage into the coffeepot when I heard someone pounding on the front door.

Mrs. Higgins! We have an eighty-year-old neighbor who loves to go for early-morning walks and sometimes forgets to take her key. Lark, petite little thing that she is, always manages to find an unlatched window in Mrs. Higgins's house and squeezes in, saving the day.

"Look, Maggie, I'll explain it when you get here, okay? Make it snappy."

"Just give me the short answer. I can't stand the suspense." The hammering on the door intensified, a maddening counterpoint to the drilling noise in my head.

"The short answer is, Guru Sanjay Gingii may have been murdered!"

With that Cyrus hung up.

I ignored the pounding, filled the pot with filtered water, pressed the red button, and padded to the door. Six in the morning, a dead guru, and a forgetful neighbor. Things couldn't possibly get worse.

They could and they did.

Standing on my doorstep, looking way too sexy for such an early hour, was none other than Cypress Grove's finest, Detective Rafe Martino.

Chapter 4

My first thought (after noticing that he looked like a million bucks) was that I was looking my absolute worst. Pale, shiny morning face, bed head, and a ratty yellow bathrobe decorated with faded blue ducks that had seen better days.

"Sorry to wake you, Dr. Walsh," he said, not looking the least bit repentant. "May we come in?"

I shielded my eyes from the glaring sunshine and noticed he had a uniformed cop with him, a gangly guy who looked about twelve in his scratchy blue serge uniform.

"Officer Duane Brown," he said, gesturing to the Opie look-alike who was shifting uncomfortably from one foot to the other and mopping his forehead with a white handkerchief. It was early morning, but they were predicting a scorcher and the day already had a hazy glow to it.

"What's this about?" I said quietly, not wanting to blast him with morning breath. (Although when you think of it, what does he expect, when he comes barging into someone's house at this ungodly hour?)

"It's about a homicide investigation," Detective Martino snapped, suddenly all business. "Could we come inside?"

I reluctantly stepped back, yanking the robe more tightly

around me. *He must be talking about Guru Sanjay!* "If this is about the guru, I don't know anything about it."

I regretted the idiotic remark the second the words flew out of my mouth. Why did I immediately assume it was about Sanjay Gingii? *Methinks the lady doth protest too much!*

Maybe Martino wasn't up on his Shakespeare, because he lifted his shoulders in a slow shrug and made a noncommittal sound.

"But you can come in, since you seem determined to," I said inhospitably. I glanced over my shoulder toward Lark's door and thought I saw it open a tiny crack. Was she standing there listening to our conversation or was I imagining it?

"Where were you last night?" Detective Martino asked abruptly. He moved past me into the living room, eased himself into the green and white wicker love seat, and whipped out a tiny notebook.

I noticed Officer Brown took a cushiony armchair and looked like he was ready to settle in for the long haul. Were they going to play good cop, bad cop? (Or have I been watching too much *Law & Order*?)

"I was here. I came straight home after my shift at WYME. I ate a pizza, watched TV, and then went to bed." Dear god, he was writing all this down! Now all of Cypress Grove would know about my nonexistent social life.

"No unusual occurrences?" Opie asked.

I had the feeling he'd piped up just to be saying something. Martino shot him a look and he sank a little deeper into the armchair. He was so slight, the padded arms engulfed him, threatening to swallow him whole like an amoeba.

"Well, just one. They forgot to put extra cheese on my pizza."

"Do I write that down?" he asked Martino, who silenced him with a look.

"So . . . you're claiming you were alone?"

"I'm not *claiming* I was alone. I *was* alone."

"I see." A beat of silence fell between us. His eyes skimmed over my terry bathrobe, and there was a wry twist in his voice. The corner of his mouth quirked, and I knew exactly what he was thinking: *No wonder she is alone!*

The notion of me having a hot date was about as likely as Mother Teresa pledging Delta Gamma.

He stared at me and I stared back. He had a strong mouth and, of course, those smoldering eyes. Wary, watchful eyes. Cop eyes.

"So," he continued, staring at his notebook as if for inspiration, "what can you tell me about Guru Sanjay Gingii?"

He stumbled over the tongue twister of a name, but I resisted the impulse to smile. I had the uneasy feeling that I was in trouble, even though for once in my life, I was completely innocent.

The only thing I could possibly be charged with was being a fashion disaster in a tatty terry bathrobe and yellow flip-flops, but as far as I knew, that wasn't a criminal offense.

"Besides the fact that he's dead?" I said wittily. My mother always said my sense of humor would be the death of me, and I wondered whether she could be right.

"You knew all about that," Martino said flatly. "It was the first thing you mentioned when we came to the door."

"Well, of course I knew about it," I shot back, feeling a little bubble of anger rising in me. "It's on all the news outlets, and Cyrus Still called me this morning to tell me about it."

I glanced at the smiling Mexican sun god wall clock over

the brick fireplace. "In fact, I'm supposed to be at the station doing a live broadcast in thirty minutes."

"Don't let us stop you," Opie piped up again. I could tell he was trying to put on a low, testosterone-charged David Caruso voice, but his voice cracked in an embarrassing squeak.

"Am I free to go, then?" I asked. If I didn't bother with hair and makeup, I could still make it to the station on time.

Martino stared at me, his face a picture of calm innocence. He made no move to get up; he just sat there, tapping his pen against the cover of his notebook. "Of course you're free to leave," he said easily; "this is your house."

He laughed at his own wit. Move over, Jay Leno!

"I mean are *you* going to leave?" I asked pointedly. Did I imagine it, or did his dark eyes flicker to the bedroom right behind me to the left? I felt as if we were playing a Tom and Jerry game, and I didn't like being Jerry.

"Just one more question," he said, dragging out the words like Columbo. "Where was your roommate last night?" He glanced down to check his notes. "Lark Merriweather."

"Lark?" I repeated, stalling for time. Opie leaned forward eagerly in his chair, muscles tensed as if he were a cougar sizing up a wildebeest, or maybe he just smelled the delightful aroma of French vanilla creme brewing in the kitchen.

The sooner I got these two out the door, the better! I planned on grabbing a cup of coffee and hitting the road in five minutes flat.

"Lark was . . ."

"Yes?" Martino said lazily. He was eyeing me carefully, and I could tell that his bullshit detector was in hyperdrive.

"Well . . ." I faltered, my chest tightening as my pulse thudded. Martino's eyes narrowed a little, and I tried to keep my expression neutral.

Did I dare tell them that Lark had disappeared for a few

hours? Why did I have the sneaking feeling that they already knew that? Was this some sort of trap? I hesitated, and then Martino frowned, something registering in his dark eyes as he looked past me. I resisted the impulse to look around and took a deep breath.

"Lark and I . . . ," I began.

Then I heard the bedroom door fling open behind me, and Lark walked into the living room. She looked pale and tired and was wearing a gray Juicy sweat suit that only highlighted the dark circles under her eyes.

"You don't have to answer that," she said quietly. "Go to work, Maggie; I'll handle this." She pulled over a bar stool from the breakfast nook and slumped into it. She looked like she hadn't slept a wink, and even her choppy blond tresses appeared limp and dejected.

Both Martino and Opie jumped to their feet.

"Are you Lark Merriweather?" Martino asked, his voice hard and metallic. When Lark nodded, Martino and Opie positioned themselves on either side of her.

I didn't like the look of this, and I wouldn't put it past Martino to slip a pair of cuffs on her. I was still smarting from the embarrassing perp walk he had put me through at the station yesterday.

"We have some questions for you, Ms. Merriweather," Martino said, "about your whereabouts last night."

"She was here," I said, my brain finally kicking into gear. "I just told you we had dinner together."

Lark glanced at me, her forehead creased. Her expression was hollow, guarded, as if she was afraid of what was going to happen next.

She was telegraphing something to me with her eyes, but all I could pick up on was an emotion I had never associated with her. Uncertainty? Dismay? Naked fear?

I felt like my brain had been taken over by alien body snatchers who had tinkered with my neurotransmitters and now I was incapable of forming a coherent thought. *Think, Maggie, think!*

I hesitated, uncertain of my next move, and Martino pounced as if he'd been reading my mind.

"Be careful what you say, Dr. Walsh, unless you want to be charged as an accessory." His voice was like shards of ice.

"An accessory to what?"

"To murder. The murder of Guru Sanjay Gingii."

My heart stuttered, but I held my ground. "That's ridiculous! Neither one of us knows anything about his death. I interviewed the man on my radio show yesterday, and that's the last I saw of him."

"Maybe that's the last *you* saw of him, but I bet Ms. Merriweather here has a different story to tell." Opie looked pleased with himself, and I felt like I'd been sucker punched.

"Lark, tell them you don't know anything about this!"

"Just stay out of this, Maggie," she said in a weary voice. "Go to work. I know they need you at the station."

"But I can't just leave you here alone with . . . Batman and Robin!" I blurted out.

Martino flashed me a cocky smile and Opie smirked. "Oh, don't worry about that, Dr. Walsh. You won't be leaving her here with us. We're taking her down to the station for questioning."

Chapter 5

"They can't possibly believe Lark did it," I moaned to Vera Mae half an hour later.

I'd just finished the rush-hour traffic report, filled in for Big Jim Wilcox on the sports desk, and then covered the breaking news of the day: "Visiting Guru Turns Up Dead."

Vera Mae peered over my shoulder to read the copy, sucked in her cheeks, and twitched her nose as if she had caught the odor of rotting fish heads. "Visiting guru turns up *dead*?" She snorted scornfully. "Oh, honey, you must be upset!"

Okay, it wasn't my best effort. I knew my writing was as flat and boring as a fried mackerel, but my creative juices just weren't flowing this morning.

Irina had come up with a breezier opening line: "Sanjay Says Sayonara!" It had some nice alliteration going for it, but Cyrus had nixed it because he felt it sounded too flippant.

Since all we had from Martino and company was radio silence, we didn't have many newsworthy details about the crime scene, and the piece about Guru's Sanjay's death took up less than two minutes of airtime.

Ray, the summer intern in the news department, had cobbled together some clips, and I'd included a quote from Guru Sanjay's publicist, who said they were rushing a posthumous biography into print ($7.99 and available at fine bookstores everywhere).

I'd been trying to call Lark on her cell every ten minutes and was frustrated that I kept getting her voice mail. "I just can't believe she's a murder suspect," I repeated peevishly.

"I can't believe it, either. What in tarnation would her motive be?" Vera Mae pondered.

"It beats me," I told her. I yanked off my headphones and we ducked into the break room to grab a whole-wheat donut and coffee (hey, fiber is healthy, right?) before heading back to the studio.

"She never even met the fella. Why would she want to kill him?"

"Exactly!" I shook my head. "The police are on the wrong track, and the sooner they figure it out, the better." Vera Mae carefully wrapped up the donut crumbs for Tweetie Bird and bought a package of peanuts for him out of the vending machine.

"And if she was at the town house all night, then I don't think those cops have a thing to go on. If they come sniffing around here asking questions, you can be darn sure I'll give them a piece of my mind. They're just spinning their wheels and wasting taxpayers' money by barking up the wrong tree. And I'm not a bit afraid to tell them so!"

She stopped as if she had run out of breath. Then she stared hard at me, her uncanny mental radar kicking in. "Maggie, is there something you're not telling me? Lark was with you last night, right?" She lowered her voice as if she was afraid that the break room might be bugged.

"Well, you see, that's the problem," I admitted. "She was home for dinner, but then she slipped out on an errand."

"Oh, lordie," Vera Mae moaned. "This is a whole different kettle of catfish. Did you tell the police this?"

"Not exactly. I hesitated and never really answered their question directly. They probably suspected I was holding something back." I bit back a sigh. You know what they say about hindsight being twenty-twenty. What if I had made things worse for Lark by fudging the facts?

"That might not have been the wisest choice, hon. But I know your heart's in the right place and you wanted to help her." Vera Mae pressed her lips tightly together, and I knew she was dying to give me a lecture on the value of truthfulness. "The police don't take kindly to folks withholding information from them. Obstruction of justice, they call it. Or maybe even an accessory to a crime."

Obstruction of justice? Accessory to a crime? I knew Martino would like nothing better than to slap those handcuffs on me again and dance me down the hallway in front of my coworkers. "Vera Mae, I may have made a tactical error, but I think it will all work out right in the end. You know what they say: The truth will come out."

I gave a good facsimile of a nonchalant chuckle, even though I suddenly felt cold inside. For all I knew, I'd be next on Martino's hit list, but at the moment, my only concern was for Lark.

"It's a done deal!" Jim Wilcox crowed, charging into the break room, startling me so much that hot coffee slopped over onto my wrist. "I just interviewed the police chief and it sounds like your roommate is guilty as sin, Maggie." He waggled his fingers at me, looking inordinately pleased with himself.

"She's not guilty," I said between clenched teeth. "No way in hell is she guilty."

"Hot damn! They're gonna nail her skinny butt to the barn door. To the barn door!" His face was bright red, and he was shouting like he was announcing a Hail Mary pass at a Cypress Grove Cougars football game. He rubbed his hands together gleefully.

Lark was guilty? Impossible! I knew I was gaping like a goldfish, but it was Vera Mae who trounced him.

"Well, my, don't you have a way with words, Jimbo," she chirped. "Nailed to the barn door? Sounds like you're the judge, jury, and executioner. I didn't realize you were a legal eagle as well as a sports announcer. And what exactly did you find out at the police station, pray tell?"

"Lark was dragged down there for questioning," he gloated. "They had her in the interrogation room, and she wasn't looking any too happy about it. If only I could've been a fly on the wall. You know what they do in there, don't you?"

"I don't think we need to hear this," Vera Mae interrupted.

Big Jim snickered. "Well, I'll tell you," he rushed on. "They turn the air-conditioning way down so the suspect starts to sweat. Then they saw off a couple of inches from both front legs of the chair. That way the poor sucker has to sit with his ass muscles tensed tight as a drum, miserable as hell, trying not to slide off onto the floor."

"Charming." Vera rolled her eyes at me.

"I saw that on *CSI* the other night." Big Jim's eyes were glazed, and his voice had a high, jittery edge to it. "I wonder if I could do a jailhouse interview and get her to confess?" he mused. "That's the kind of thing that can get you on *Dateline*. I can see it now: 'Women Who Kill! A Jim Wilcox Exclusive.'"

Jim spread his beefy hands out in front of him, as if he could see a brilliant career in big-league broadcasting unfolding before his bulging eyes.

"I can't believe Lark's down there right now in a jail cell," I said miserably. "I need to talk to her right this second and find out how I can help her. Maybe I can finally reach her on her cell." A horrible thought hit me. "Unless they took it away from her." I pictured Lark in a lonely, dark cell with nothing but a thin gray blanket and a Roller Derby queen named Killer to keep her company.

"We need to get over to the jailhouse right now," Vera Mae said.

"Well, there's no point in you two playing Thelma and Louise, because the fact is, she's probably on her way home by now," Big Jim huffed, taking his voice down a notch.

"What? She's on her way home? You had us thinking she was on death row!" Vera Mae glared at him, her hands on her hips.

Big Jim shrugged. "They released her—but that's just for now," he added darkly. "She's their number-one suspect, though. They're probably biding their time, building a case. I tried to get a statement as she was getting into her car, and she darn near ran me over with that little foreign number of hers."

He brushed at an imaginary piece of lint on his powder blue polyester jacket. "It could have been a case of vehicular homicide. She's lucky I'm such a nice guy. Anybody else would've pressed charges."

"Oh, vehicular homicide, my patootie," Vera Mae exclaimed. "Is the girl all right? That's all we want to know."

"She seems to be," he said, helping himself to the coffee, ignoring the "honor jar" filled with quarters. "She's a feisty little thing, isn't she? But stay tuned, folks," he said, his good humor restored. "That girl's in a heap of trouble."

Chapter 6

I finally managed to catch up with Lark during a thirty-second commercial break on my show ("The Last Call Funeral Home! We're dying to please you!"). She sounded tired and listless, as if all the energy had been sucked right out of her. She said she was going directly to bed, and I promised to pick up some of her favorite Chinese takeout for a late dinner together.

Veggie stir-fry for her, veggie lo mein for me, and a heart-healthy dumpling for Pugsley—steamed, not fried, no soy sauce, no MSG. It's probably significant that the dog eats healthier food than we do, but this wasn't the time to dwell on it.

This also wasn't the right time for a heart-to-heart talk with Lark, I decided.

I needed to get through my shift and then do some investigating before getting the lowdown from her. If Detective Rafe Martino was determined to zero in on the wrong person, that was his business. I would outmaneuver him and outfox him every step of the way, and I knew exactly where I had to start.

It was a no-brainer.

I needed to scope out the place where the guru had met his untimely end, or his "transition" into the cosmos, as he would call it.

So that meant I needed to see Ted Rollins, general manager of the Seabreeze Inn.

"Maggie, good to see you!"

"You, too." He pulled me into a gentlemanly hug and kissed me on the cheek.

Ted is the proverbial nice guy, the kind your mom and all your friends wish you would marry. He's tall and ruggedly handsome, with sandy brown hair and a terrific smile. He was wearing a crisp white shirt with a wheat-colored blazer that set off his deep tan, along with some expensive-looking Italian loafers.

Ted has been asking me out ever since I moved to Cypress Grove, and I've always turned him down. What can I say? I always pick bad boys, the kind the nuns warned me about. You know, the guys who don't call, trample on my heart, and wreak havoc with my emotions. And naturally I pursue them relentlessly, doomed to fail, like a salmon swimming upstream only to dash itself against those pesky rocks hidden underwater.

Which probably explains why I'm still single at thirty-two and Ted and I will never be more than good friends.

"Terrible news about the guru," I murmured as Ted ushered me into the empty breakfast room off the lobby and poured coffee for us. I shot a sidelong glance at him. He was acting very calm and collected, as always. How much did he know?

It was a cheerful place with a high ceiling, blue chintz tablecloths, and a wide bay window that offered a dazzling view of the hotel gardens. The polished heart-pine floors were scattered with handmade yellow and blue braided rugs that gave it an upscale yet cozy feel.

I heard the chatter of cicadas and glanced outside as we sat down. It was early summer, and the garden was spectacular, a riot of blooms and color. Delicate yellow roses and day lilies vied for attention with flashy hibiscus and purple bougainvillea. A Casablanca fan swirled lazily in the breakfast room, and a faint scent of honeysuckle wafted in from an open window.

If I hadn't been feeling so wired, it would have been a great place to relax.

Breakfast was served from seven to ten every morning, but Ted always keeps free coffee, juice, mineral water, and muffins available for the guests all day long. That's just the kind of guy he is.

"It's awful," he said, pulling his chair close to me. "I still can't believe it happened right upstairs," he added, shaking his head. "I've been fielding questions from reporters all morning, and we've already had a few guests cancel their reservations."

"Really?" I kept my tone neutral, but my pulse skittered.

"It's very upsetting for them, you know. To think that someone died under suspicious circumstances, right here at the Seabreeze. I tried to reassure them, but what could I say? No one really knows what happened to Guru Sanjay. I guess they're considering the possibility of foul play, but they're not giving out much information. His team is going ahead with the conference, but they're all pretty shell-shocked. They're upstairs right now in the Magnolia Ballroom. A pretty good turnout."

"Is that so? I'm surprised they didn't just cancel it." So Team Sanjay was still here. In the Magnolia Ballroom. That gave me an idea. I could start my investigation immediately.

"Miriam Dobosh—she seems to be in charge now—said it's what the guru would have wanted. They're going to head back to South Beach to arrange for the funeral right after the closing ceremony tomorrow morning. Of course, there's always the possibility they'll have to return to Cypress Grove for questioning. I guess it all depends on what the police decide to do. They haven't even released the body yet."

"I'm sure it's very unsettling for everyone," I said demurely, wondering how I could find out what else he knew. He'd mentioned suspicious circumstances and foul play. Was that an educated guess, or had he heard something? I needed to find out exactly what he knew—fast.

"Of course, he could have died from natural causes," he said, breaking into my thoughts.

"Oh, absolutely." I smiled brightly at him, hoping he would say more.

"I heard your interview with him yesterday," he said, resting his hand lightly on mine. "You did an excellent job, as usual. It made me want to run out and buy his book, and I'm usually not into that self-help stuff." He gave a little self-deprecating smile.

I nodded. Ted listens to my show every single day. *Just like my mother*, I thought wearily, and then realized that Freud would have a field day with that one.

"I'm not into all that cosmic stuff, either," I admitted, slathering a blueberry muffin with honey butter. *I'm into calories and cholesterol*, I thought, resisting the urge to slide a cheese Danish onto my plate. And those tiny banana-nut minimuffins at the Seabreeze—they're the best. I poured two Splendas into my coffee to even out the calorie count.

"I suppose it was very hard for you to get the news," he went on. "You know, I've been worried about you, Maggie. I'm glad you stopped by today. I was going to call and see how you were doing." (See what I mean? He's not only kind and good-looking; he's sensitive and worried about my feelings. Maybe I *am* insane not to take our relationship to the next level!)

I nodded, trying to look properly somber. "It was certainly a shock." I toyed with my teaspoon, wondering how to broach the subject. "Do the police have any leads?" I asked innocently.

"I'm not sure," Ted said, his tone grave. "They were here late last night interviewing the staff, and the lead detective was back again this morning. He's sort of an annoying guy," he said, his face clouding.

"Really?" My heart rate bounced up a notch. *Annoying, irritating, and impossibly sexy.*

"Yeah." His blue eyes glinted and his smile was sardonic. "He came on pretty strong and tried to steamroll his way over everyone. I guess he was only doing his job, but I'm not looking forward to seeing him again. And I have the feeling he'll be back."

"Detective Martino?" I blurted out without thinking.

Ted looked surprised. "Yes, how did you know?"

"I think I may have heard his name mentioned at the station," I said glibly, not wanting to explain the early-morning visit. "You know, Big Jim Wilcox usually covers the crime beat. But he was tied up this morning, and I think I saw Martino's name on a news report Jim had filed."

"Well, he certainly grilled Carmela, who was working the front desk last night." Ted frowned. "She's not completely fluent in English, and I think she was intimidated by him. If I'd been thinking straight, I would have insisted on having an interpreter there for her. He can be something of a bully, and I don't appreciate him manhandling my staff."

"He can have that effect on people." I allowed myself a small, derisive snort.

"So you know him?"

"No, of course not. But that's what I've heard. You know, around the station," I said, backpedaling quickly as Ted's eyebrows shot up. "So, what did she tell him?"

"He wouldn't let anyone sit in on the interview," Ted said morosely. "But I know that Carmela told him a young woman visited the guru in his room last night. Someone slim and blond who was carrying a big tote bag. I guess it was a purse, but Carmela said it was so big, she thought it might be an overnight bag."

Lark and her yellow Coach bag! That clinched it. Lark was at the Seabreeze, but when? And why? She hadn't paid a surprise visit to her idol, had she? My thoughts were scrambling like a gerbil on steroids. But Carmela must have been mistaken. Maybe Lark had just left a note for the guru at the front desk, I decided. There was no way she would go up to his room, was there?

"Did Carmela know the girl's name?" I asked, trying to keep my voice bland.

"I don't think so, but I know that Martino took down a description and Carmela said she's seen her in the neighborhood. Very slim, shaggy short blond hair, about five-two. Funny, but if I didn't know better, I'd say she could be Lark's twin."

Lark's twin. My spirits sank like a stone, but I managed a wan smile. "Hey, wouldn't that be something?" I said, joining in the fun. "Maybe Lark has a long-lost twin who has a thing for gurus, but I guess that only happens in detective novels." I bit back a nervous laugh that ended in an embarrassing squeak.

"I guess," Ted said, looking puzzled.

"So," I said, clearing my throat, "it sounds like Martino

may have a lead. But did anyone else visit the guru last night? Did Carmela mention any other suspects? I mean guests?" I corrected myself quickly.

"Carmela didn't see anyone else."

I glanced out into the lobby. "Yes, but someone could have slipped by the front desk if things were busy. See how easy it would be? All they had to do was follow that hallway toward the garden, and then they could take the back stairs and walk right up to his room."

"I guess it's possible."

"Or maybe it was someone in the guru's own party; you know, one of his staff members. He could have had some sort of confrontation with him, and maybe he accidentally killed him." I paused, thinking it over. "I bet lots of people had access to his room. He was on the second floor, right?"

"How did you know that?"

"Well, he told me he hated elevators. He said he refused to use one. We were talking about claustrophobia during the commercial break yesterday, and I just couldn't picture him hoofing it up several flights of stairs. So I figured he'd ask you for a room on the lowest floor."

"Maggie Walsh, ace detective," Ted teased me. "You know, you sound like you're conducting a homicide investigation. For all I know, you could be working undercover as Martino's partner."

"No chance of that."

He grinned and gave me a searching look while I busied myself pouring more coffee for us. "Is there something you're not telling me, Maggie? You're not here on assignment, are you? Covering the story for WYME?"

"Oh, no, nothing like that," I rushed on. "It's just that . . . well, you know, I interviewed Guru Sanjay, and I feel terrible that he died. Or was murdered. Right here. In this hotel."

I felt my face flushing, and I could feel a trickle of flop sweat crawling down my spine. I knew I had said too much. Was Ted suspicious? My mental 8-Ball said: "Signs point to no." He was slipping his arm around me, big-brother style.

"Hey, Maggie, honey, you can't let this get to you." He pulled me close to him for a moment, his voice warm with concern. "Just let the police do their job, and it will all come out right in the end, you'll see. They'll find out who killed Guru Sanjay."

Manuel, the busboy, suddenly materialized next to us. "Señor Rollins," he said softly. He pointed to the front desk, where Carmela was pantomiming that Ted had to take an important phone call.

"Oops, that's a call from Corporate I've been expecting. I've got to skedaddle." He smiled into my eyes before sliding back his chair and standing up. "I don't want you worrying over this anymore, Maggie. The police will get to the bottom of it; they're the professionals, you know."

"I know."

He playfully touched the end of my nose, his deeply tanned face breaking into a wide grin. "So I want you to promise me you won't give it another thought."

"I promise." I fake-smiled back at him and for the first time in my life raised three fingers in the Girl Scout sign, even though the closest I've ever gotten to the world of Scouting is scarfing down an entire box of Samoas at one sitting.

Somehow I knew he would like the three-finger salute, though, and sure enough, he gave me a big thumbs-up. I made a show of leaning back and reaching for that luscious cheese Danish, the one that had been sitting on the plate all that time, calling my name. I did it just to show Ted how relaxed and worry free I was (even if mildly carbohydrate addicted and maybe even insulin resistant).

I watched Ted hurry over to the front desk and allowed myself a sad little sigh at the way his brown hair looped sexily over one eye and his broad, muscular shoulders filled out his blazer. There he was: smart, handsome, successful, kindhearted, and single. Cypress Grove's most eligible bachelor, everything you could want in a man.

And he wanted—me!

There's nothing he wouldn't do for me. This is the guy who surprised me by ordering a special "Beefy Liver doggy birthday cake" for Pugsley from the Sweet Cakes bakery over on Main Street. He sent over the hotel gardener with a bouquet of yellow roses last week, and hand delivered a pot of chicken soup last month when Lark had the flu. He even power washed my deck when I said it was looking a little grungy.

Hell, he'd probably paint my bathroom if I asked him to.

So what's the problem? Okay, maybe I'm crazy. But here's the hitch.

Call me shallow, but can you imagine having hot monkey sex with a guy who says things like "skedaddle"?

I rest my case.

Chapter 7

I waited until Ted disappeared into his office behind the front desk and watched while he shut the door behind him. There was one person who might hold the key to the puzzle.

Miriam Dobosh, right hand to the guru himself.

After taking another quick peek to make sure Ted's office door was still firmly shut, I bounced to my feet and trotted along the back hallway to the stairs to the second floor and the Magnolia Ballroom. The double brass doors were closed, but I could hear the soft murmur of voices inside, along with some ethereal music. At least I think it was supposed to be ethereal. It sounded like whale sounds, a mournful elegy punctuated by a series of squeaks that reminded me of Pugsley's squeeze toy.

Cautiously, I opened the door a crack, only to find myself face-to-face with yet another of the *Sopranos*-type bodyguards. He was a Goliath. I'm five-ten, and I had to crane my neck to look up at him.

"This is a closed workshop," he rasped, all set to slam the door in my face like I was the Avon lady offering him a free lip gloss.

"But I've been invited!" I protested.

"Yeah?" His eyes slid over my short-sleeved salmon-colored Tommy Bahama blouse and tan pencil skirt. "If you're a registered conference guest, go down to the front desk and pick up your name tag." His tone was brusque and his black eyes glittered as cold and hard as river rocks.

"I've got a press pass," I said quickly. I reached for my pass and found to my horror it was missing. Hoping for the best, I pulled out my laminated Cypress Grove Public Library card and waved it at him. A beat of tense silence fell between us.

He ignored the card, so I shoved it back in my bag. Either he doesn't read a lot or he was on to me.

"Look, I'm with WYME, and I interviewed Guru Sanjay on my radio show yesterday. We were going to continue our conversation last night and I was shocked to learn he had died."

This earned me an even icier glare. *Oops!* Nix the word "die." I'd forgotten that death doesn't exist in the world of Sanjay Gingii. Time for damage control.

"I mean before he . . . um . . . transitioned to another dimension. He asked me to attend the conference today as his special guest."

"I don't know nothing about that." He had a rough New York accent (maybe Bed-Stuy?) and looked like his nose had been broken a few times. His beefy arms were bulging out of his black Team Sanjay T-shirt, and I couldn't take my eyes off his neck. It was as thick as a sequoia and decorated with a creepy weird tat that looked like a forest of kudzu vines gone wild.

"The guru and I bonded with each other," I went on quickly, "and he was going to explain more of his metaphysical theories to me. Today. At this workshop."

My stomach was pricking with anxiety, and I tried to ignore the stream of pure adrenaline shooting through me. If this Neanderthal wouldn't let me in, how would I ever gather any information?

"Do we have a late arrival?" A tall woman dressed from head to toe in navy blue polyester appeared behind him. A navy pillbox hat balanced tipsily on her frizzy gray hair, and she looked ghostly pale, either because she was grief stricken or because she wasn't wearing a smidgen of makeup. She pushed past bouncer guy to give me a quick once-over. From the pinched expression on her face I could tell she didn't like what she saw.

She was pretty hefty and looked as if she had bought out the entire "slimming collection" from the Home Shopping Channel. Not a natural fiber anywhere on her body.

I hoped no one lit a match around her—she'd go up in flames like a human torch.

"Maggie Walsh from WYME," I said quickly. I extended my hand, and she reluctantly shook it. A hint of alarm registered in her eyes, but she said quietly, "I'll handle this, Bruno," waving the thug away. I tried to peer into the ballroom, but she closed the door behind her and stepped into the hallway.

"Is there something I can help you with? I'm Miriam Dobosh, executive assistant to Guru Sanjay."

Miriam Dobosh! I had hit pay dirt on the very first try. An amazing piece of luck. The detective gods were with me.

"I just have a few questions to ask you," I said, gesturing to a pair of cushy wicker armchairs arranged in a conversation nook a few feet away. I whipped out a notebook and pen before she could change her mind.

"We're right in the middle of a seminar—"

"It'll only take a second, honest!" I put on my most winning smile, but I knew that this was going to be a hard sell. "We're putting together a eulogy for the guru—"

"A eulogy? That's for dead people," she snapped.

"Sorry, I meant to say a retrospective." I paused for a beat, and she lowered herself into the chair next to me. "I just wanted to get a few quotes from you. Something that the guru's followers would want to know—you know, a personal anecdote or two. I'm sure you have some wonderful memories of him."

I pulled out my tape recorder and slid it onto the coffee table in front of us.

"I'll be taking notes as well; this is just to refresh my memory," I said, catching her frown. I know that people feel intimidated when you whip out a tape recorder, which is why I never taped my psychotherapy sessions with my clients back in New York. But I thought it might give me some journalistic cred (since my public library card clearly wasn't cutting it).

Miriam was already drawing away from me, leaning back lightly in her chair with her arms folded over her cushiony chest. Uh-oh. Closed body language. I knew I had to act fast to reassure her or she'd snap shut like a North Atlantic clam.

"I want to make sure I capture every word." I looked straight into her eyes and hoped that she fell for the bait. The guru's words preserved for generations to come! Who could resist the offer? Apparently Miriam couldn't.

"Well, I suppose I could tell you a few things . . ."

I let her ramble on for a few minutes, hoping she didn't notice that the red light on my tape recorder wasn't blinking. I'd slapped a WYME sticker on it so it would look official but never remembered to buy batteries for it.

"In the last five years, Guru Sanjay's appeal has skyrocketed. He's made esoteric metaphysical concepts accessible to a mass-market audience," she droned, as if she were reading from a press release.

"Hmm." I nodded, encouraging her.

"He's become such a pop-culture icon, he's known all over the world. If you say the name Sanjay, everyone knows who you're talking about, just like Oprah, Bono, or Deepak."

Or Flipper, I added silently.

I sneaked a look at my watch. There was something oddly flat about her voice, and underneath all the hype, I wondered whether I sensed a note of something sinister in her tone. A touch of jealousy? A flare of resentment? I knew that all was not right with the head of Team Sanjay, and I decided to foster a guess.

In psych terms, they would call this an "interpretation." You ignore the surface of the speech and go for the subtext, the meaning behind what the client is saying. On *The Sopranos*, this is the point where Dr. Melfi would say to Tony, "So, what I hear you saying is . . ."

"Miriam, it sounds like you practically ran the whole organization. You were the real power behind the throne, the person responsible for his success. I hope that he appreciated you."

Her eyes flickered with surprise and then clouded. Bingo. Then I realized that I had been as subtle as a brick to the forehead. Time to rephrase or I'd lose her again. "I mean, it's obvious that the guru relied on you to keep things going smoothly."

"Well, he did," she admitted, smoothing an imaginary wrinkle in her polyester skirt. "I've been with him from the beginning. When he was just starting out."

"Really?" I pretended to make a note of it. "Can you tell

me something about those early years? When it was just the two of you building his empire?"

"It wasn't much of an empire back then," she said, her mouth tightening. "Sanjay was giving seminars to civic groups at community centers. Sometimes there were only thirty people in the audience at a fire hall out in the boondocks in some Podunk little town. Sanjay self-published his first book, and we used to sell copies out of the trunk of his car."

"But somehow people were drawn to him and he became famous. I bet that had a lot to do with your promotional skills."

"Oh, I wouldn't go so far as to say that." She shook her head, her double chin quivering. "It was Sanjay's gift that drew people, his understanding of the cosmos and human emotions. I just handled all the administrative details for him. You have to remember, Sanjay was the greatest thinker of this generation, not someone who could be bothered with the mundane details of running a business."

Hmm. So it seemed that she'd hitched her star to the guru's many years ago. But where had it gotten her? There was something about her tone that made me think she wasn't thrilled with being relegated to an outer ring of the Planet Sanjay. I wondered whether her fortunes had risen as rapidly as his. Judging from her shiny polyester suit, they hadn't.

"So all the books and the podcasts and the teleseminars came later?" I tried to look awed. "You must be a marketing genius. There's a lot of competition in the motivational field. I know plenty of psychologists who can't get a book deal or attract a national audience. They have the academic credentials, but they don't know how to get their name out there or how to connect with people who can guide their careers." I managed a bashful smile. "I wrote a self-help book myself, and it sank like a stone."

She looked at me with new interest, as if I had finally said something intelligent. "Most people have no idea what it's like," she said, her face hardening. "It's a lot tougher than it looks. The books and tapes drive the speaking deals, and you have to top yourself each time. It's all about the numbers, and these tours are murder. There are a million things to think about."

"I was surprised Guru Sanjay agreed to offer a workshop in our little town," I said, watching her closely. "I know that he usually speaks to thousands of people at a time in big venues."

"I'd heard he had a connection to Cypress Grove," she said hesitantly. "The story was someone from here helped him in the past, and he felt obliged to return the favor." She stood up and gave me a little smile. "I better get back to the seminar now. Can I have your card?" Her tone was definitely warmer than it had been in the beginning. I fumbled in my bag and handed her my card. "We'll be here till tomorrow morning," she said as she turned and left.

I thanked her and sat there for a few minutes, going over my notes. So Guru Sanjay was here in Cypress Grove once before? And Miriam might feel unappreciated by him? Maybe she had put in years of hard work for nothing? Who benefitted from his death? Had he left his fortune to Miriam? Would she be running his empire now that he was in a galaxy far, far away?

These were all issues worth investigating, the "story behind the story," as Cyrus is fond of saying. But at the moment, I had a more urgent matter on my mind. I needed to make a pit stop at the Seabreeze ladies' room before heading back to the station.

I was surprised to find a weeping Sanjay-ite huddled in a love seat in the cozy anteroom that led to the actual restroom. She was young and blond, probably in her early twenties. It looked as if she'd been crying for quite a while, because her face was blotchy and her eyelids puffy. She was clutching a tear-stained copy of *Heal the Cosmos* and swiping her nose ineffectively with a paper towel.

"Oh, sorry," I said, obviously intruding on a private moment. "I'm just going to use the . . . uh . . . facilities," I said, heading for the tile-walled room with the sinks and toilets. She nodded, sniffling, and then my psychology training kicked in—how could I leave her there in distress?

I heard myself saying, "Is there anything I can do to help you? A drink of water?"

She shook her head, drew her knees up on the couch, and gave full vent to her grief. "I can't—I can't believe he's gone," she said between sobs. She obviously hadn't finished reading *Heal the Cosmos* or she'd know he wasn't really "gone," just transitioned, but I decided not to point this out to her.

"Did you know the guru very well?" I said softly, slipping into an armchair next to her.

She nodded. "For over five years. I've read all his books and I've gone to all his seminars."

Wow, quite the devoted little acolyte, I thought.

"So you're a follower . . ."

"Oh, I meant more to him than that," she said miserably. "He has millions of followers, you know."

I nodded sagely. She meant more to him? What was she talking about? Had I struck pay dirt again?

She leaned forward, her eyes locking on mine, her voice soft and full of tears. "I was going to take over the number-one spot in his organization." She dabbed her eyes. "He was going to announce it this weekend, and now it's all gone." She threw one arm out in a hopeless gesture, railing against fate. "It's over!" she said, jumping to her feet. "Now that dreadful woman will run his empire right into the ground, and there's not a damn thing I can do about it." She turned and stormed out into the hallway.

I sat back, stunned. This was more than I'd bargained for. The dreadful woman had to be Miriam Dobosh. Was there really going to be a change in command? Or had Guru Sanjay been toying with this sweet (and pretty) young girl? And did Miriam Dobosh have an inkling about what was going on?

I stood up shakily, pondering my next move. First a pit stop and then—I jumped back in surprise when a tall, stocky figure came barreling out of one of the stalls.

Miriam Dobosh. It was like the scene in *Fatal Attraction* when Glenn Close suddenly pops up in Anne Archer's bathroom, and I staggered backward in shock.

"She's insane," she hissed, her face close to mine. "Insane!" At this angle, with her flat, broad features and glittery eyes, Miriam looked a little demented herself.

"The girl who was just in here?" I said stupidly.

"Her name is Olivia Riggs." She shook her head up and down, nearly dislodging her Jackie Kennedy hat. "Completely delusional. She was infatuated with Sanjay. Sanjay wanted nothing to do with her. She's an annoying little pest."

She glanced in the mirror, grabbed the hat pin, and viciously jabbed it into her pillbox to anchor the hat more firmly on her head. Our eyes met for a moment in the glass, and her mouth was tight, her face contorted with rage.

"So you're saying there never was any chance that she was going to—" I wasn't sure how to tactfully finish the sentence.

"Take my job? Oh, please." Miriam gave a sardonic chuckle. "The girl has the IQ of a pigeon. She could never do what I do, not in a million years." She tapped her gray curls in a self-satisfied way. "It was all in her head," she said meaningfully. "She has a vivid imagination."

I did my business and scurried out, not sure whether I could take any more surprises.

Chapter 8

Of course I knew I had one more big surprise waiting for me back at the town house.

Lark. I glanced at my watch. In just a few hours, I'd know what really happened the previous night with Guru Sanjay.

But first I had another show to do. Two shows in one day, but this was an easy one—no callers, just a guest interview. We'd rerun this show for a holiday broadcast—a girl has to get some time off. I peeled out of the Seabreeze parking lot in a cloud of blue smoke, heading straight for the station. My guest was Dr. Hyram Rosenkrantz, author of *You and Your Colon: A Fragile Alliance.* We were low on mental health experts and Vera Mae had the bright idea of adding some shows on wellness and lifestyle issues.

I waggled my fingers at Irina, who frowned at me and pointed to the giant wall clock over the reception desk. "You are cutting it close to the bone," she said reproachfully. "Vera Mae is going pecans, wondering where you are. And your guest, he is looking to be losing it."

"I'm running a little late, sorry!" I tossed the apology over my shoulder as I sprinted down the hall. Grabbing a donut out of the break room barely broke my stride, and I kept on running straight into the booth, just as Vera Mae scurried to her spot at the board.

She glared at me through the window. "Holy buckets, girl, where've you been? Big Jim was going to rerun one of his sports broadcasts to fill the time slot."

I slapped my headphones on as Ray, the intern, hustled Dr. Rosenkrantz into the booth and settled him in a chair. My spirits sank when I got a look at my guest. He was a Pillsbury Doughboy of a man with a mass of yellow-white facial hair that nearly obliterated his pudgy features.

No time to offer him mineral water or coffee, not a moment to introduce myself or to make any attempt to put him at ease. The eminent doctor treated me to a scowl as I gave him a breezy smile. He was going to be a disaster on the air—I just knew it.

No time to worry about that, though, because we were going live in ten seconds!

I'd like to say the next two hours flew by, but really, how much can you say about colons? Dr. Rosenkrantz wasn't the most scintillating guest in the world, but in all fairness, he had a pretty grim topic—flatulence, constipation, and diverticulitis, all leading to the dreaded IBS, or irritable bowel syndrome.

The thrill of it all nearly sucked the air out of the booth.

His message was primarily cautionary: Be kind to your intestines and they will be kind to you. A sort of gastrointestinal Boy Scout oath.

I waved my whole-wheat donut at him to show I was with the program, but he seemed unimpressed and looked mournfully over his notes during the commercial breaks. Perhaps he needed a little more roughage himself?

Note to self: Ask Cyrus to find more entertaining guests.

Something to ponder: Did the fact that Guru Sanjay turned up dead after doing my show hurt my chances of getting A-list guests?

Later that evening, after stopping at Johnny Chen's for our take-out order, I cautiously unlocked the front door to the town house. I tiptoed inside, wondering whether Lark was awake and functioning, and was pleased to see her curled up on the sofa watching television with Pugsley at her side.

Then I noticed that she was staring blankly at the Weather Channel, and I knew her mind wasn't on rainstorms in Topeka or the blustery Santa Anas in Southern California.

"Hey," I said, setting the little white cardboard cartons with wire handles from Johnny Chen's on the coffee table in front of her.

"Is that dinner?" she asked listlessly.

"No, I adopted a bunch of goldfish from Mike's Marine World."

I took a close look at her and saw that her eyes were red rimmed from crying.

"Bad joke," I apologized, handing Pugsley his steamed dumpling on a napkin. He swallowed it in one gulp, and I took the remote out of Lark's hands to kill the distracting chatter about cumulus clouds forming in the Pacific Northwest.

"We need to talk," I said gently. It was dim in the room, and I switched on the ginger-jar lamp on the end table, flooding the room with soft pink light.

"Okay." A tiny, ghostly voice and a hopeless shrug.

"But we can eat first if you want," I added, taking in the stricken expression on her face. Her mascara was smudged from crying and she looked very small and vulnerable with her blue and white vintage afghan tucked around her legs.

She reached for her carton of veggie stir-fry and stabbed at the contents in a desultory way with a plastic fork. We ate in uncomfortable silence side by side for a few minutes, with Pugsley hovering around us like a hungry jackal, watching our every bite, his little feet tapping a staccato on the polished oak floor.

Finally Pugsley curled up under the coffee table. The town house became very still except for the solemn ticking of the grandfather clock in the entryway. Why wasn't Lark speaking up, telling me she was innocent? I was convinced she had nothing to do with Guru Sanjay's death, but for some reason, I needed to hear her say the words.

Then I gave myself a mental head slap. What in the world was wrong with me? How could I even think Lark could be capable of violence? She's so softhearted, she even rescues ants, carrying them outside in an envelope and setting them down gently in the garden.

The idea of her killing someone was ridiculous. Even someone as odious as Guru Sanjay.

Yet, something wasn't right. My stomach started to prick with anxiety, and my nerves were strung as tight as piano wire.

I drew in a long, slow breath, hoping to relax, and found that my chest ached from the effort. I shoveled in more veggie lo mein to soothe my jangled nerves with a little carb rush. Chinese food therapy: works every time.

"Okay," Lark said finally, breaking the silence. She shot a sidelong glance at me, pushed the afghan aside, and sat up straighter. "I think I'm ready to tell you what happened last night."

Finally, the moment of truth! I knew what was coming next. Lark would tell me what I already knew—that she had nothing to do with Guru Sanjay's death and it was all a case of mistaken identity. The kind of thing that could happen to anybody—right?

"Okay, let's hear it."

She took a long, shuddering breath, and then she let out a little sigh. Her blue eyes were shining with intensity and her pupils were dilated. Her gaze dropped to her hands, folded primly in her lap.

"Maggie, I think I may have killed him."

I felt like I'd been sucker punched and nearly dropped my carton of noodles on the polished oak floor, causing Pugsley to yip with excitement. My breath caught in my throat, as if it couldn't make it all the way down to my lungs.

"What? This is a joke, right?"

"It's no joke. It never should have happened this way. I never meant to hurt Guru Sanjay."

"I believe you, but start from the beginning." I tried to rein in my rampaging emotions. So much for eight years of psychoanalytic training! I was an emotional wreck, and my thoughts were swirling like dry leaves in the wind as I struggled to make sense of what she was saying.

"I'll try, but some of the evening is a blur. I think I must have blocked part of it out of my memory. I told that to Detective Martino, but he didn't believe me," she added ruefully. "He thinks I'm guilty, you know."

"Don't worry about Detective Martino right now. He thinks everybody's guilty. Just tell me what happened," I said firmly, "and don't leave anything out." I gave her a sharp look. "That bit about going out to the drugstore last night wasn't true, was it?"

"No, it was just an excuse," she said, flushing a little. "I went straight next door to the Seabreeze as soon as I left here. I knew you'd think it was crazy, so I felt too embarrassed to tell you the truth."

So Carmela was right, I thought grimly. I wondered whether Lark knew she'd been spotted in the hotel lobby and had probably already been positively identified by the front-desk clerk. That must be why Martino had dragged her down to the station this morning. Otherwise, why would he have reason to suspect her?

"I was going to call Guru Sajay on the house phone to ask him to autograph my copy of *Heal the Cosmos*—"

"You had it with you, right? That's why you were carrying that big yellow Coach knockoff; you had the book in there."

Lark nodded, drawing her knees up to her chest and wrapping her arms around them. With her choppy blond haircut and winsome features, she looked about twelve years old.

"Yes, and I brought along a little gift for him, a bottle of my Calming Essence." Lark makes her own herbal essences from dried flowers, and, generous soul that she is, she loves to give them out to her friends. You just add a few drops to a glass of water and instant nirvana.

"Go on." I was beginning to wish I had poured us both a glass of wine before hearing what Lark had to say. A hefty flute of Pinot Grigio would hit the spot about now. I looked longingly toward the kitchen but didn't want to interrupt Lark's train of thought.

"Well, I was heading for the front desk when I spotted him walking down the hallway to the back stairs. I don't know how I got up the nerve to speak to him, but I did. I ran right up to him and told him I'd read all his books and had brought him a little present. I told him I'd love to have him autograph his book for me."

"And of course he agreed," I prompted. I could just picture it. A fat middle-aged man meeting a devoted follower who just happens to be a gorgeous young blonde. It didn't take much to connect the dots.

"Yeah, he agreed all right, but I got more than I bargained for," she said, letting out her breath in a whoosh. "He invited me up to his room for a minute, and that's when things got crazy."

Despair laced her voice, and her tiny hands were knotted in fists, clutching the afghan as if it was a lifeline. Pugsley gave a nervous little nip, probably tuning in to the desperate tone in her voice.

"Crazy how?"

Lark blushed, a slow red burn that crept up her neck. "Well, first I asked him a lot of questions about his philosophy, and he seemed really interested in explaining it all to me."

I nodded, remembering how much Guru Sanjay liked to talk about himself.

"And then suddenly he gave me a funny look and his whole attitude changed. He was like a different person, Maggie. He lunged at me and tried to kiss me. I couldn't believe it! How could I have been so stupid? He was a complete lech. He didn't want to talk about metaphysics; he just wanted to get into my pants!"

"Ah." A beat of silence passed. "Okay, so he was a jerk and he made a pass at you. What happened then?"

"I tried to leave," Lark said slowly, "and he blocked my way. He was standing right in front of the door, trying to put his arms around me." She gave an involuntary little shudder at the memory, and her voice suddenly became high-pitched and girlish.

"He sounds like a creep! What did you do?" Pugsley's

eyes darted back and forth between us, as if he was following the conversation with rapt interest.

"I managed to slip past him and get my hand on the doorknob, but he caught me. So I turned around, put my hands against his chest, and pushed him as hard as I could. Maybe he tripped or maybe I'm stronger than I thought, but he stumbled backward."

"Onto the floor? Or onto the bed?"

"I don't know," she admitted. "I didn't wait around to find out. I ran out of there as fast as I could and took the back stairs down to the gardens." Her blue-eyed gaze locked onto mine.

"But I swear he was alive when I left, Maggie, honest!"

"I know," I said quickly. "But we've got to figure out what happened next. How long were you in his room?"

"I don't know . . . maybe forty-five minutes or an hour. Why?"

I bit my lip, thinking. "Lark, you came home sometime around midnight. What did you do after you left the Seabreeze?"

"I walked along the boardwalk for a long while. I think I lost track of time. I was so upset, and you know how I like to walk to clear my head." She pulled in a breath that fluttered on the edge of tears. "But Detective Martino doesn't believe a word of this. He thinks I killed Guru Sanjay! The only reason he hasn't charged me yet is he doesn't have enough evidence to make the charges stick. But he's keeping his eye on me and I know he'll be back. He made it pretty clear I'm his number-one suspect."

"We have to think this through, Lark," I said, my analytical side finally kicking in. If I was going to help Lark, I had to push my emotions aside and focus on the details of the case. "Do you know how Detective Martino connected you to the crime in the first place? Why did he zero in on you as a suspect? How did he even know you visited the guru last night?"

I wondered how much Martino had told her when he'd interrogated her, and I figured he was keeping the main details of the investigation to himself. Still, he might have given her a hint of what sort of case they were building against her. I had the horrible, sickening feeling that Lark was right. She was their prime suspect. Their only suspect.

"It was the bottle of Calming Essence," she said, surprising me. "That's what did it." A mirthless smile crept across her face. "As they say, 'No good deed goes unpunished.' If I hadn't brought it with me, none of this would have happened."

"What in the world are you talking about?" I was flummoxed.

"You know, the gift I brought Guru Sanjay. I put it down on his dresser when I first walked into his hotel room, and then I just forgot about it. When he attacked me, all I wanted to do was get out of there fast!"

"The Calming Essence!" I said, light dawning. "It had one of those handmade labels on it, didn't it?"

Lark nodded miserably. She does beautiful calligraphy work on handmade paper and attaches a tag to each gift bottle. With her name and address and an inspirational quote.

Bingo.

What a terrific bit of luck for Martino. He didn't have to be Adrian Monk to track her down with a clue like that staring him in the face!

"Tell me what happened down at the police station. Did you ask for a lawyer?"

She shook her head. "No, nothing like that," she said quickly.

"Did that detective—Martino—offer to get one for you?"

"Oh, yes, that's the first thing they told me. That I could have a lawyer and that I was free to leave anytime I wanted. Of course, they said since I hadn't done anything wrong or committed a crime, I wouldn't be needing a lawyer."

Hmm. Clever move. Nice bit of forensic psychology at work here. I knew Martino was smart enough not to jeopardize his case by denying Lark her rights, but he wasn't going out of his way to protect her interests, either. "So they interrogated you for a while and then let you go?"

Lark nodded, stifling a yawn. "It seemed like hours. I told them exactly what happened, and at first they seemed to believe me." She shook her head. "Then another detective came in and asked me a couple of times if I'd been really angry with Guru Sanjay for coming on to me."

"And you said—"

"I admitted that I'd been really angry and disappointed. But I certainly didn't kill him. Why would I?"

Why, indeed? I needed to know what Martino's next move was going to be. Had he accepted Lark's explanation, or was Big Jim Wilcox right? Were they really focusing on Lark exclusively? It certainly looked that way.

And what about Miriam Dobosh and Olivia? Did Martino even know about their connection with the guru and what his death might mean to them? Why was he focusing on Lark and ignoring some other hot leads? And what was the cause of death? Had that been determined? It sounded like the cops knew that Guru Sanjay was the victim of foul play, but they were still hazy on the details. Or they weren't ready to show their hand just yet.

At midnight, I decided to turn in, leaving Lark and

Pugsley curled up together, watching *Sense and Sensibility*. Ideas were flying inside my brain, but I put on a CD of *Soothing Ocean Waves*, snuggled under the comforter, and tried to make my mind go blank.

Tomorrow was another day, and I had a good idea where to pick up my investigation.

Chapter 9

The next morning I called a reporter friend, Nick Harrison, from the *Cypress Grove Gazette* and invited him to lunch. Nick, who is in his early twenties, covers arts and entertainment for the paper, and I'd heard he was planning a big piece on Guru Sanjay for the Sunday supplement. He's a good-looking guy, tall and athletic looking, with a boyish smile and dirty-blond hair worn on the longish side. Today he was wearing what I call Cypress Grove Casual, a snowy white golf shirt and pressed khakis with Reeboks.

Nick and I have sat through a couple of local press-club dinners together, and I figured meeting him for pasta would be the quickest way to get some background information on Guru Sanjay. Nick's laid-back, a nice complement to my type-A personality, and there's enough of an age difference that he thinks of me as an older sister, not potential date material.

We met at Gino's, a tiny Italian restaurant close to the station. Gino's is so much like the Italian bistro in Billy Joel's song it's almost a cliché, with red-and-white-checked tablecloths and photos of long-dead Italian opera singers lining the walls. The only thing missing is a Chianti bottle on each table, with multicolored strands of candle wax dripping down the sides. The food at Gino's is first-rate, the prices reasonable, and the service fast, so it's popular with the business crowd. After settling ourselves into one of the red leather booths and making an agonizing choice between vodka penne and fettuccine Alfredo, we got right down to business.

"Guru Sanjay was quite a piece of work," Nick said, reaching for his icy mug of draft beer. "I'm just getting into the story, and no one has anything good to say about him. Of course I'm saving the corporate people for later in the week; right now I'm concentrating on his personal life. The guy sounds really loathsome. I don't know how he attracted such a big following."

"Tell me about it," I agreed. "I had to sit through two hours on the air with him, remember?" I sipped my mango iced tea and tried not to look enviously at Nick's frosty glass of beer. I would have joined him, but I had a show to do that afternoon.

"So what was your take on him?"

"Well, at first I couldn't see how he managed to become a New Age superstar. I guess I just didn't get his appeal. But somehow, once he was live on the air, he changed. He was like a different person. He was magnetic, almost mesmerizing. I can see how people want to believe in him, and how they're taken in by his message."

"Sucked in, you mean," Nick said wryly.

"Yeah, definitely sucked in. The phones were ringing off the hook. It's hard to explain; the guy has charisma. I hate to admit it, but he does. He's almost like a religious figure, a cult figure."

"I think he tells people what they want to hear," Nick said. "Maybe he plays on their vulnerabilities, their insecurities."

"That he does," I agreed.

"I think I'm going to use a lot of quotes from his ex-wife in the opening of the piece," he went on, his brown eyes soft and reflective. "Or maybe highlight them in a sidebar. The problem is, her quotes are going to be pretty inflammatory, so I'll have to edit out the expletives." He patted a thick file next to him on the table. "In fact, I better run some of the material by the managing editor before I turn in my article. I don't want Sanjay Gingii, Limited, to hit us with a defamation suit—I've heard they have a crack legal team on retainer."

"Wow, is it that bad?" I was so excited I nearly forgot my fettuccine. So the guru had an angry ex-wife, and she was ready to tell all. Was there anything here that could further my own investigation?

"Worse than you think. Hell hath no fury like a woman scorned, you know."

"Are you telling me Sanjay left her for someone else?"

Nick nodded. "He got involved with another woman, and the timing couldn't have been worse. He cheated on Lenore right after she made him famous. She's the one who created the whole Guru Sanjay persona, you know—the seminars, the tapes, the talks. Before he met her, he was nothing."

The story was getting better and better. "So he wasn't always a guru? How does someone get to be a guru, anyway?" I mused. "I've always been puzzled about that. I wonder if it's like being a psychic or a ghost whisperer. There's no qualifying test—if you say you're one, that's it. You're in."

The corners of Nick's mouth quirked, and I noticed a couple of girls at the next table giving him the once-over. He really did have an adorable smile, complete with dimple. "Well, the first thing you do is latch on to someone in the motivational field who has a national audience, along with

Ivy League academic credentials and some big commercial
appeal. Someone with a platform. Someone like Lenore Cooper, Sanjay's ex-wife."

"Lenore Cooper? Why does that name sound familiar?"

"Lenore is a psychotherapist, and she was the one with
the big career when she first met Sanjay. And he wasn't calling himself Sanjay Gingii back then. His name was Lenny
Vitter, and he spent his time selling used cars and writing
bad checks back in Sioux Falls, South Dakota."

"You're kidding!" This was even better than I'd hoped.
Not only was Guru Sanjay a fake; he was a criminal!

"He has a long rap sheet, and I'm amazed that the tabloids haven't picked up on it."

"A rap sheet? What sort of crimes are we talking about?"

"Petty crimes. Forged checks, a couple of stolen cars that
he claimed he borrowed, things like that. The guy's slippery,
and my contact with the Sioux Falls PD said trying to pin a
charge on him was like trying to nail Jell-O to a wall. Everyone knew he was a lowlife, but it was hard to prove.
There were a few widows who lost their life savings to him.
Sounds like he must be some sort of sweet-talker. He'd be-
friend lonely old ladies and convince them that he should be
handling their investments for them. The investments would
go belly-up, but it was hard to prove that the money went
into his pocket."

"Wow." I was stunned. "You know, there was something
very slick about him. I felt it right away. Underneath the
phony charm, I thought I saw the soul of a sociopath. It was
really odd."

"Well, didn't they say that Ted Bundy could be pretty
charming if he wanted to be?" Nick raised his eyebrows.

"Yes, they did. The shrinks call it superficial charm. It's
all an act, but somehow there's something compelling about

it. That's how Ted Bundy lured his victims into his web, and I guess that's what Sanjay did. On a much smaller scale, of course."

"Sanjay was strictly small-time," Nick added. "People lost their money, not their lives."

"Tell me more about Lenore Cooper," I said, suddenly feeling energized. I attacked my fettuccine with gusto while Nick flipped open the folder in front of us.

He began to read from the first page. "She's a licensed psychologist—"

"Now I remember! I heard her speak at a regional psychology conference back in Manhattan. But she wasn't into metaphysical mumbo jumbo; she was talking about bipolar depression in adolescents, I think. I know she was the real deal, and she certainly wasn't a con artist like Sanjay." I paused for a moment, remembering the confident woman in the black Armani suit standing at the podium, giving a Power-Point presentation.

Nick quickly riffled through his notes. "Apparently she gave up private practice when she made it big with the books and seminars. Sanjay met her, and the next thing you know, he was up on stage with her. They coauthored a few books, and then they both were reeling in the big bucks. But there's no doubt about it; Lenore was the brains of the operation. Lenny was just along for the ride, and he knew a good opportunity when he saw one—Lenore Cooper was the best thing that ever happened to him. They got married six months after they met."

"Sounds like a sweet deal for him."

"It was until he got involved with Lenore's eighteen-year-old assistant. The two of them had a thing going, and Lenore found out. She kicked Sanjay out of the mansion that same night and divorced him, but he bounced right back. By that time, thanks to Lenore, he had a national platform. He got an A-list agent and started making his own book deals and giving his own seminars. He was speaking to crowds of five thousand people in big venues, and his CDs were selling like crazy. Last month, his agent was angling for a television deal for him with one of the networks—he figured he'd be bigger than Oprah."

"All thanks to Lenore," I muttered. "He probably stole all her best material."

"Exactly. And he was certainly quite the showman. She had more substance, but he had the flash and the charisma. The audiences loved him. It's hard to believe, but his books were hitting the best-seller lists, and Lenore's star had already started to fade." Nick stopped to savor his vodka penne. "I guess it's a case of the student surpassing the master."

"Which can be pretty damn annoying for the master," I pointed out. But the big question was, Was Lenore Cooper furious enough to kill Sanjay? "Can you give me some contact information on Lenore?"

Nick scribbled a phone number on a paper coaster and passed it across the table to me. "You didn't get this from me."

I widened my eyes. "Absolutely not."

"That's her cell," Nick said helpfully. "She lives in New York, but she's traveling in Florida right now, promoting her latest book."

My pulse ratcheted up a notch. "She's here in *Florida*? Right now?"

"Just thirty miles away," Nick said placidly, "over in Lakeville. You could probably catch her at her book signing tonight. Bargain Books—it starts at six o'clock."

"I'll be the first in line for her autograph," I said, my heart thudding with anticipation. Lenore Cooper, here in

Florida. Now I had three suspects to investigate—Miriam Dobosh, Olivia Riggs, and Lenore Cooper—and they all had good reasons for wanting to see Guru Sanjay dead.

Or rather, "transitioned," I reminded myself.

It was obvious from the small turnout in Lakeville that Lenore Cooper didn't have the same devoted fan base as Guru Sanjay. I'd called Lenore at six and said I'd be at the bookstore in an hour or so. Traffic was light and it was nearly seven when I parked on a narrow side street lined with little shops and family restaurants and walked two blocks to the address she'd given me.

Bargain Books was a tiny bookstore wedged between a pizza joint and a shoe store, and, like most of Lakeville, it looked like it had seen better days. Even the palm trees at the curb looked dejected, their fronds sparse and tinged with yellow at the tips. The bookstore had a faded green awning that hung limply over the transom and a concrete planter filled with wilting pink impatiens marking the front entrance.

There was an entire window display devoted to Lenore Cooper, and someone had made a pyramid of copies of her latest title (*Imagine It, Dream It, Do It!*) along with a hand-lettered sign announcing: MEET THE AUTHOR TONIGHT!

Lenore was sitting at a card table, talking on her cell when I walked in. It took a moment for my eyes to adjust to the dim lighting, but it was obvious that she hadn't drawn a huge crowd.

In fact, she hadn't drawn any crowd at all—the book signing was a bust. A dozen or so folding chairs—all empty—were arranged in front of the card table, presumably so the author could entertain her fans, if she felt so inclined. Two young female clerks wearing Bargain Books T-shirts were sitting on the floor, chewing gum and stripping books headed back to the publisher.

One of them started to scramble to her feet, but I motioned that I was waiting to see Lenore, and she immediately plopped back down on the floor, returning to her task. It was deathly quiet in the store, except for the lazy whirring of a Casablanca fan, and the narrow aisles and low lighting gave the whole place a claustrophobic feel.

After a moment, Lenore snapped the cell shut, and just for a second, her features slumped in disappointment, like one of those mournful Weimaraners you see on greeting cards. She had an angular face with very pale skin and looked to be in her mid-fifties, with a dramatic streak of white running through her shoulder-length dark hair. I caught myself staring at it, wondering whether it was some sort of genetic mutation or she had actually paid her hairdresser to create it.

"Maggie Walsh?" she said tentatively. She focused her dark eyes on me, and her expression was sharp and speculative. She had a Kathleen Turner voice, so sultry and whiskey smooth, she must have practiced to bring it down to that low register.

"Thanks for seeing me, Lenore," I said, moving forward to shake hands. Her grasp was limp and clammy, and she quickly dropped my hand to wave me to a seat next to her.

"It's wonderful to meet you. I've heard all about your show." She was smiling into my eyes, and I had the feeling she was being deceptively friendly, the way many celebrities are when dealing with reporters.

"Having a radio show is a nice change of pace for me," I said carefully. "I interviewed Guru Sanjay on my radio show, and I want to offer my condolences. His . . . um . . . passing must have been a terrible shock to you." I just couldn't bring myself to say "transition" one more time. As far as I'm concerned, dead is dead.

"Thank you," she said, her lips tightening almost imperceptibly. "It's been several years since we've been divorced, but of course it's still a shock." She took a little breath and let it out, but she managed to keep her tone even and not break eye contact. I had to admire her; she was a pro.

A beat of silence fell between us as I pondered my next question. Asking her how the book signing was going would obviously be too unkind, so I picked up a copy of her latest release. "Your tenth book! Quite an accomplishment."

"Have you read it?"

"Not yet," I admitted. I fumbled in my shoulder bag for my wallet. "I'd like to buy a copy right now, though."

"Oh, don't be silly. I'll give you one. Here, let me sign it." She scribbled her name on the title page with a black Sharpie and handed it back to me. "Not much chance we'll run out of books tonight," she said wryly, looking at the empty store.

"I suppose it's hard to predict how these things will go," I said diplomatically, "and with all the news coverage of Sanjay's death—"

"Yes, exactly," she said, interrupting me. "Who would think he'd find a way to upstage me, even from beyond the grave. Some things never change!"

"What did you say?" She'd blindsided me with that remark, and I didn't have time to cover my shock.

Her eyes widened, and she flushed with embarrassment as she touched my arm. "Oh, god, I never should have said that, Maggie. What was I thinking? You won't use it in your feature, will you?" She rubbed a hand over her eyes for a moment and blinked several times, struggling to compose herself. "The stress of this book tour is really getting to me, I guess. Twelve cities in fifteen days. And as you can see, the turnout has been less than stellar. My publicist was supposed to get me signings in fabulous bookstores like City Lights in San Francisco and Murder on the Beach in Delray. I never thought I'd end up in this burg!"

"It sounds pretty grueling," I agreed.

She grabbed my arm. "Please say you won't use my awful comment about Sanjay. My readers would be horrified to think I could say something so cruel and mean-spirited."

So she was thinking about sales . . . interesting. Maybe she was more like the guru than she wanted to admit.

"Don't worry, I won't use it," I said slowly. "Now, tell me about your book." I whipped out a small notebook and nodded encouragingly. I figured I'd get her talking about her latest self-help tome and then gradually move into her history with Sanjay. Talking about herself would be a good way to get the conversational ball rolling.

I listened while she described her latest inspirational book and how she'd integrated solid psychological concepts with real case histories to make the material come alive. None of it seemed exciting or compelling, and I wondered whether she longed for the days when she and Sanjay wrote books together. Books with legs, as they say in the industry, books that fly off the shelves, skyrocket to success, and make all the best-seller lists.

Who wouldn't long for that? And how angry she must have been when her dreams fell apart and her career took a downward spiral.

I asked a few perfunctory questions about her publishing history, wondering how I could encourage her to talk about Sanjay, when she surprised me by mentioning him.

"I divide my books into BS and AS," she said cryptically.

A wry smile flitted across her sharp features, and her face flushed with amusement.

BS and AS. I was blank for a moment and then grinned. "BS and AS. Got it!" I exclaimed. "Before Sanjay and after Sanjay." She visibly relaxed, enjoying her own joke, and I waited a beat before adding, "All the books you cowrote with Sanjay are still in print, aren't they?"

She frowned and pivoted in her chair to grab a hardcover book from a nearby shelf. "They're all doing well, still hitting the best-seller lists," she said ruefully. "I hate to admit it, but the numbers are much better than the numbers I'm getting on my own. And look at the covers! I'm afraid this says it all. It's beyond insulting!" She held up a copy of *Healing Hearts*, cowritten with Sanjay Gingii.

She tapped the glossy cover with a long magenta-colored fingernail, and her chin jutted forward, the muscles in her jaw tightening. Something in her expression made me go cold inside.

"*Healing Hearts*," I said mildly. "I remember this one. I read it when it first came out. In fact, I used it in one of my couples' counseling groups. This is the first book you wrote with Sanjay, isn't it?"

"You've done your homework." She looked pleased, and then her face clouded, her dark eyes turning stony. "But as you can see, they've repackaged it. It's the same book, but they gave it a completely different cover and a new design."

"Ah," I said, wondering where she was going with this. "Still the same title . . ."

"Yes, but look at our names!" she prodded. "It's simply outrageous." She arched an eyebrow and her lips thinned, giving her a strangely predatory look. "It certainly shows who's the top dog, doesn't it?" She leaned toward me, her voice sliced with bitterness, and I found myself drawing back in my seat.

I glanced at the book. Sanjay's name was plastered across the cover in giant letters, taking up the top half of the book. The title was in the middle. And Lenore's name was tucked way down low at the bottom, in tiny letters. It was as though she was an afterthought, like a ghostwriter. It must have been irksome for her, to say the least. "They seem to have put your name in the smallest font possible," I said sympathetically.

"That's an understatement," she snapped. "If my name were any smaller, it would be on the inside of the book!" She turned the book facedown on the table as if she couldn't bear the sight of it.

"And your agent can't do anything about it, I suppose?" I was eager to keep her talking, hoping her anger at Sanjay might cause her to slip up and reveal something I could use.

"Nothing. The man is useless. Sanjay kept my original agent when we parted company." She snorted. "Along with a big chunk of my corporation. He might as well have rolled a Brink's truck right up to my bank account and emptied it. He took two of the houses and three of the cars." Her right eye twitched, a nervous tic, I decided. "And a large portion of my career and following. I've never regained the momentum I had in the old days."

I raised my eyebrows. Now that Sanjay was gone, I wondered what would happen to the royalties on those earlier books. Would they revert to Lenore, or would they become part of the Sanjay Gingii estate? I couldn't think of any diplomatic way to ask her, so instead I said, "Is Lakeville the first stop on the Florida section of your book tour?"

"Oh, heavens no," she said carelessly. "I was in a department store in Boca earlier in the week and a big chain bookstore in Palm Beach yesterday. Of course, none of it really mattered, because I didn't get any good crowds. I didn't sell a single book in Boca. An old lady came up to me at the book signing and asked me where the ladies' room was." She snorted derisively. "I suppose the publisher won't make the mistake of sending me on a book tour again."

So Lenore was in the area the night Sanjay was killed. Could she have slipped up the stairs at the Seabreeze to confront him, and had the meeting turned deadly? It was certainly a possibility. I wondered whether Sanjay's death would breathe new life into her stalled career. Maybe she could even write a tell-all book about life with the guru. Who knew?

We chatted about books and the self-help movement for another twenty minutes, and I told Lenore I would include her in a self-help weekend we were planning at the station. She seemed to accept my cover story and thanked me warmly for driving over to see her.

I was saying my good-byes when her cell phone rang. She turned away from me to grab it, and I immediately sensed that the call was important.

"Sorry, I have to take this; it's my agent," she said, excitedly hitting a button.

"I'll be in touch." I started to gather up my things but took my time, hoping I could hear a little of the conversation.

"Oh, really?" she said into the cell, her voice vibrating with excitement. For the moment, she sounded young and girlish. "I'm just amazed. This certainly changes everything. This is more than I could have hoped for. It's a really good sign, don't you think?" She suddenly noticed that I was dawdling and flashed me an irritated look.

I gave her a cheery wave and quickly made my exit.

So Lenore had just received some very good news, I decided on the drive back to Cypress Grove. The call had been from her agent, so that meant it had something to do with her career.

I had absolutely no proof, but I just knew that somehow or other, Lenore was going to profit big-time from Guru Sanjay's death.

Chapter 10

It was dusk when I pulled up in front of my town house, and I sat in the car for a moment with the windows wide-open, enjoying the soft evening air scented with honeysuckle and roses.

I reached into the glove box and added Lenore's name to my notebook. I was keeping track of everyone I talked to—describing their relationship to Sanjay, why they might be involved with his death, and how they could profit from it. At the moment, all I had was a handful of names and a few suspicious comments, probably not enough to interest Martino.

My only hope of clearing Lark's name was to connect the dots and point the cops in the direction of the real killer. I was chewing on the tip of my ballpoint, mulling over the possibilities, when I spotted Ted Rollins striding purposefully into the Seabreeze Inn next door.

"Ted!" I cried, bounding out of my car. I slammed the car door and hurried to catch up with him.

He frowned, peering into the darkness, and then his face broke into a welcoming grin. "Maggie! Come in for a nightcap." He gave me a quick hug, wrapped his arm around my waist, and ushered me into the wide veranda of the inn. His touch felt warm and comforting, but as always, I marveled at the complete lack of chemistry between us.

Hugging Ted is a lot like hugging Pugsley, except Ted smells like breath mints and Pugsley smells like liver snacks.

"Are you busy with something? You don't usually work in the evening." Ted has an oceanfront condo, and he makes it a point to leave everything to the inn's night staff once his workday is over.

"Something came up tonight," he said lightly. "That annoying detective—"

"Martino?" I kept my voice level, but my heart did a little flip-flop just the same.

"That's the one. He called me at home half an hour ago and asked me to save some audience evaluation forms from the conference. I figured I'd better find them and put them someplace safe before Housekeeping throws them out tomorrow. Martino's coming by first thing in the morning to pick them up. I don't feel like having him prowling around the hotel, so I plan on leaving them at the front desk. With any luck, I won't have to talk to him at all."

"Audience evaluation forms?" I was baffled. "Where did they come from? And why would Martino care about them in a murder investigation?"

"Beats me. He seems to think they're important, though. The conference organizer passed them out with the registration packets, and then in all the confusion over the guru's death"—he shrugged—"no one ever thought to collect them. They're probably still up in the Magnolia Ballroom."

He paused for a moment, gesturing to the cushy wicker gliders and rocking chairs on the wide-planked porch. It was a peaceful spot, with baskets of lush ferns hanging from the rafters and porcelain pots of primroses artfully arranged between the graceful chairs and end tables. "Want to sit out here and have some wine? It's a nice night."

"Sure." I dropped gratefully into the glider, my mind whirling with possibilities, while he hurried inside to get our drinks. So Martino was coming by the Seabreeze tomorrow morning—interesting! And I'd read in a WYME news report that there was going to be a sunrise memorial service for Sanjay, right before everyone headed back to South Beach.

I'd have to make sure Cyrus agreed to let me cover it for the station. I wondered whether I could find a way to interview a few more members of Team Sanjay at the memorial service. With any luck, Olivia would be there and I could find out whether she really was next in line to be Sanjay's assistant, or whether this was just wishful thinking, as Miriam Dobosh had suggested.

"Found them!" Ted said, breaking into my thoughts, waving a sheaf of papers. "I don't think Martino's going to find them very interesting, though. I only glanced at a few, but they seem to be positive. It looks like the audience really loved Sanjay."

"Somebody didn't," I said thoughtfully. "Can I take a look at them?"

"Help yourself," he said, laying them on the glass-topped wicker coffee table. I'd just started to leaf through them when Ted was called away to deal with a late arrival, a middle-aged couple named Parker, in matching Florida T-shirts, who insisted on seeing both of the garden rooms before checking in. Ted shot a helpless look in my direction and herded them up to the second floor. I smiled at him and went back to my reading.

Ted was right: The audience evaluation forms were all wildly complimentary, except for one that chilled me to the bone. It was unsigned, and the writer clearly wasn't a fan of Guru Sanjay—hatred and venom practically rose off the paper. It was hard to read in the dim light of the porch, but a few words jumped out at me, followed by a flurry of exclamation points. "Charlatan! Con Man! Fraud!! Your day will come!!!"

I sat back, stunned. I had to get a copy of this piece of paper—and fast. Once Martino got ahold of it, it would officially become evidence and I'd never get a peek at it again.

Ted was still busy with the Parkers, and no one was manning the front desk. I slipped the form into my pocket, strolled into the lobby, and, after making sure no one was in the office, slapped the page on the copy machine. I heard Ted coming down the stairs just as the copy rolled into my hands, and I shoved it into my pocket, along with the original.

"I was looking for some munchies," I said by way of explanation.

"I've got a jar of those pistachio nuts you like in the kitchen. Make yourself comfortable. I'll bring them out on the porch, along with a bottle of wine."

I returned to the glider, slipped the original form into the pile with the others, and swung back and forth a little, lost in thought. I was pondering my next move when Ted joined me.

"Finally got them settled," he said, easing himself into a chair. "What a pair! They couldn't decide if they wanted the white room with the blue-tiled bathroom or the yellow room with the green-tiled bathroom. She wanted white; he wanted yellow. It was like trying to hammer out a Middle East peace accord."

I smiled to show I absolutely understood the craziness of hotel guests.

"Interesting reading," I said, patting the pile of audience evaluations. "But nothing out of the ordinary." Ted nodded. "I didn't think you'd find anything significant." He paused to sip his wine, looking out at the darkening sky. "You didn't happen to come across one from Kathryn Sinclair, did you?" he said, sitting up a little straighter.

"No, who is she?" I pulled the papers onto my lap and began riffling through them a second time. I heard a scuffling sound in the darkness and wondered whether one of Ted's many cats was out there. Funny, but I had the eerie feeling someone was watching me.

"She's the proverbial fly in the ointment. Probably the one person in the group who isn't a Sanjay fan. I forgot to tell you about her, but she was having a screaming match with that woman who was Guru Sanjay's assistant. Miriam something-or-other."

"Miriam Dobosh," I said excitedly. "Why was Kathryn Sinclair arguing with Miriam?" I finished flipping through the evals but didn't see anything from her. Either she hadn't attended the conference or she didn't bother filling out the audience evaluation. Or . . . she'd written the threatening anonymous note I'd just copied. In any case, I needed to find Kathryn Sinclair and talk with her.

"I didn't get all the details, but apparently Mrs. Sinclair's daughter went to one of those weekend marathons Sanjay puts on. The ones out on the West Coast."

"Get Real and Feel It!" I murmured. "I've heard about them; they sound awful. They've been condemned by all the mainstream psychological associations, you know. The weekend marathons were probably big moneymakers for Sanjay, but they can be a disaster for people who are emotionally fragile. They can actually be very dangerous."

Ted nodded. "Well, this one sounded like it was pretty confrontational. Mrs. Sinclair said that her daughter wasn't allowed to have anything to eat or drink all day, even though she's a diabetic. Plus, the leader and the group members verbally attacked her. She was in tears the whole time."

"It always amazes me that anyone would pay to go to them," I murmured. "And not only do they deprive you of food and water; they don't even let you take bathroom breaks." I shuddered at the thought.

"What's the point behind it?" Ted asked. "It sounds wacky."

"The idea is that if you're miserable and in physical distress, all your defenses will be down and you'll have some sort of epiphany. At least, that's the philosophy behind it. It's an old idea; it goes back to the California encounter groups in the sixties. Guru Sanjay was the only person who still offered them."

Ted raised his eyebrows. "Does it ever work?"

"Not as far as I know." Sanjay's encounter weekends sounded like a Gilligan's Island version of psychotherapy. *No phone, no light, no motor cars, not a single luxury . . .* I turned my attention back to Ted, who was giving me a speculative look. "So tell me what happened with Mrs. Sinclair's daughter. Did she walk out?"

"Not quite. It seems that she already had some pretty serious emotional problems to begin with and the marathon weekend just put her right over the edge. She collapsed from the strain and had to be rushed to a hospital for hypoglycemia and dehydration. Mrs. Sinclair is still furious over it and was talking about a lawsuit against the corporation. You know, hit them where it hurts, and everyone knows Sanjay Gingii, Limited, has deep pockets."

"Is Mrs. Sinclair still here at the hotel? I'd love to talk to her." I tried to keep my expression neutral, but my nerves were zinging with excitement. Had I just found suspect number four?

"I think so," Ted said slowly. "You can probably see her if you attend that sunrise service tomorrow morning."

"I'll be there!" I assured Ted.

Chapter 11

I spotted Nick in the garden of the Seabreeze Inn the next morning. He was squinting into the bright sunlight and scarfing down a bran muffin without spilling a drop of the frosty mimosa balanced on top of his notebook. (Reporters and free food—what can I tell you? Yin and yang.)

It was a beautiful clear day, the sky enamel blue with a couple of fat clouds on the horizon. The perfect day for a funeral. Er, transition.

Ted and Team Sanjay had gone all out to make this a memorable memorial service, planting a podium and microphone in front of a flamingo pink hibiscus bush at the back of the garden. The flagstone walkway was strewn with ivory rose petals, and a white silk tent was set up to protect the Sanjay-ites from the morning sun. Two giant pots filled with white calla lilies flanked an oversize photo of Guru Sanjay, who looked twenty years younger, had a body like Mark Wahlberg, and was Photoshopped down to his fluorescent white teeth. At least Sanjay had kept his veneers up, right till the end.

The perfect photo op, I decided. The whole garden had a

stagy look to it, as if it were part of a theatrical set. *Sayonara Sanjay, the Musical*. At least fifty chairs were arranged on the grass, and almost all of them were already occupied by grieving followers. Most of them were clad in snowy white, reportedly Sanjay's favorite color.

Miriam Dobosh was flitting around like a bird of prey, planting poles with bright silk banners flying from them at the perimeter of the garden. I noticed that she was wearing a white cotton pique pantsuit with purple trim, and I wondered whether the wardrobe choice was driven by some unconscious desire to attain royal status. After all, purple was the color of kings in ancient times, so perhaps she figured she was next in line for the Sanjay throne. (Or maybe my psychology training was getting the better of me and the purple trim meant nothing at all. After all, even Freud said that sometimes a cigar is just a cigar.)

I was puzzled by the banners—fluttery squares of orange and yellow silk with strange words stenciled on them. Words from a foreign language, known only to Sanjay-ites? Or maybe they were just acronyms. I made a mental note to check them out.

A towering pyramid of Sanjay's books was artfully displayed on an antique refectory table covered with a bright blue Indian batik, and people were lining up to buy them. One of the acolytes was thoughtfully sticking an autographed bookplate inside the front cover of each volume. I'm sure if there was a way for Sanjay to sign autographs from beyond the grave, he would have done so. From a marketing point of view, the bookplates were the next best thing. CDs and workbooks were stacked in a neat pile, and a price list was helpfully displayed on an easel nearby.

Sanjay the guru might be gone, but Sanjay the brand was still going strong.

"What's with the banners? It looks like a Renaissance fair,"
I said to Nick, who had finished the muffin and moved on to
the basket of tempting little orange and walnut scones, another of Ted's specialties. I noticed that Nick had loaded his
plate with pastries and sliced kiwi and mango, as if he hadn't
eaten in three months.

Nick caught my glance and sheepishly put three almond
tarts back on the tray.

"It's Kabbalah," he said between mouthfuls, looking mournfully at the scones as if they were calling to him.

"Kabbalah? As in Madonna-wearing-a-red-string-bracelet
Kabbalah?"

Nick nodded. "I think so. See that one over there? It says
'tikkun.' That's from the Kabbalah. It means two opposing
desires."

"Like the superego and the id," I murmured.

"You got me there." Nick took a hefty swig of mimosa
and practically smacked his lips in enjoyment.

"Freud," I said absently. "It's the basis for his psycho-
dynamic theory. The id represents all our unconscious wishes
and hidden desires—it's what drives us to act, sometimes irre-
sponsibly, or even self-destructively. If you have dark secrets, they'd be found in the id. The superego is what keeps
us in check. It's all the rules and regulations society imposes
on us, plus, of course, our own moral values and conscience.
So the id and the superego balance everything out. Sort of
like this *tikkun* you mentioned."

"Whatever you say, professor." Nick politely stifled a yawn.

"Sorry," I said, flushing a little. I have to remember that
most people don't find psychoanalytic theory as fascinating
as I do.

"Speaking of dark secrets," Nick murmured, moving a
little closer to me and lowering his voice, "there's something

you should know about your friend Lark." He shot me a speculative look. "Or maybe you already do."

I felt a little twinge in the pit of my stomach. Whatever Nick was about to say, it couldn't be good. Nick's hazel eyes had clouded, and a muscle in his jaw was starting to give a little telltale twitch. Uh-oh.

I shook my head wordlessly, and I felt my stomach tighten with trepidation.

"I didn't think you did." He drew in a long breath and let it out slowly. "Okay. She has a police record."

"What?" I reached for a flute of cranberry juice, and my hand trembled, sloshing a few drops of wine-colored liquid over the ivory tablecloth. "That's impossible. If Lark were a criminal, I'd certainly know it. I see her every day, for heaven's sake." I looked around quickly to make sure no one had overheard him. "There must be some mistake, Nick. She's as wholesome as white bread." Okay, not the best analogy, but my mind was reeling at the news that I'd been living with a female Charles Manson.

Nick quirked an eyebrow. "Sorry, but there's no mistake." His tone was tinged with sympathy, and his eyes locked onto mine. "I'm an investigative reporter; that's what I do, Maggie. I dig up facts people would rather have stay buried. I know you're her friend, but you can't hide your head in the sand on this one. I've got the goods on her, so that means Cypress Grove's finest do, too."

"Oh, no," I moaned. Lark a criminal? Was Lark even her real name? Come to think of it, I'd never seen her driver's license, and all her mail was addressed to L. Merriweather. Why would you go by an initial?

A neon sign over my head flashed: ALIAS. ALIAS. ALIAS.

But her name wasn't the issue; the crime was. What had she done?

Nick was more than ready to fill in the blanks. "I did a quick background check and came up with some interesting facts." He put down his plate, handed me his mimosa, and whipped out a tiny notebook, just like the one Martino used. My blood froze. Suddenly, it all seemed real, not hypothetical.

"Let's start with her name. You knew her name wasn't Lark, right?"

"Not really."

"C'mon, Maggie, who would name a kid Lark?"

"Have you heard about Moon Unit Zappa and Pilot Inspektor? Or Apple and Moxie Crimefighter?"

"Whatever," Nick said dismissively.

"Lark's real name is Lilith Merriweather."

"Lilith?" My mouth gaped open like a flounder's. "She doesn't look like a Lilith," I said idiotically.

"That's the least of her worries. She's from Flint, Michigan, and she was arrested on an aggravated assault charge five years ago. She slugged a guy in a bar, and because of the victim's character she was able to plea-bargain down to simple assault. Really did a number on him—dislocated his jaw and knocked out three teeth." Nick squinted to read his scribbled notes. "Plus multiple contusions and lacerations when his head hit the mirror hanging over the bar. The vic had surgery on his temporomandibular joint, had three herniated disks, and was in traction for a week."

"Lark did all that?" My mouth was so dry I could hardly force the words out. "She's so tiny, so petite. I just can't believe it."

Nick gave a little laugh. "Believe it. She may be tiny, but she's tough. Did you know she has a black belt in karate?"

"Karate?" I gulped. "I knew she had training in martial arts, but I thought it was tae kwon do. The whole idea is passive resistance. Lark always says the trick is to use your opponent's strength against him. It's not aggressive at all; it's a self-defense technique."

"Believe me, there was nothing passive about the attack. The only reason she didn't have to serve serious jail time is that the guy was a drug runner and the jury didn't have much sympathy for him." Nick slapped the notebook closed and grabbed a fizzy peach cocktail from one of the servers who was walking around with a tray. "I'd hate to meet your roommate in a dark alley."

Nick wandered away to interview some Sanjay-ites, and I was alone with my whirling thoughts. Words were flying through my brain like a meteor shower. Aggravated assault. Contusions. Lacerations. Was Lark really capable of harming another human being? How was that possible? She picks up worms from the sidewalk and places them gently in the grass, so they don't broil to death in the Florida sun. She lets Pugsley sleep in her bed even though she's so allergic to dog fur, she has to use an inhaler.

Lark involved in a barroom brawl? Impossible!

I remembered how she'd described the scene with Sanjay in the hotel room. She said he'd lunged at her and made a disgusting pass, and she'd pushed him away. But it had been an act of self-defense, and it had seemed completely justifiable to me.

Or had she just been putting a good spin on it? Was she really that calculating and manipulative? How could I have missed that trait in her personality after all the long heart-to-hearts we'd had?

I was still trying to wrap my mind around the idea that Lark had a criminal record when a middle-aged woman approached me. She was attractive, probably early sixties, but thanks to some surgical enhancement, she could have easily passed for late forties. Her face and neck were smooth and unlined, but the hands are always the giveaway. Ask any cosmetic surgeon.

She was wearing a beige custom-tailored Armani suit paired with a white silk blouse and Frappuccino-colored Chanel pumps, and she carried a clutch bag probably made from an endangered reptile species. Her thick auburn hair was pulled back into a loose chignon at the nape of her neck, an excellent choice for south Florida weather. If it hadn't been for the anonymous dead reptile, the outfit would have been perfect.

"Dr. Walsh? Mr. Rollins pointed you out to me." Her voice was low and husky, feminine but with a touch of authority. I immediately thought, *Steel magnolia*.

"Yes, but please call me Maggie."

"Kathryn Sinclair." She extended a delicate hand. She had long, French-manicured nails and was sporting an emerald ring the size of a walnut.

Kathryn Sinclair! I nearly swooned. The investigative gods were surely with me, because she was next on my list of subjects to interview. I couldn't wait to pick up where Ted Rollins had left off. My mind darted back to our conversation on the porch of the Seabreeze. Ted had told me that a guest named Kathryn Sinclair detested the guru and had argued with Miriam Dobosh.

I could hardly believe that a new lead was dropping into my lap.

"Can we talk for a moment? I heard your radio interview with that man, that dreadful man," she said, her voice faltering. "I wanted to call in, but I didn't trust myself to speak." Just for second, her eyes blurred with tears and her mouth trembled.

"You heard my show with Guru Sanjay?"

"Guru Sanjay," she said sarcastically, her eyebrows arching. Her mouth twisted and she permitted herself a ladylike little snort, deep in her throat. "Well, Maggie, he can call himself whatever he likes, but that wasn't his real name, you know." She paused, not making eye contact, gazing into the distance, and her lips quivered a little. I could see that she was making a monumental effort to compose herself, and I nodded encouragingly, hoping she would go on.

This is the strategy I always used with my clients when they were about to divulge sensitive material during a session. Timing is everything. Jump in too fast with a comment or an interpretation and the moment is past. Then they clam up on you and whatever they were about to reveal is pushed back into the murky depths of their psyche and lost forever.

A long beat passed between us. "You knew him?" I ventured. I spoke softly, not wanting to interrupt the story she seemed so eager to tell me.

"I know quite a bit about him." She looked directly at me then, and her pale green eyes suddenly blazed with an inner light. She grabbed my hand and squeezed my fingers so tightly, I winced. "You see, Maggie, Guru Sanjay killed my daughter."

Chapter 12

"He killed her?" I blurted out. This was the last thing in the world I was expecting, and I took a quick breath, my chest tight. A chill snaked up my spine and my pulse ratcheted up a notch. I had to resist the impulse to yank back my hand.

"Well, not physically." She finally released my fingers from her death grip and gave a dismissive little wave. "In some ways, what he did is even worse, because he killed her spirit, her soul," she said, her eyes drilling into mine. "Do you know what I mean, Maggie?"

"He harmed her in some way psychologically." I remembered what Ted had told me about the marathon encounter group session and what an ordeal it had been for her.

"Yes, that's it. He ruined both our lives, because I'll never be the same, either. Sometimes I don't know how I'm going to go on. There are days I can hardly drag myself out of bed."

Her words ran together and ended in a wrenching sob. Suddenly she reached out, her jeweled hand leaning heavily on the buffet table. The color had suddenly faded from her cheeks, and she'd turned such a deathly shade of white, I was afraid she might pass out.

I grabbed her elbow to steady her. "It's the heat, Kathryn," I said tactfully. "Let's sit down somewhere where we can talk privately." I motioned toward the umbrella tables set up on the flagstone patio outside the Seabreeze breakfast room. It was secluded, and the lush wall of arborvitae muffled the sounds of the Sanjay-ites who had started some eerie chant in a minor key.

"I don't know where to start," she said, settling herself on a black wrought-iron patio chair. A waiter stopped, and I ordered two club sodas with lime.

"Start anywhere," I prompted her. I knew the important thing was for her to tell the story in her own way and her own time.

"I had such high hopes for Sarah when she first told me about the guru," she said ruefully. "Sarah was in her first year of college and having a hard time adjusting. I thought it was just the usual adjustment that most kids go through, you know, first time away from home. She's an only child, and I suppose I've been a bit overprotective with her." She shot me a challenging look, as if daring me to disagree with her.

"It's normal for mothers to want to protect their children," I said lightly. "What happened exactly?"

Kathryn drew in a long breath, her green eyes filled with sadness. "She had read one of Sanjay's silly books, and she was just enthralled by him. I figured it was harmless, the sort of psychobabble that you see everywhere." I figured this wouldn't be the right time to tell her I had written a pop-psych book myself. Unlike Sanjay's tome, it had plummeted to well-deserved obscurity.

She propped her chin on her elbow and fixed her gaze on me. "But then it got out of hand. She seemed almost obsessively devoted to him. She bought all his books and tapes and even had a poster of that loathsome man in her room. As if he were a rock star! Can you imagine such a thing?"

I shrugged. "He seems to attract some pretty devoted followers." *And he certainly loved publicity*, I added silently. I noticed that garden was thick with mourners, mostly women, all wearing virginal white dresses. They couldn't all have attended the conference. Word must have gotten out about the memorial service, because I saw Ted hastily setting up a few more rows of folding chairs, and the catering staff was bringing out more trays of cakes and fruits.

"She went to a weekend retreat on the California coast. It was over her summer vacation from college. It sounded harmless enough, although it did have a rather retro flavor to it. It reminded me of one of those encounter groups, you know, the kind that were popular back in the sixties?" Kathryn gave a sad little smile. "I told Sarah I thought she was wasting her money, but she swore it was just what she needed. She said it would 'open up her spirit' and that she would be completely transformed by the experience."

"What happened?" The server silently placed our club sodas on the table. Kathryn was so caught up in her story, I don't think she even noticed.

"I'm still not clear on the details." She blew out a little puff of breath. "Well, for one thing, Sarah is a diabetic; did I tell you that?" I shook my head. "She has juvenile diabetes, type one."

"That can be serious," I murmured sympathetically.

"Very serious," Kathryn said. "She's what they call a brittle diabetic, and her blood sugar can suddenly plummet with no warning, you know? It can be life-threatening."

"And they knew all this? The people organizing the meals at the conference?" I immediately thought of liability issues.

Had she told them she was a diabetic? Had they provided the proper food for her? Was medical help available on the site? It seemed surprising that such a well-oiled machine as Team Sanjay wouldn't have explored all those possibilities and taken legal steps to protect themselves.

"She wrote it all out on the form. I insisted she make a copy of the contract before she submitted it with her check." A smart move, I thought. My instincts had been right about Kathryn—she was definitely someone to be reckoned with.

"And then something happened? She had some sort of medical crisis at this retreat?"

"They deprived her of food and water. Can you imagine? She had taken some diabetic granola bars with her, but they took them away from her, as if they were contraband!" Her eyes blazed at the memory. "And then she and the others were all forced to sit in a circle for hours without moving, without even taking"—she paused delicately—"a bathroom break."

"Sounds awful." *And dangerous. Especially for someone with health issues.*

"It gets even worse," she said darkly. "After hours of this silly navel-gazing, or soul-searching, or whatever they call it, everyone had to get up on a stage one at a time. The rest of the group would shout at them, taunt them, tell them they were worthless. Verbal abuse. Each person had to just stand there and endure it, until the leader finally decided they 'got it' and could step down."

"What were they supposed to 'get'? I wonder."

Kathryn shook her head. "I have no idea. But you see how crazy the whole thing was. Sarah ended up collapsing onstage and being rushed by ambulance to the local hospital; she's been ill ever since. Both mentally and physically."

"I've read about those groups, but I've never been to one."

"Well, it was very irresponsible, and I called Guru Sanjay to tell him so. Naturally, he has a wall of people around him, and I had to talk to one of his underlings, that dreadful Dobosh woman. She was completely unsympathetic and said there was nothing they could do. She even suggested that my daughter must have had emotional problems to start with, and reminded me that Sarah had signed a liability waiver."

"So you never had a chance to talk to Sanjay directly?"

She hesitated. "No. I never did."

I leaned back in my chair then, while Kathryn sipped her club soda. The sunlight was filtering through the banyan trees, and the white jasmine creeping over a wooden trellis was giving off a delicious scent. It would have been a beautiful scene if it hadn't been completely overrun with those annoying Sanjay-ites.

Olivia Riggs approached me, looking considerably more cheerful than the last time I'd seen her, crying her eyes out in the ladies' room. "Maggie Walsh? A reporter told me your name. I'm Olivia Riggs. I'm so sorry for the meltdown the other day," she said in a low voice. "I was just in shock at Sanjay's death. He was my mentor, and I thought my career was over. I thought my whole life was over." She shook her head as if trying to dispel negative thoughts.

"No apology necessary. It must have been very difficult for you," I murmured.

"It was." She looked glum for a moment, but then her expression brightened. "But something amazing happened. Remember what Sanjay always said—when one door closes, another one opens? That's exactly what happened for me!" She gave a wide smile. "I met somebody at the Seabreeze who offered me a marketing job with a string of health spas in California. I'll be based in Laguna Beach and making twice the salary I was making here. Is that lucky or what?"

"I'd say that's very lucky indeed."

"Thanks for being so understanding." Olivia touched my arm and flitted away, looking young and carefree in her flirty cotton sundress. *From the depths of despair to Laguna Beach*, I thought. Interesting.

I could see Miriam Dobosh fiddling with the microphone on the podium, probably preparing to make some sort of address, and I figured this might be a good time to make my exit. Kathryn and I had exchanged business cards, and there didn't seem to be any reason to prolong the interview. There were probably more questions I should ask her, but they could wait.

But there was one last thing I had to know.

"Kathryn," I said slowly, "I'm puzzled about something. Why did you come here today? If Guru Sanjay was the person responsible for harming your daughter, why would you turn up at his memorial service? Surely not to pay your respects?"

I let the question dangle while I pushed my hair out of my face. I could feel a thin sheen of perspiration forming on my temples, and I wished I could look as cool and collected as the woman sitting across from me.

Kathryn drained her club soda and stood up. I was relieved to see that a hint of color had returned to her face. Maybe telling me the story had been cathartic for her, because her expression had brightened, and just for a moment, she seemed almost lighthearted.

"Pay my respects? Oh, you can be damn sure I didn't come here for that, Maggie." She tossed her head back and I saw a look of defiance cross her pale green eyes. She leaned

across the table, her eyes fixed so intently on mine, I was starting to feel nervous. "I just wanted to make sure that bastard
was really dead."

"Well, butter my butt and call me a biscuit! She really said
that?" Vera Mae was bustling around the studio, doing her
usual sound checks before the afternoon show. I'd come back
to the station early and was munching on a cinnamon bagel
(proving once again, you can never have too many carbs!)
before checking my notes for the day's show.

"Kathryn Sinclair really said it, but that doesn't prove anything, you know. She was speaking metaphorically, and even
if she wasn't, making sure someone's dead isn't exactly an
admission of guilt."

"I still think you should call that Martino fellow and tell
him to check out her alibi, if she even *has* one," Vera Mae
said. "It's a well-known fact that murderers often attend the
funerals of their victims." Vera Mae is a big fan of *CSI*, *Law
& Order*, and *Criminal Minds*. "Another thing—it's a darn
shame you didn't get her comments on tape. Haven't I been
asking you to get batteries for that little recorder you carry
around?"

"Guilty as charged," I agreed. "You've asked me about a
dozen times. I'm not sure what the Florida law is on taping
conversations without permission, and anyway, she didn't
really say anything incriminating." I finished the last crumbs
of the bagel and flipped through my day planner..

The afternoon show was going to be a snooze, I thought,
spirits sinking: Cecilia Gregg from the Cypress Grove Hor-
ticultural Society on the psychological benefits of gardening. I saw from her bio that her specialty was tubers. I had
no idea what a tuber was and had even less desire to hit
Google and find out.

My experience with gardening is somewhat limited. When I first moved into the condo, I planted some luscious pink and white begonias in the long wooden box sitting on the edge of the patio. They looked adorable, but the little darlings must have made a suicide pact during the night, because they all were dead by morning. Lark swears they picked up negative vibes from me, but I don't think that's possible. I'm thinking they were psychologically unstable from the start and when I transplanted them from their little garden-store pots it pushed them right over the edge.

"Sounds pretty suspicious to me," Vera Mae continued. "Going to a funeral just to make sure someone's dead. Besides, it would give you an excuse to call that nice young detective, not that I think you really need one. A young feller like that, single and all, could probably use a home-cooked dinner. If I were thirty years younger, I'd invite him over myself. There's nothing like a platter of chicken and biscuits to win a guy over, with a mess of greens on the side and a nice blueberry cobbler for dessert."

"I'll keep that in mind," I murmured.

"You young girls never learn," Vera Mae retorted. "The way to a man's heart really is through his stomach. Ask any gal over fifty, and she'll tell you."

An inner office line buzzed and Vera Mae turned to answer it. She clamped the handset to her ear, listened to a voice on the other end, and frowned. "You don't say. Well, that's a fine kettle of fish. All righty, I'll tell Maggie and we'll come up with something else. We always do."

"Bad news?"

"That was Irina. Cecilia has the flu and can't do the show today. She plumb forgot to cancel," she said, raising her eyebrows. She was glancing out the big double window that looked out onto the parking lot. It was cracked open at the bottom, and the buzz of cicadas drifted into the studio. "I figure we can always do an open call-in show, or maybe do a repeat of one of your last shows, or . . . Oh, lordie, is that who I think it is?"

Vera Mae broke off suddenly, her voice tripping into an uncharacteristic falter. She wrenched her gaze away from the window and stared at me.

Her eyes were bulging as if she were auditioning for a Wes Craven flick. If this was a slasher movie, this would be the point where Vera Mae would have just learned the terrifying phone calls were coming from *inside* the house.

"Vera Mae, for heaven's sake! Who's out there? What did you see?" For some reason, Vera Mae's anxiety was infectious. I sat frozen to my chair, heart pounding, a horrible feeling of impending doom spreading over me. Either all those grande lattes with cinnamon had set my nerve endings atwitter or I was teetering on the edge of a major panic attack.

"Maggie, I don't know how to tell you this," she began.

A wild gulp of laughter rose in my throat, and I tamped it down. "Just spit it out, Vera Mae. You're making me nervous."

"Brace yourself, Maggie, and take a look outside." I reluctantly pulled myself out of the chair and walked shakily to the window. "See that woman in the pink halter dress and those big Jackie-O sunglasses? Goshalmighty, I think that's your momma come to pay us a visit."

I peered out the window and my heart dropped into my stomach. The platinum hair, the swaying hips, a voluptuous frame delicately balanced on four-inch stiletto sling-backs.

Goshalmighty, I think Vera Mae was right.

Lola was back in town.

Chapter 13

"Kisses, everyone! Kisses!" Lola burst into the studio the way she did everything.

Full throttle.

She leaned in to give a startled Vera Mae an air kiss before enveloping me in a quick hug and love bombing me with a choking cloud of Arpège. Then she folded her fifty-eight-year-old—but still gorgeous—legs into a swivel chair and checked out the studio.

I know the tabloids are fond of saying some celeb or other is a "force of nature," but in Lola's case, it is absolutely true. My mother, Lola Walsh, has the style and panache of one of those long-dead heroines of the silver screen. The ones you see late at night on Turner Classic Movies, when it's just you in your jammies with a pint of Chunky Monkey watching those feisty heroines of yesteryear.

Think Dorothy Lamour, Jane Russell, or even Lola's icon, Marilyn (Monroe, not Manson).

Everything about Lola is big. Big hair (Clairol Blissfully Blonde), big lips (Sally Hansen Lip Plumpers), and a big voice. ("I'm not loud, dahling, I'm *projecting*, as we theatre folks like to say. As the great director Hal Prince once told me,

'They have to be able to hear you all the way in the back row of the mezzanine, Lola.'")

Talk about larger than life. Take a Barbie doll's measurements, calibrate them to human scale—voilà! Lola in the flesh. Her shocking-pink dress, very retro, very seventies, was hugging her body as if it were liquid polymer.

"What brings you to town, Mom?" My mother lives north of Miami and ventures to Cypress Grove only when she feels a compelling need to shop the outlets at Sawgrass Mills. After a tough day of shopping, she sometimes jumps back in the car, heads north on A1A, and spends the night at my condo.

"I have some big auditions coming up, my love, and all my clothes are hopelessly out of date. Well, what I really mean is, they make *me* look out of date. Positively matronly. I have a new agent now, and Edgar thinks that I need to present a more youthful image."

A more youthful image. Vera Mae and I exchanged a look. My mother has never come to terms with the fact that she's "of a certain age," and her wardrobe is either early Nicole Richie or late-night Lindsay Lohan.

She paused, looking around the studio hopefully, and Vera Mae filled the gap.

"My stars, Lola, if you looked any more youthful, you'd be jail bait. What does this Edgar know, anyway? Is he anyone I've heard of?"

Lola wrinkled her nose. Even she knew when a compliment was over the top, although she would certainly give Vera Mae an A for effort. "Edgar Dumont," she said loftily. "He's been a theatrical agent for many years and has only recently become involved with film and television. I believe his first client was James Dean."

"James Dean!" Vera Mae chortled. "That must make him

older than Methuselah. Are you sure he's the right agent for you? And where does he get off telling you that you should look more youthful? He must be pretty long in the tooth himself."

"Well, he's been around for a while," Lola admitted. "But that's a good thing in an agent, being seasoned, I mean. He takes on very few clients, and I was thrilled when he agreed to represent me."

She gave her Victoria's Secret push-up bra a little tug, and her assets threatened to spill out of her sundress. "I had to audition for him in a loft in South Beach last week, surrounded by all these sweet young things. I felt like I'd stumbled into a Hannah Montana look-alike competition." Just for a moment, a sour expression passed over her face. "Anyway, I did Portia's speech from *Merchant of Venice* and blew everyone away. As Edgar said, I really nailed it. I was the only actor he signed that day."

"Really." Vera Mae busied herself with the pile of commercials scheduled for that day. "I don't mean to break up this gabfest," she said, glancing at the clock, "but what do you want to do for the show today? We go live in seven minutes."

I swung around to my desk, suddenly all business. In the excitement of Lola's arrival, I had forgotten all about the missing Cecilia and her tubers.

"Is there a problem?" Lola asked.

Vera Mae grunted. "I'll say. Our guest canceled at the last minute and we don't have anything scheduled for today."

Lola clapped her hands together. "No guest? No problem!" She smiled winningly, like the host of a cheesy late-night infomercial. "Let me be your guest. I can talk about my life in the theatre. I've met all kinds of people, some famous and some not so famous. I've worked with some real characters. I bet your listeners would be fascinated."

"Mom, the topic has to be related to psychology," I protested. Well, at least vaguely related, I thought, thinking of the "You and Your Colon" show we did a few days earlier.

Lola looked stumped. "Psychology? That sounds like a snooze."

"Mom! It's what I do, remember? Or what I did," I said, between gritted teeth.

There was a brief silence, and then Vera Mae snapped her fingers. "You know, we could try something different today. Stir things up a bit, just to keep it interesting. How would you like to be part of the show, Lola?"

"I'm going to be the guest? Fabulous!" Lola was already out of her chair and heading toward the visitor's seat next to the control board.

"Not so fast." Vera Mae blocked her path, clutching a pile of tapes in front of her like a shield. "You know, Lola, I was thinking about all those famous people you've worked with and how you had to get along with them. How would you like to cohost the show today? It'll be a call-in show, and you and Maggie will field questions from the listeners."

"What's the topic?" I asked, feeling alarm bells going off in my gut. I looked at the clock. Three minutes till we went live. Live!

Vera Mae gave a little smile. "Relationships, ladies. Relationships. The good, the bad, the ugly."

Lola's smile lit up the studio. "I love it!" she exclaimed. She was wriggling with excitement like Pugsley does when he hears the telltale crinkly sound of an open bag of potato chips.

Suddenly she gave a little moue of concern and rested her hand lightly on mine, her eyes serious. "But maybe you better let me do most of the talking, Maggie," she said huskily. "After all, I've had three husbands, six fiancés, and more gentleman callers that I can count, so this is really more my area of expertise than yours. No offense, darling."

Gentlemen callers? I vaguely remembered that line from *The Glass Menagerie*, when Mom had played Amanda Wingfield in summer stock in Provincetown many years ago.

Lola gave a breezy smile as Vera Mae handed her an extra headset and I settled down next to her, fiddling with the mike. I noticed the board was already lighting up; we always have a few die-hard fans who are determined to be first in line, even if they don't know what the day's topic will be.

"Live in five!" Vera Mae yelled, dashing around to the production room. I sat up straighter in my chair as Vera Mae pointed at me and silently mouthed, "Go!"

"So the way I look at it, men are like shoes," Lola was saying twenty minutes later in her smoky, theatrical voice. "They may look adorable, but if they don't fit in the beginning, they'll never fit right. Nothing you do will help. You'll curse the day you saw them. I'm afraid the only thing to do, sweetie, is to toss them out and find yourself a new pair." She gave a musical little laugh and paused for a beat. "Does that answer your question, Naomi?"

"It sure does, Miss Lola. Men are like shoes. Gee, I've never looked at it quite that way before."

I bet, I said silently. It was annoying to admit, but all my years of psychological training couldn't match my mother in action—she was a huge success with the audience. Warm, accessible, and witty, she managed to make an immediate connection with each listener. How did she pull it off?

I was in awe—and green with envy. Maybe it was her acting ability, maybe she was genuinely empathic, but Lola was a hit.

If anyone was measuring her Q Score that day, it would have been off the charts.

Meanwhile, my loyal followers were deserting me in droves. After the first few minutes, they didn't bother directing their questions to me; they turned to Lola for help with their problems.

Or maybe I just wasn't at my best. My mind was still going over Guru Sanjay's murder and my meeting with the formidable Kathryn Sinclair. Her anger at Guru Sanjay was palpable, and beneath her stylish exterior, she reminded me of a tigress protecting her young.

Was she capable of murder? My trusty 8-Ball would say: "Signs point to yes." But what did she have to gain from his death, besides revenge? I drew a blank on that one.

And then there was Lenore Cooper, whose A-list shrink status had been usurped by her ex-husband. She might profit from his death, especially if she decided to write a tell-all book. The only trouble with that theory was that Guru Sanjay had dumped her several years ago, so why would she take so long to do him in?

There seemed to be no immediate motive to murder him, or was I missing something? Wouldn't there be more money and more buzz in a tell-all book if Sanjay were still alive? So why would she kill the golden goose, if writing an exposé was her aim?

I was pondering my next move in the murder investigation when I suddenly realized there was a tiny sliver of dead air. Now was the time to jump in with a pithy comment, some keen psychological insight. Nothing came to mind, so a platitude would have to do.

"Um, you know, sometimes it's a mistake to bail out too quickly on a relationship," I fumbled.

Vera Mae locked eyes with me for an instant and then jabbed a button. She must have decided that my inane comment didn't even deserve a follow-up. "Abigail on line three. She has a question for Lola."

Foiled again!

"Lola, I think you were on my favorite soap a few years ago," a female voice raced across the line. "You played Martina on *Troubled Hearts*, didn't you? I'm so excited that you're on the radio today, I can hardly breathe! I watched every single episode of that show."

I rolled my eyes. Forget about *On the Couch with Maggie Walsh*. We had morphed into *Soap Watch with Lola Walsh*.

"Yes, indeed, I played Martina Saint Pierre on *Troubled Hearts*, and it's always nice to be remembered." Lola gave a happy little sigh. "You know, I've been so busy with the theatre lately, I haven't had the chance to do any soaps."

"You were wonderful. And so beautiful," Abigail said in an awestruck tone.

Lola put her hand on her heart, her eyes welling up a little. "I'll always look back fondly on those early days in New York. Acting in the daytime dramas was my first entrée into show business."

"I loved that whole story line with Root and Sledge," Abigail continued. "I cried when Sledge had an affair with the Romanian nanny and didn't tell anyone about it. Not even his own brother, Root."

"Yes, that Sledge," Lola said fondly. "He was quite the scamp. And of course I'm sure you remember that a baby resulted from"—Lola paused delicately—"that dalliance." A long beat. "Baby Giuseppe."

Baby Giuseppe? I raised my eyebrows, but Lola ignored me.

"Hey, I remember that scene!" Vera Mae's face lit up.

"Sledge was stranded at a cabin in Big Sur with the nanny and he had to deliver the baby himself. I always wondered why he never told anyone about it. It was like he forgot the whole thing ever happened."

"Delivering your own baby in a mountain cabin? That seems like a pretty big thing to forget," I interjected. Out of the corner of my eye, I could see Lola perched on the edge of her chair, her mouth open wide like a seagull hoping for a flying carp.

"A lot of our viewers wrote in about that plotline," Lola said disarmingly. "You're right, they did think it was a little far-fetched. Delivering a baby isn't like delivering a pizza, you know." Again, the girlish laugh that sounded like temple bells.

"Exactly!" Abigail agreed. "And it would have stayed a secret forever, except for that whole episode with Carlotta in Genova Hospital. She was out for revenge, right, Lola?"

"She certainly was," Lola said sweetly. "Carlotta never learned that revenge is a dish best served cold."

Hmm. A dish best served cold. My mind had been playing with the notion of revenge, secrets, and the idea of waiting to put the screws to someone. Would that explain Lenore Cooper's timetable for polishing off Guru Sanjay? After all, she had years to watch his meteoric rise to fame while her own career faltered, book sales dropping, speaking gigs tapering off. So was she biding her time, secretly plotting his demise?

Time to get back into my own show. "You know, sometimes we block things from our consciousness," I began. "It can be a defense mechanism, or it can be the result of—"

"And does anyone out there remember how Carlotta finally got her revenge?" Lola asked her new fans in radioland. "This was a key plot point," she explained helpfully.

Vera Mae, who was standing behind the glass window in the control room, chewed on a pencil nub, deep in thought. She looked so intent, you would think Alex Trebek were standing by with a big fat cash prize for the right answer.

"I remember!" Abigail yelled. "Carlotta had a baby with Sledge's twin brother."

"Getting back to our original topic—," I cut in.

But once again, Vera Mae was too quick for me. "Well, folks, we just have time for one more call and then . . . oops, we have to take a commercial break right now!" Vera Mae punched a button on the control panel, yanked off her head-set, and skittered around to our side of the window.

"What a show!" She hugged Lola and said happily, "You know, this past hour just flew by. I think this is the best *Maggie Walsh* show we've ever had!"

I was trying to think of a clever comeback when Cyrus stuck his head in the door, grinning from ear to ear. He gave a big thumbs-up. "Great show, kids! Keep up the good work, Lola. We just may have to hire you! You'd be quite an addition to the WYME team."

Lola was beaming. "Wouldn't that be fun, honey? The two of us working side by side."

Chapter 14

Mom followed me back to the condo, and after arming each of us with an ice-cold Corona with a wedge of lime, I decided to tell her about the murder investigation. She was still flush from her stint as a radio host and was dancing around the room with Pugsley in her arms, doing a modified tango to a Ricky Martin number. Pugsley was thrilled at the attention and licked her nose rapturously at every twirl, glancing at me over her shoulder. He was practically drooling with happiness and was wriggling so hard, I was afraid she might drop him.

Mom was only half listening to my story, but when I got to the part about Lark being pulled in for questioning, she came to an abrupt halt, turned off the radio, and plunked an annoyed Pugsley down on the parquet floor. Shrugging at the fickleness of humans, he trotted off to his dish of kibble.

"And the really shocking thing is that they aren't even looking at other suspects. They've zeroed in on Lark."

"They suspect Lark? Everyone knows that sweet little thing isn't capable of murder! Who's in charge of the investigation? Maybe I can pull some strings. Or at the very least,

I can march down there and give that detective a piece of my mind."

"Mom, that's not a good idea," I said hastily. I could just picture my mother confronting Rafe Martino and shuddered at the visual. "This is a police matter. There's nothing you can add to the case. I only got involved because I'm Lark's roommate. And her friend."

"I did a couple of *Matlock*s, you know," she said, settling herself into a rattan basket chair I'd picked up at a yard sale. It had a green and white cushion silk-screened with palm trees and could have been a knockoff of one of the pieces in the Humphrey Bogart Collection.

"I'm not sure what you're getting at," I prompted her.

"I'm simply saying that I'm clued in to how the legal system works." She was all set to stroll down memory lane, but before she could do a riff on Andy Griffith in his blue and white seersucker suit, I whirled around to cut her off.

"You did some *Matlock*s?" I raised my eyebrows. "This is the first I've ever heard of it."

It's a standing joke in Hollywood that whenever actors want to beef up their résumés, they use *Matlock* as a credit because they figure no one will ever check. After all, they must have taped a zillion *Matlock* shows, so who would know? It's not like anybody's going to call the producer and double-check.

"Well, maybe it was just one *Matlock*," Mom said, back-pedaling quickly. "And it was a guest shot, so I had very little screen time." Now we were getting closer to the truth. If Mom said she had very little screen time, that meant it was a walk-on; she was probably an extra. Or maybe she was an "under five," meaning she had fewer than five lines. An "under five" might be a waitress in a diner, yelling something like, "Two corn beefs on rye, extra mustard and hold the mayo!" Or a receptionist in a medical drama saying, "The doctor can see you now." It's not usually something you highlight on your résumé. In fact, mentioning such a tiny part on your résumé smacks of desperation.

I raised my eyebrows and she chewed thoughtfully on a sourdough pretzel stick. "Actually, I may take *Matlock* off my résumé. It makes me seem a little . . . mature, you know. Maybe I should put *The O.C.* down instead. That sounds much better, doesn't it?" she said, taking a swig of her Corona.

"*The O.C.*?"

"Yes, Maggie, *The O.C.* It sounds young and hip. Don't you keep up with these things?"

"Of course I've heard of *The O.C.*," I said, but I couldn't stop her. Mom was on a roll.

"*The O.C.*," she continued, "*One Tree Hill*, *Laguna Beach*, and all those reality shows filled with beautiful young people. I can hardly keep up with them. It's a youth-oriented culture, darling, a youth-oriented culture. You have to stay on your toes. No one cares about classical training anymore; they care about cheekbones and hair extensions. In my day, it was all about the work. Trodding the boards, studying with the great masters like Stella Adler and Sanford Meisner. The most important thing in those days was honing one's craft."

She put the beer bottle down on a WYME coaster, and her expression clouded for a moment, as if she were contemplating the dismal state of her acting career. I hated to admit it, but she had a point. Outside of old favorites like Helen Mirren, Meryl Streep, Goldie Hawn, and Diane Keaton, how many working actresses are there over the age of fifty? Things are tough in Tinseltown, and she knew it.

Still, it was time for a reality check.

"Mom, you were never on *The O.C.*"

She waved a hand dismissively. "Oh, don't be such a stickler for details," she said. "A minor point. I would have been terrific on that show, but I didn't have Edgar then, and my agent never even sent me over to meet the producers."

"A pity." I sneaked a peek at my watch. I tried to be surreptitious, but Mom was too quick for me.

"Well, let's get back to Lark," she said, switching gears. "How did her name even come up? What's her connection to this guru who was murdered?"

"It's very circumstantial. She was the last person to see him alive, but she did have a good reason to be angry with him. She gave him a push and it's not certain if he fell and hit his head. Nothing seems really certain except that foul play was involved. They don't even have the autopsy results yet, but that doesn't seem to matter to the Cypress Grove PD. Lark is their main suspect. Their only suspect." I quickly filled her in on the incident in Guru Sanjay's hotel room but stopped short of mentioning Lark's criminal background. I decided it would be best to let Lark bring up the subject herself, when she felt the time was right. I still had trouble believing it, and I wondered whether somehow Nick had left out part of the story. Not deliberately, of course, but maybe there were some details that he didn't know about.

We moved out onto the tiny balcony, sitting side by side on a couple of navy canvas deck chairs, my latest find from "Tarzhay." The balcony is probably only fifty square feet, but it overlooks a shady garden and a pretty little fountain spilling into a pond. I watched the copper green metal dolphins twirling in the spray, the droplets looking like tiny crystals as they landed on the terra-cotta tiles edging the pond.

It was late afternoon, and now that the haze of the day had burned off, a golden glow was settling over the scene. The scent of freshly mowed grass mingled with the fragrance of the white magnolia bushes rimming the edge of the garden. The sun was hanging low in the sky like a big orange lollipop, and a soft breeze was ruffling the fronds on the coconut trees. If it hadn't been for this pesky business of a murder investigation, all would be well with the world.

Half an hour later, I decided to throw together a quick dinner on the balcony—quesadillas roasted on the grill, sliced tomatoes with raspberry vinaigrette, and a corn and black bean salad from the deli. The doorbell rang just as I slapped some crumbly cheddar cheese and roasted red peppers into the last tortilla.

"I'll get it," Mom sang out from somewhere inside the condo.

"Probably Lark forgot her key again," I called out. "Tell her dinner will be ready in fifteen."

Except it wasn't Lark.

My barbecuing fork froze in midair and my heart skipped a beat when I heard Mom say, "Well, hello, gorgeous!" Hardly original. This was one of her favorite lines. And not even original. She stole it from Barbra Streisand's acceptance speech on Oscar night.

A friendly yip from Pugsley, and then I heard a sexy male voice that I immediately recognized as Martino's.

Martino? Here? Now? The possibilities burst in my head like fireworks when Mom trilled, "Maggie! Turn down the grill and get in here. We have a guest."

I quickly closed the lid on the grill, wiped my hands on a towel, and paused for a moment, flipping a mental coin. Play it cool? Light? Sardonic? A small voice in the back of my head reminded me to ignore how incredibly hot he was and not fall to pieces at the sight of him. *Note to self: Play it cool, Maggie; play it cool.*

Of course, my resolve crumbled like a Thin Mint when I saw him. My hormones had stormed into high gear and my mind was running willy-nilly in a thousand directions. Let's face it: I was a lost cause whenever I was around him.

"Dr. Walsh," he said in that sexy baritone. "I hope I'm not intruding." He looked from Mom to me, a slow grin flickering at the corner of his mouth.

"Intruding? Don't be silly," Mom babbled, practically dragging him into the living room and pushing him into a basket chair. "What would you like to drink? I make a mean mojito. Or there's beer, iced tea, or lemonade." Mom had once played a flight attendant in a B movie, and she seemed to be reprising her "Coffee, tea, or me?" role. Was I imagining it or did she just give him a saucy wink?

He gave her a level look and then nodded. "Some lemonade would be nice. Or just a can of diet cola. Don't bother with a glass." *Don't bother with a glass? Was he afraid she might try to slip him a roofie?* "I'm here on police business," he added, just to let her know it wasn't a social call. *Uh-oh.*

"Maggie told me you're a detective," Mom gushed. "That is just so exciting. You know, I played a forensic investigator years ago in a movie we shot in Tijuana. *Pasiones peligrosas. Dangerous Passions.* Of course, the script was in English, so it had to be dubbed into Spanish and had limited distribution, but—"

"Mom," I said sharply. "The lemonade?" The moment she sashayed to the kitchen, Rafe turned to me with a disbelieving look.

"Your mom is a movie star?"

"In her own mind. When she said it had limited distribution, she meant three people might have seen it in a drive-in in Kentucky. Before it went straight to video." I paused. "So you're here to see Lark?" Not a sparkling conversation opener, but the best I could do, under the circumstances.

He looked like a million bucks, a crisp white shirt showing off his Florida tan, sleeves rolled up, his dark hair boyishly falling over one eye. He wore it a little long, at least compared to other cops I had known, but maybe the detectives had more leeway. He gave me a neutral look I couldn't quite read, and my mind flipped through the possibilities.

"I do want to ask Lark a few more questions. But I really came here tonight to see you, Dr. Walsh." His tone made it clear that passion, romance, or even sheer animal lust wasn't in the cards. Bummer. He wasn't mixing business and pleasure, after all. Rafe Martino was all business.

"Maggie," I said automatically. "You can call me Maggie."

"Maggie." He managed to make it sound like a caress, and a little hum began in my head. My heart started to pound like crazy, but there was still that cool-cop look that I couldn't quite decipher.

I stalled for time and sat down on the love seat, with the wicker coffee table between us. I was definitely feeling uneasy. Freud would probably say I was out of my psychological safety zone so I was overcompensating by keeping the coffee table between us. Like a barrier. Hmm. I considered the Freudian hypothesis for about two seconds, and then I reminded Uncle Siggy that sometimes a cigar is just a cigar.

"So what do you want to see me about?" I noticed I was crossing and uncrossing my legs the way perps do on *Law & Order*, so I made a conscious effort to stay still. My hands felt clammy and I folded them in my lap. I took a deep breath, forcing myself to lean back in the chair, as if I had memorized the entire first chapter of *Secrets of Body Language 101*.

He probably didn't buy it for a second, because he fixed me with those amazing dark eyes and gave a sad little head shake. "I'm afraid you've been playing detective." His voice had suddenly turned serious. "Not a good idea, Maggie. Poking into things that don't concern you, looking for trouble."

"Looking for trouble?" I wrestled with my conscience for a moment, wondering whether I should come clean.

He looked me square in the eye, as if I were a convicted felon who had violated parole and was heading back to the can. "You're playing a dangerous game, Maggie."

I was struggling to come up with an answer, and Mom chose that moment to pop up from the kitchen like a prairie dog. For an actress, she has an incredibly bad sense of timing. "One lemonade coming up," she said, putting the glass in front of him with a flourish.

She gave him a big smile and handed him a little cocktail napkin and beer nuts like she was auditioning for the role of World's Oldest Living Flight Attendant.

"Thanks." He smiled back at her and I swear she melted. He took a sip and nodded approvingly. "Very nice. Tart, not too sweet." Mom was all set to hover, but I sent her a death glare and she got the message and scurried away.

Rafe waited until she disappeared back into the kitchen before continuing, and I sat perfectly still, heart pounding. What was coming next?

"I hear you've been asking questions about Guru Sanjay," he said coolly. "Interviewing potential witnesses, visiting the crime scene . . ." He let his voice trail off as if he was disappointed in me.

I immediately felt on the defensive. Was he checking up on me? And how did he know I'd visited the Seabreeze? Since I hadn't gone up to Guru Sanjay's bedroom, I could hardly be guilty of visiting the crime scene, but I didn't think this was the time to mention it. I'd hung out on the front porch, talked to Ted Rollins, and swiped one of the audience evaluation forms, but Rafe had no way of knowing that. And this wasn't the time to mention it. And I hadn't tampered with any evidence; I'd copied the form and put the original back in the pile.

"Well, I may have asked a few questions, here and there." I hesitated. "And why shouldn't I? He was a guest on my show, and it's only natural that I'd be interested in finding his killer."

"It's only natural," he echoed in that eerily flat tone. And just the touch of a sardonic smile. His sangfroid act was putting my nerves on edge, and I found myself wishing I could wrap my hands around another frosty Corona.

"Well, yes," I faltered. "Of course it's natural. I'm not just being nosy, if that's what you're hinting at. The sooner I find the real killer, the sooner you can eliminate Lark as a suspect. It should be pretty obvious to you by now that she had nothing to do with it."

The words spilled out in one rush of breath, and I felt a little ripple of anger spreading through my body. Who was Rafe Martino to tell me what to do and who I could or couldn't talk to?

I wondered which "potential witnesses" he was referring to. Was it Lenore Cooper, the disgruntled ex-wife, or Kathryn Sinclair, the angry mother? They were the top two on my suspect list, even if they weren't on the Cypress Grove PD's radar screen yet. If I didn't hunt for the real killer, who would? As far as Rafe was concerned, it seemed to be "case closed."

"Did it ever occur to you that you might be compromising an ongoing investigation?" His voice was low and calm, and he didn't seem to be the tiniest bit upset by my outburst.

He took a long swig of lemonade and looked at me. "Doesn't that bother you? To think that you might do or say something that would interfere with police business and make our job a lot harder?"

He leaned forward, elbows on his knees. The air between us hummed with tension. Why was he criticizing me for doing a little freelance detective work?

I felt a surge of heat rise to my face, and my voice lifted a little. "I wasn't interfering with anything. I have every right to ask questions," I began, but he cut me off, and a flicker of something cold went through his eyes.

"And you went to his memorial service. We were there, too, you know." He leaned forward, his eyes never leaving my face.

"You were there?" Too late I remembered that cops often went to victims' funerals because often the perpetrator was dumb enough to show up. "I didn't see any of Cypress Grove's finest at the service."

"We were there undercover. We tried to blend."

"Oh, yes, of course." I felt chastised. And moronic. "Then you saw me talking to Kathryn Sinclair," I said without thinking. I regretted it the moment the words were out of my mouth.

"Yes, we did. It looked like the two of you were pretty chummy." He paused, looking at his hands for a moment. "Would you care to tell me what the conversation was about? Had you known her before the service?"

"No," I said quickly. "I never met her before she came up to me in the garden." I neglected to say that Ted Rollins had tipped me off that she'd been making waves about the guru and his dangerous "therapies."

"What did you talk about?"

"Her daughter," I said slowly. "Her daughter, Sarah, was

a client of Guru Sanjay's. Well, not exactly a client. She went to one of those encounter groups his organization runs, and she had a bad experience there."

Rafe nodded. "Go on." I had the feeling he already knew all this and was testing me. But why? I had no idea what his agenda was, and it was making me uncomfortable. Like all shrinks, I like to be the one in control, the one asking questions. Rafe Martino was upsetting the natural order of things, and I found it unsettling.

"Kathryn was unhappy with the way her daughter was treated. It sounded as though she was bullied, and eventually"— I paused, trying to be precise—"she had to be hospitalized. Her experience at the encounter group hurt her psychologically and actually damaged her health. It sounded like reckless behavior on the part of Guru Sanjay's organization, and I was surprised to hear about it." I bit my lower lip, wondering what Rafe was thinking.

"Did you ever wonder why she was telling you all this?"

I gave a careless shrug. "No, I didn't even think about it. She knew he'd been a guest on my show and I suppose she thought that I would find it interesting. And as a psychologist, I could understand how destructive the whole experience had been for Sarah." I paused. "I think she just wanted someone to talk to. You know, to vent."

"So you're saying she was angry with him?"

"Venting isn't exactly the same as anger; it's more like letting off steam," I sidestepped neatly. A quick lesson from Psych 101.

"And it never occurred to you to tell me about this?"

He was beginning to remind me of Sam Waterston, the prosecutor on *Law & Order*.

I struggled for a light touch. "Hey, I'm a talk show psychologist, remember? I listen to people's problems all day long. Most of them are calling to complain about someone in their lives, so I wasn't too surprised when Kathryn told me about her daughter and the encounter group. She was just one more person with a gripe, that's all. It happens all the time."

"Yes, but the people they're complaining about don't usually end up dead, do they?"

Touché. "In your professional opinion," he said, barely containing a smirk, "would you say that Kathryn Sinclair was mentally unbalanced or potentially violent? Could she be delusional?"

"What? No, of course not," I said hurriedly. Why was he slapping her with a medical diagnosis? Was he on a fishing expedition, or did he really have some cold, hard facts that made her a viable suspect? "She's none of those things. She's just a mother who was upset over the way her daughter was treated." I hesitated, trying to choose my words carefully. I had the feeling that he was mentally ticking away everything I told him, even without Opie and his ever-present notebook.

Rafe shot me a wry look that told me he guessed I was uncomfortable with the line of questioning. "Go on." I had the feeling he was keeping his voice deliberately even, trying to lull me into a false sense of security.

"I don't know why she chose to confide in me, but she did. She'd heard me on the radio. Sometimes it gives people the idea of a connection, even though they're total strangers to me." I shook my head. "I know it sounds strange, but that's the only explanation I can think of."

"Interesting," Martino said. He finished his lemonade and slowly stood up. Every move he made was relaxed, fluid, and he walked with an air of easy confidence. Very sexy. "I'll be back in touch with you; we may want to take a deposition."

"A deposition?" So he really considered Kathryn Sinclair

a suspect? I suddenly felt uneasy, as though I had ratted her out, all on the basis of a brief interaction at the memorial service. "About my conversation with Kathryn, you mean?"

He didn't answer, and I found myself trotting along behind him like Pugsley pursuing his chew toy. My confidence was wilting like one of the quesadillas heating on the grill. I decided I better say something—fast—both to maintain my dignity and to set the record straight.

"I hope you didn't get the wrong impression from what I told you about Kathryn Sinclair. She was upset, that's all, and people say things that are out of character when they're under stress." I wanted to sound professional and just a touch conciliatory, but would he buy it?

I heard a little noise in the kitchen and suspected Mom was peeking around the door to spy on us, but I didn't dare turn to look. The fact is, I couldn't take my eyes off Rafe. There was something wildly attractive about the broad shoulders, the chiseled features, the flashing dark eyes. I could sense my earlier annoyance with him starting to soft-shoe toward the shadows, and my heart melted a little.

Then he frosted me with a look that killed the warm little buzz building up in my veins and stilled the pitter-patter in my heart. Rafe had his cop face on, and he was back to cop-speak.

"Thanks for the heads-up," he said, his voice laced with sarcasm. "I'll be sure to remember that the next time I'm interviewing a felon. Nothing like a little nugget of advice from a talk show shrink to keep me on track."

Ouch.

As Rafe walked to the door, his hand grazed my arm, and my traitorous skin tingled a little when I felt the touch of his warm fingers. I blanked on a snappy retort, and he turned to face me as he opened the door. "Oh, and that deposition I told you about? The one I may need you to give, down at the station?"

"Yes?"

"Just to clarify things, it's not about Kathryn Sinclair." He paused. "I'm going to be asking you some questions about Lark Merriweather." He hesitated for a moment, his hand on the knob. "Oh, and in the future? Leave the investigating to us, Nancy Drew. Okay?"

And then he was gone.

Chapter 15

When Lark showed up at the condo a few minutes later, Mom was nearly swooning from her all-too-brief encounter with Detective Martino.

"Maggie, you never warned me how good-looking he was," she gushed, spooning salads onto our dinner plates. The quesadillas from the grill were a little overdone but still edible with a hefty dollop of Lark's homemade salsa spooned on top. "Can you imagine? I opened the door and nearly fainted. That young man could have quite a film career if he ever decides to leave police work. He's drop-dead gorgeous."

"I don't think a film career is in the cards for him, Mom. I think he's pretty invested in his detective work. Maybe even obsessively so." I thought ruefully about Rafe and his dedication to the Cypress Grove PD. The thought of him ditching it all for a movie career was about as likely as Horatio Caine flashing his badge to cadge a free donut and coffee at the Krispy Kreme in north Miami.

Some things are inviolate.

"Well, so was Dennis Farina, and look what happened to him. One moment he's a cop in Chicago and the next thing you know, he's a movie star. All because he was a technical adviser on a film set and Michael Mann noticed he had acting potential."

Mom is an expert on Hollywood trivia and loves to recount stories of people making it against all odds in the film trade. I'm sure she thinks that it's not too late for the Hollywood gods to smile on her someday.

We were eating dinner on the tiny balcony and I could see that Lark was more than a little unnerved to hear about Rafe's surprise visit. She barely touched the vegetarian version of a key lime pie I'd whipped up earlier that day. It's laced with fresh lime juice along with vegan cream cheese, and it's usually a big hit with her.

"But what did he want, exactly?" Lark lowered her voice to a near whisper as if Rafe was lurking somewhere in the magnolia bushes under the balcony or had planted a bug in the salt shaker. "Why did he show up here at the condo?"

I shrugged. "Um, I'm not really sure," I hedged. *Later*, I mouthed. I glanced over at Mom and raised my eyebrows a fraction of an inch, and Lark got the message. We'd talk privately after dinner when we took Pugsley for his evening stroll.

We finished our coffee, and as always, Mom pivoted the spotlight back to herself. The talk turned to WYME, and I could see Mom was angling for another guest-host spot on my show. She said she planned to spend a few more days in Cypress Grove, and I wondered whether she was staying with us out of concern for Lark or because she hoped to revive her flagging acting career.

Doing a radio talk show on WYME is certainly the bottom rung of the show business ladder, but Mom believes in trying every avenue to further her career. Holding on by her fake, French-manicured fingernails if necessary. Anything it takes to "get her name out there," as she calls it.

She is nothing if not persistent, and I admire that quality in her. I wondered whether she'd told Edgar about her latest gig and whether he'd encouraged her to bug Vera Mae for another chance. Or maybe I was reading too much into it, and she had just enjoyed being on the air with me.

Right after dinner, Lark and I took Pugsley out for his walk. Pugsley is a big fan of evening walks and has developed a cute trick of tugging his leash off the door knob and dragging it across the rug until we hook it to his collar. Then he runs in manic circles until we rouse ourselves from the sofa and head outside with him. It's obvious who's the master and who's the slave in this relationship.

Lark was uncharacteristically quiet as we started out, and I was lost in thought. We live on a leafy street in a quiet, residential neighborhood that's canopied by banyan trees. The only commercial enterprise is the Seabreeze Inn next door. With its pale lemon exterior and glossy white gingerbread trim, the big Victorian looks more like a private house than a B and B. Only a discreet, hand-painted sign made from white birch announces that guests are welcome. When the inn is full, Ted simply brings the sign inside. It's all very casual, and he has the same guests stay with him year after year. After the disaster with Guru Sanjay, I doubt he'd ever be willing to host another conference.

I glanced up at the wide veranda to see whether Ted might be outside chatting with the guests, but the porch was empty, the hanging baskets of ferns swaying in the gentle evening breeze. I suddenly remembered those audience evaluations Ted had shown me. Had Rafe stopped by to pick up them up the morning of Guru Sanjay's memorial service?

I made a mental note to ask Ted the next time I saw him. Of course, I had my own copy of the threatening evaluation tucked away in my underwear drawer. I had copied it impulsively and had no idea what I was going to do with the information, but I just had a gut feeling it might come in handy.

Was it simply a negative evaluation written by a disgruntled conference-goer, or was it something more sinister? A note from the murderer? But why would anyone who was planning a murder want to advertise the fact? Was it written by a man or a woman? Presumably the police would analyze it, and that would be one of the first things they might try to determine.

I didn't dare tell Rafe Martino that I had made my own copy; he might accuse me of tampering with evidence.

I was a little rattled by the idea that Rafe and company had attended Guru Sanjay's memorial service and that I'd been watched so closely. *I hadn't even noticed*, I thought ruefully. I'd played down my conversation with Kathryn Sinclair when I spoke with Rafe, and I wasn't sure why. Was I biding my time because I was too caught up in my own investigation? Did Rafe really have any justification for telling me to back off?

I was still smarting from the crack about Nancy Drew.

I didn't really think Kathryn Sinclair had murdered Guru Sanjay, but I didn't like the idea that Lark was still the number-one suspect. I was mulling this over when Lark broke into my thoughts.

"There's a couple of things you don't know about me," she began. She tossed me a nervous glance, and her blue eyes clouded with an emotion I couldn't quite place. Doubt? Apprehension? Her voice wobbled a little and she bit her lower lip, scuffing her flip-flops on the packed-oyster-shell pavement. We were standing by a banyan tree, which Pugsley was sniffing with such intensity, you'd think he was looking for work as a bomb-detecting dog.

I decided to cut to the chase. "Look, if you're talking

about the brawl in the bar in Michigan? I already know about it, Lark. But I'd be interested in hearing your side of it. If you want to tell me, that is. It's entirely up to you."

Lark let her breath out in a slow puff of air. "I was going to tell you the truth right away, Maggie, and then things just got crazy. You know how you just put things off and then you can never find the right time to say something?"

"Yes, I've done that myself." I felt a tug at the leash. Pugsley had finally decided there weren't any nuclear explosives tucked between the lush leaves of the banyan tree, and now he was ready to head on down the street. Pugsley is a creature of habit and insists on making his appointed rounds, going down the same streets in the same order and stopping at various points of interest.

"The whole incident in the bar—it's not what you think," she said, stealing a quick look at me.

I raised my eyebrows. "It sounds like it was pretty serious."

"He had it coming, believe me," she blurted out. She slapped her hand over her mouth in a girlish gesture and gave a rueful smile. "I know that's a terrible thing to say, but he really did, Maggie. There's more to the story than meets the eye."

"There usually is." I plastered a nonchalant look on my face. I was still having trouble imagining Lark as a crazed woman attacking a guy in a bar and wondered what possible explanation there could be. Temporary insanity? Hormonal imbalance? There was no way to reconcile violent behavior with this gentle soul walking beside me.

"Okay, here's what happened." She took a deep breath. "The guy I attacked? He wasn't just some jerk in a bar who made a pass at me. I knew the guy. He'd been dating my sister and he nearly destroyed her."

I widened my eyes. This added a new dimension to the story.

Lark's voice quivered with emotion. "She was so messed up, I practically had to do an intervention with her. When I saw him there, laughing and having a few beers with his friends, I just lost it, that's all. I thought about all the pain he had caused, and I guess I just went ballistic. I can barely remember what happened. It was like a red haze in front of my eyes, and then it was all over and he was just lying there." She shivered a little at the memory and wrapped her thin arms around herself.

I shook my head, confused. "You were angry with him because of something he did to your sister? Did any of this come out at the trial?"

"Not really. But it's probably why I was allowed to plea-bargain to a lesser charge. The jury wasn't allowed to hear about his past offenses, and my sister's record was sealed because she was a juvy. But you know how it is in a small Michigan town; everyone knew who he was and what he was."

"And what was he?"

"The guy was the local drug dealer. Scum of the earth." Lark's tiny hands were clenched into fists, and her mouth had tightened into a thin line.

I raised my eyebrows. "How long was your sister mixed up with him?"

"Nearly a year. I can't explain it. She's a smart girl, but she just made some really dumb mistakes with men." Lark shook her head as if she shared my bewilderment.

As Vera Mae would say, "When love flies in the window, common sense walks out the door."

I paused, thinking. "You said she was a juvenile. So this is your younger sister?"

"Yes, my kid sister. She was barely seventeen when she met this guy. She was very young and impressionable. She was working at a Dairy Queen, saving money for college. You can't get more middle American than that, can you? He told her he was a performance artist from New York. A performance artist, can you imagine?" She made a little snorting noise. "I wonder where he came up with that line."

"He probably wanted to explain why he didn't have a nine-to-five job, like the rest of us working stiffs," I said dryly.

While living in Venice Beach one summer in my early twenties, I learned that the term "performance artist" is often code for "unemployed." I met a few guys who spent their days panhandling and their nights sleeping in their cars, and they all called themselves performance artists. "So she met this guy and she was completely taken in by him, maybe even fell in love with him?"

"Big-time. She was always into the arts, and he filled her head with crazy ideas that the two of them would escape to New York or L.A. Just crazy, drug-fueled dreams. I never thought she'd get into drugs, though. She just got into the wrong crowd, smoked some grass with them, and then she got hooked on X and crystal meth. The heavy-duty stuff."

"What happened next?"

"I got her into rehab and she did the twenty-eight-day thing. It worked. Then she came home and the judge ordered her to a twelve-step program. Ninety-ninety. Ninety meetings in ninety days and she had to have a little card stamped to prove she really went every day."

"Sounds like she was compliant with treatment. A lot of drug addicts aren't."

Lark nodded. "I know. They warned me that there was always the chance of relapse, but Rain knew a good thing when she saw it. And she was grateful for getting a second chance. She said she learned a lot in rehab and she's stayed off drugs ever since. She's a good kid."

"Rain?" I smiled.

"Short for Rainbow. What can I say? My parents were hippies."

"It could have been worse; they could have named her Mango. Or Kiwi."

"Exactly . . . I just wanted you to know the whole story, Maggie. You know I didn't kill Guru Sanjay, but I bet the cops will try and use this against me."

Pugsley guided us through the last stretch of the evening's walk, and we headed for home after he'd enjoyed a long, leisurely sniff at a neighbor's bougainvillea bush. A dog behaviorist appeared on my radio show last month, and he explained that a dog sniffs a bush or tree the way you and I read the newspaper. It's endlessly fascinating to him. Who would think so much drama could be found on the base of a tree trunk or a lamppost? Love, hate, revenge, betrayal, all the makings of a Shakespearean play sitting within sniffing distance of Pugsley's shiny black nose.

It's his way of scoping out the local news. Who's been on his home turf? Are they fearful? Friendly? Aggressive? Apparently dogs can tell all this from one sniff. He might pick up the scent of some familiar neighbor dogs and the occasional new dog on the block. My guest expert told the listeners never to hurry their pets through this little ritual, and said, "Remember, it's only a walk around the block to you, but it's the highlight of your dog's day."

Mom had made hot chamomile tea for us, and we sat companionably around the table, munching almond biscotti. I glanced over at Lark, petting Pugsley, who was happily curled up in her lap munching one of his organic dog biscuits. Lark looked more composed and relaxed than she had before we took the walk together, and she bent down to nuzzle him. When our eyes met over the top of his furry head, she gave me a guileless smile, her expression radiating sweetness and innocence.

Except now I knew there was another side of Lark, a dark side of her that could turn violent if provoked. This is the kind of thing a prosecutor could have a field day with. I shuddered at the image of Lark in a prison jumpsuit with a chain around her waist and willed it out of my mind.

There was no way Lark could have killed Guru Sanjay, and I was going to have to prove it. And I had to do it quickly, before the Cypress Grove PD could ask the DA to slap her with a murder charge.

Chapter 16

It was almost eight thirty when Mom had a sudden craving for a cappuccino float from Sweet Dreams, a trendy little ice cream shop that's just a few blocks away on Magnolia Street, the main drag in Cypress Grove. "It's still open, isn't it?" she asked, grabbing her purse.

"It closes at ten; we have plenty of time." Lark fastened Pugsley's leash and pulled on her running shoes. "Let's walk. It's still light out and it's a nice night." She glanced at me. "You're coming, right, Maggie?"

I hesitated for about two seconds, reminding myself that I needed to prepare for tomorrow's show, and then I caved. Sweet Dreams' signature dish, a tangy lemon sorbet topped with fresh raspberry sauce, was calling my name.

We'd walked only a block when I suddenly remembered I had agreed to do a pre-interview with one of my upcoming guests, Dr. Cornelius Abramson, a psychology professor from the local junior college. He was teaching an evening class and I'd promised to phone him at nine o'clock sharp tonight.

I'd been putting off calling him for days, partly because I was so involved with the murder investigation and partly because I'd met the professor socially a couple of times and the guy was mind-numbingly dull. But since he and Cyrus, the station manager, are golfing buddies, I couldn't think of any polite way to wriggle out of it.

Cyrus had promised the professor that he could speak on his favorite subject, Jungian archetypes. Since I was confident my entire listening audience wouldn't know an archetype from an armadillo, I felt fairly certain the show was doomed to be a total snooze. The purpose of the pre-interview was to try to encourage him to come up with some interesting anecdotes. Wildly entertaining would be even better, but I didn't want to press my luck. This guy wasn't Jay Leno.

A show about the mind of a serial killer would get good ratings, I thought wistfully, but I had no idea how that would fit in with Jungian archetypes. And I doubted that the good professor would, either.

I decided to call him from Sweet Dreams but patted my pocket and sighed when I realized I'd forgotten my cell phone. So after I made my apologies to Mom and Lark, there was nothing for me to do but head back to the condo. I made it back in a record four minutes flat and was panting a little when I turned the corner to my street. The sky was darkening but the humidity was still high, and my short-sleeved blouse was clinging to me.

I had just bolted up the front stairs and stepped into the hallway when my heart skipped a beat.

The front door to the condo was open a crack.

I stared at it for a long moment, thinking. My breath caught in my throat. If it really was open, I should scurry down the front steps and get help, right? But was it really open? I was torn with indecision. I took another look.

There it was. Hardly noticeable, but yes, there was the tiniest sliver of light spilling out onto the darkened landing. I felt a prickly sensation creep up my spine and forced myself to take a deep breath to steady myself.

Was it my imagination, or just a trick of the light, or did I see a shadow moving inside?

Time seemed to stand still, and I hesitated, inching forward. It was like a freeze-frame in a movie. A hyperawareness had kicked in. I was suddenly aware of the crickets chirping in the hibiscus bushes in the front garden, the sweet fragrance of the magnolias drifting into the hallway. And the hammering of my own heart in my chest.

Everything seemed normal, and yet different. I took another look, squinting in the semidarkness, my heart beating like a rabbit's. Yes, the door was definitely open. A fraction of an inch.

I remembered I had left the radio on, tuned to an oldies station, and the melancholy sounds of "Moon River" were wafting under the door. My heart lurched as I tried to make sense of the situation. I was the last one out; had I simply forgotten to pull the door shut?

The wood on the doorjamb is warped from the Florida humidity, and it takes a pretty hefty tug to close it properly. I must have been careless when I barreled down the steps with Mom, Lark, and Pugsley. That was the only logical explanation. In my eagerness to get to Sweet Dreams, I'd stupidly left the door unlocked.

Nearly giddy with relief, I felt my pulse ratchet down and I gave the door a tentative little push. It swung open immediately. The first thing I noticed was that the living room was a little darker than usual. Funny. The table lamps were turned off and the only source of light was the bright overhead fixture in the kitchen. Lark calls it the "operating room light" because it casts a harsh white glow over the breakfast table, tingeing everything a fluorescent blue. I thought I remembered leaving a reading lamp on, the big ginger-jar one next to the sofa, but I wasn't really sure.

I shut the door quietly behind me, taking stock of the situation. Everything looked normal, the dinner dishes still sitting in the sink, the sliding door opening onto the balcony, Pugsley's chew toy lying on the Navajo rug.

And of course, the silky notes of "Moon River" drifting out from the radio.

I was fumbling for the light switch when suddenly a figure clad all in black dashed out of the bedroom and rushed straight toward me. Instant panic. A scream froze in my throat as my mind scrabbled in a million directions, trying to come to terms with the unthinkable.

I was going to die. Or suffer horribly, or be torn apart, or maybe even be eaten alive. (I'm embarrassed to say that being threatened with death tends to bring out the drama queen in me. It would probably take years of analysis to explain this annoying personality quirk.)

Images of every slasher flick I'd ever seen flipped crazily through my mind, like I'd uncovered a giant Rolodex of B movies. Freddy Krueger, Jason Voorhees, Michael Myers, all whizzed by at twenty-four frames a second.

The intruder leapt toward me like a panther. My heart lurched as I jumped to one side, but I was too slow and I slammed my knee against the sharp edge of the end table. It was like being trapped in one of those awful anxiety dreams when you try to run but your legs have suddenly turned to concrete and you flail helplessly, rooted to the spot.

I felt a powerful body pinning me against the wall, and then I dimly saw a hand raised in the air, followed by a crashing blow to my head. A stick? A baton? A baseball bat?

Whatever it was, it hurt like hell.

I was down for the count, my nails scrabbling the length of the wall as I crumpled to the floor. I was vaguely aware of the front door opening and shutting.

The intruder had left. I knew that I had to get up, find the phone, and dial 911. But somehow, it all seemed like too much trouble, and I could feel my eyelids fluttering like butterflies as the darkness started to close in on me, warm and comforting.

As I drifted into oblivion, the song played on, the lyrics blending with my scattered thoughts, just below the level of consciousness. Who had just broken into the condo? Who had hit me over the head? I took shallow breaths, kept my eyes tightly shut, and listened to the final stanza of "Moon River," trying to figure out the puzzle. It's a beautiful song, but Andy Williams was no help at all, crooning about dream makers and heartbreakers.

Because whoever had hit me over the head certainly wasn't my huckleberry friend.

"Ohmigod, ohmigod, ohmigod," I could hear Lark chanting. I was still flat out on the floor, and she was bending over me, while Pugsley swiped me with his fat tongue, treating me to a blast of doggie breath. "Maggie, are you all right?" she shrieked.

"Of course she's not all right," I heard Mom say. "She's got a lump on her head the size of a golf ball. Somebody must have really walloped her."

I made a halfhearted motion to sit up and was immediately hit by a wave of dizziness and nausea. "Just stay still, Maggie," Lark implored as she eased me back down. "The paramedics will be here any minute."

"Para . . . ?"

"Paramedics."

"Don' need para, para, whatever you said," I mumbled. My voice sounded as thick as if I'd been on a weekend bender, and I could hardly get my tongue around the words. I gingerly touched the tip of my tongue to the roof of my mouth and tasted blood. Was I missing any teeth? Maybe my jaw was dislocated. I had a sharp pain on the left side of my face, and it felt like someone was jamming me in the ear with a screwdriver, the remnants of an old TMJ problem.

"Who could have done this?" Lark wailed. "Maggie, did you see who it was? Was it just one person, or was there a gang? And how in the world did they get in?"

"Shhh," Mom said, kneeling down next to me and taking my hand. "She's not supposed to talk."

"Why noth?" I gurgled.

"Well, because . . ." Mom shot me a quizzical look. She thought for a moment, idly rubbing my hair back from my face. "That's what they told us on *Stolen Passions*. I played a nurse and Marco was brought into the ER with a concussion, remember? I said to him, 'Don't try to talk.'" She used her throaty television voice and played the line as if she was doing a final taping. "It was just one line, but I put my heart and soul into it." She paused for effect. "Don't try to talk."

She looked at me. "I said it just like that, with that exact intonation."

"Thass amazing. How dith you rumembah dat?" I said with an effort. "The parth 'bout not tawking if you haf a concuss'n."

"Rumembah? Oh, remember. You always remember your first line in the business, dear," she said cheerfully. "Three years of waiting tables and finally my big break. A speaking part in a soap!"

I tried to get up but sank back to the floor. It was easier to think lying down, I decided. At least the living room had stopped twirling like a Cirque du Soleil dancer on a silk streamer, and I could feel myself drifting off to sleep.

It was only later, when I was being lifted into an ambulance on a stretcher, that I realized Lola was still holding my hand, her face a mask of worry. "Sho whah happened to Mahco in the hoshpital?" I said gamely, trying to lift her spirits. "On *Shtolen Pashions*. Did he evah talk aftuh you ashed him not to?"

Mom smiled. "Mahco?" She looked blank. "Oh, Marco. No, dear, Marco never talked again. Well, not after Rinaldo broke into Seabrooke General and shot him in the head." She turned to the paramedic, who was a dead ringer for Edward Norton. "Memory loss," she said in a stage whisper. She tapped her own temple to demonstrate postconcussion amnesia. "Could be the sign of a head trauma, you know. Probably something you'll want to mention to the doctor." He nodded, hopped in after me, and closed the ambulance doors behind him.

Just before I drifted off to sleep again, I saw Mom waving a hanky at me through the window.

When I woke up half an hour later, I was in Mayberry.

There was Opie at my side, staring at my IV pole. Just the two of us. I blinked twice. Yep, he was still standing there, in full cop regalia, looking a little pale around gills, his freckles standing out like a bad case of chicken pox against his white skin. Either I looked worse than I imagined, or he just had a thing about hospitals.

Then I realized we weren't alone and we probably weren't even in Mayberry. The hunky-yet-annoying Rafe Martino was standing in the corner of the cubicle talking to Mom and Lark, who seemed to be hanging on his every word.

Then I heard a soft woof and glanced down at the floor.

Pugsley! Sitting in his oh-so-chic yellow and black tartan dog carrier, a knockoff of an Abercrombie and Fitch model I saw at a doggie boutique at the Sawgrass Mills. He was pawing at the mesh door to get out, his little feet tapping a sharp staccato that set my teeth on edge.

"How'd you get the dog in here?" I said slowly. Every word was an effort. I was surprised to find that my voice was thin and hollow, hardly more than a whisper. I sounded like I was a hundred and ten years old. I felt strangely distant from everything, one level removed, as if I was watching a not-very-entertaining movie.

And I wasn't really in a hospital room, I realized, doing a quick survey. But it was definitely some sort of medical center, maybe an emergency room. It looked like a holding area, because I was lying on a hard metal table with a canvas curtain drawn for privacy. From the horrible sounds coming from outside the curtain, I'm glad I didn't have access to the visual. I heard a series of piercing wails, a few muffled Spanish curses, and what sounded like somebody coughing up a lung.

"The dog," I repeated in a stronger voice. "What's he doing here?"

This time three faces turned to me, and Mom rushed over to cover my forehead with kisses. "You're awake! Thank god! We've been so worried about you. They think you might have a concussion."

"The dog," I said with great effort. "How did you ever sneak Pugsley in here?"

Mom looked puzzled. "Well, we didn't have a choice. We had to bring him with us," she said, glancing at Martino, "because your whole apartment is a crime scene. Just like on *CSI*."

"A crime scene?" I vaguely remembered being hit on the head. Maybe I had a brain injury.

And it must have been a hell of a wallop, because I couldn't stop thinking about Andy Williams.

She couldn't keep the excitement out of her voice. "They have people dusting for fingerprints and looking for trace evidence." *Trace evidence?* She lowered her voice as if she was about to reveal the secrets of the universe. "I overheard them talking. They're doing a BOLO on a guy in a Ford Mustang. BOLO means 'be on the lookout for.' It's cop talk."

I nodded. "That's nice." I had no idea what she was talking about.

"Your neighbor, Mrs. Higgins, saw the Mustang parked down the street. And she's never seen it there before so we think it might belong to the perp."

I tried not to smile. *The perp? What perp?*

Mom would have loved to have been deputized by Martino and been part of the team. She'd never make it as a cop, though. She had to shoot a .357 Magnum in a B movie once, and she said it felt as if she were shooting a toaster. The producer brought in a firearms instructor for her, and after squeezing off a few dozen rounds at the range with a twenty-two, Mom managed to get through the scene with a prop gun.

Opie cleared his throat. "Um, ma'am, if you're feeling up to it, we have a few questions we need to ask you about the events that occurred tonight."

"Okay." I shivered a little and sank back into the pillows. Someone had jacked up the air-conditioning, and the cubicle was as cold as Montauk in December. Mom hurried to cover me with a white blanket that was as thin as tissue paper. "But first, I want to hear about Pugsley," I said stubbornly. "How did you get him past security? And where are we, by the way?"

"Cypress Grove Memorial. The emergency room. We didn't

have to sneak Pugsley in here," Mom said confidentially. "I said he was a helper dog. They have to allow them in public places, you know. It's a federal law. I said we'd left his harness and identification back in the apartment in all the confusion."

Twenty-two-pound Pugsley a helper dog?

"But he's not a helper dog." I glanced over Mom's shoulder and saw Opie rolling his eyes, obviously eager to get on with the Q and A.

"Yes, dear, but he's not going to tell them that, is he?"

"What exactly do you remember about the events that transpired?" Opie whipped out his notebook, ballpoint poised. I remembered Rafe introducing him as Officer Duane Brown, but he'd always be Opie to me.

"Not very much." I reached up and touched a sore spot on the back of my head and winced. "I hit my head," I said slowly, "because it was so dark in the apartment."

I saw Lark and Mom exchange a look. Wrong answer. Funny how fuzzy my mind had become. My brain felt like it was stuffed with wet Kleenex, and my thoughts were skittering in all directions. It was hard to focus. Maybe I really did have a concussion.

"You're saying you tripped in the dark?" Opie raised his sandy eyebrows.

"No, wait, I remember now!" I said, sitting up straight in bed. "The door was open, and the apartment was very dark. I was trying to figure it all out when somebody came barreling out of my bedroom. He was dressed in black, I think, and he pushed me against the wall and clobbered me." My heart beat a little faster, just remembering the scene.

Opie was dutifully writing this all down when a nurse came in to take my vitals. A cell phone jangled, and out of the corner of my eye, I saw Rafe slip out into the hall.

"Can we bring her home now?" Mom asked the nurse. "It's been a long night."

"We're waiting for the results of the CAT scan; the doctor will be in soon." The nurse stifled a yawn before vanishing through the curtain.

Opie was chafing at the bit, eager to get back to his questioning. "So the intruder in your apartment was definitely a male?"

"I couldn't tell." I squinted my eyes and tried to recall the menacing figure. I had no idea whether it was a man or a woman; my heart was in my throat at the time.

"You said 'he,'" Opie pointed out. He looked pleased with himself, as if he had made a deduction worthy of Hercule Poirot.

"I guess I just assumed it was a guy," I said, trying to focus. "He was about five-ten or -eleven, and really strong. I remember that because he sort of picked me up and slammed me against the wall. And then he hit me with something; I don't know what."

"Oh, my poor baby," Mom moaned.

"What happened next?"

I shook my head. "That's all I remember. Until now." I paused and looked over at Mom and Lark. "You put me in the ambulance," I said smiling. "We were talking about Rinaldo shooting Marco in the head."

"A shooting?" Opie asked, puzzled. "When did that happen?"

Mom quickly explained the complex plot points of *Stolen Passions*, and Opie listened politely, eyes glazed. I looked over at Lark and grinned. We both knew that once Mom got started talking about her soap career, she would be good for hours. I sighed and put my head back on the pillow. Maybe there was time for a quick nap before Rafe came back.

"I can't believe they don't have any suspects," Mom said a couple of hours later. It was after midnight, and I'd been discharged from the hospital in record time, with a few ibuprofen and a copy of my CAT scan. My instructions were to relax, drink plenty of fluids, and call my own doctor later that day. I thought longingly about slipping into bed, but Mom insisted on making me a cup of herbal tea, a vile concoction laced with sassafras root.

"They think it's just a break-in," Lark said, "maybe neighborhood kids looking for money or something to pawn."

I thought of the powerful figure in black. This was no neighborhood teen. Whoever was in the apartment wanted something, but what?

"Was anything taken?" I looked around the living room. Everything looked fine.

"The silver candlesticks are gone." Lark gestured to the distressed oak mantelpiece over the fireplace. It was completely bare except for a wilting fern in a ceramic pot.

Oops, somehow I'd missed that. I'd picked up a pair of candlesticks at an estate auction a couple of months ago. They were British and very nice, but they had a few dents and weren't really that expensive, which made me doubt the theory of it being just a botched robbery.

"Why would anyone break in and just take a pair of candlesticks? There are a few other things here that are more valuable," I said. "Cameras, jewelry . . ."

I suddenly remembered my jewelry box in the bedroom. I'm not into baubles, but I do have a nice set of pearls and an antique cameo that I'd hate to lose.

Lark must have read my mind, because she said, "Relax, he didn't take anything from the bedroom. Maybe he just ran in there to hide when you opened the door." She paused. "He did knock over a few files, though. Did you have anything important in there? There was a whole stack of papers lying on the floor by your briefcase. It looked like he might have been going through them, or maybe he just tripped over them when he ran out. The cops aren't sure."

"Any fingerprints?"

Lark shook her head. "They didn't say anything. I know they dusted for them." She thought for a moment. "You're sure there wasn't anything important inside your briefcase?"

"I'm positive. Just some show ideas. Certainly nothing worth stealing." My head was throbbing and I popped a couple more ibuprofen, but I might as well have scarfed down some M&M'S. I was already regretting my trip to the hospital. It would have made more sense to go to the local drugstore and buy a bottle of Advil.

Plus, Rafe had never reappeared, and Opie had finished his questions just as the doctor appeared to sign my discharge papers. All in all, it had been a wasted evening. I could only hope that my health insurance covered the cost of the ambulance ride and the ER visit.

I decided to call it a night, ignored the open briefcase and the tangle of papers fanned out on the floor, and fell into bed. Everything could wait till morning. Just before drifting off to sleep, I remembered that I'd never called Dr. Abramson, my prospective show guest. I'd have to make my apologies in a few hours.

Chapter 17

"Land sakes, you look a mess, girl," Vera Mae greeted me when I zipped into WYME that afternoon. "You're so pale you could be one of those Goth chicks, you know, the ones with the black lipstick and the body piercings? It looks like you've already got the black eye shadow thingy goin' on." She leaned over to peer at me. "Upper and lower, I'd say."

"Thanks," I said dryly. I glanced in the mirror. I was dead white, with the same ghostly pallor Helena Bonham Carter sported in *Sweeney Todd*. Except on her it looked sexy.

"How're you feeling?"

"Like I've gone three rounds with Mike Tyson," I moaned. A wave of dizziness came over me and I sat down abruptly in the reception area, wishing I could bag the show and go back to bed. I felt like my head was stuck in a vise. "So what's on the agenda for today?"

"You are, sweetie; you're the big news," Vera Mae said, showing me the call book. "There's a lot of buzz about the break-in, and your fans want to make sure you're okay. The phones have been ringing off the hook, and I thought Irina was going to have a psychotic break."

Then she handed me the spot log, which lists all the commercials scheduled for my time slot that day. "I asked Big Jim to tape the live ones for you, and the rest are already in the can. I didn't think you'd feel like messin' around reading cemetery ads or plugs for Dora's House of Beauty."

"Thanks, Vera Mae. You are so right. I don't know what I'd do without you. Don't ever leave this place, okay?" I stifled a low moan. My head felt like a trick cigar; it was threatening to explode at any moment.

Vera Mae grinned. "Don't worry, honey. I'd never leave WYME. I'm a lifer."

I'd already called in my apologies to Dr. Abramson, who wasn't the least miffed with me about the missed phone interview. Tossing around the words "blunt-force head trauma" garners one a lot of sympathy, I'd discovered. We decided to go ahead with the show on Jungian archetypes without any preparation. I could only hope that he'd be mildly entertaining in person and that we'd get some interesting questions and comments from the listeners.

"So did they get him?" Vera Mae asked a few minutes later in the break room. She poured me a cup of hazelnut coffee, and we decided to go over a printout of some of some of the listener e-mails. She pushed a box of Dunkin' Donuts at me and I ate half of a powdered old-fashioned.

And then I ate the other half. Plus a jelly donut. A bear claw was calling to me, but I managed to ignore its sugary little voice. Who says I have no self-control?

"Afraid not. I couldn't give much of a description, and one of my neighbors saw a car parked outside, but who knows? They may never figure out who did it." I went for a sugar cube and then poured a packet of Splenda into my coffee instead. Two donuts versus a packet of Splenda. If you do the math, it doesn't make any sense at all. "And the more interesting question is not who, but why? God knows there's nothing in my condo worth stealing."

"But maybe he didn't know that," Vera Mae said, resting her chin on her hands. "It was a he, right?"

I nodded. "I think so. Or it might have been a very strong woman. Someone tall with a powerful body build." I shuddered, remembering how the intruder had picked me up like a rag doll and tossed me against the wall.

"Well, the station is going to follow this closely. They're doing hourly updates."

"But there's nothing new to report. I haven't even talked to the police today." I'd been idly thinking about calling Rafe Martino but decided to wait another day. If he had any news, he would have gotten in touch with me. And I didn't want to get stuck shooting the breeze with Opie, who was probably better at hooking marlins than solving neighborhood robberies.

"This is Cypress Grove, honey. The break-in will be the talk of the town, trust me."

I'd called Vera Mae earlier that morning to fill her in on most of the details of the break-in. She'd told me the latest buzz. Cyrus wanted to feature the break-in as a Crime Watch Exclusive, "Talk Show Host Mugged and Robbed in Her Own Apartment!" I thought it was over the top, but he thought that my loyal viewers would be fascinated by the case and it would boost the ratings.

The reaction among the rest of the staff had been mixed. Big Jim Wilcox had given me a speculative look as I checked my mailbox, probably wondering whether I had masterminded the break-in as a publicity stunt.

Twyla in Human Resources told me that if the break-in was related to my work at WYME, the station would consider picking up my medical bills. Since I had no idea who had hit me on the head, or why, I didn't expect to collect on her offer.

Irina shyly handed me a bunch of violets and a card when I walked past her desk. It read, "I was deluged to hear you were hit on head. Your faithful friend, Irina."

"Deluged? What do you think she means?" I asked Vera Mae, who read the note and giggled.

"Devastated? Or desolated? Something like that. Her heart's in the right place even if her English isn't up to par."

I picked through the phone messages. Nick Harrison, my reporter pal at the *Cypress Grove Gazette*, had called a few times. I zipped into my cubbyhole/office to call him back, and he told me he was already writing a front-page piece about the attack.

I scrambled in my briefcase while we chatted, trying to find my day planner. No luck. It was probably buried under the mountain of papers on the desk and stacked up against the wall. The office was a mess, but here's my defense:

Being a radio talk show host—even in a small town like Cypress Grove—puts you on the radar screen of every publicist in south Florida. I got a ton of press kits and promotional materials every single day. I gave up on the day planner and turned my attention back to Nick.

"And it's going to appear above the fold," he was saying excitedly. *Above the fold?* Apparently getting thwacked on the head was big news in my small Florida town.

I asked Nick for an update on the guru investigation. He told me he'd already talked to Rafe Martino and learned there weren't any hot leads in the case. I guess the cops hadn't found fingerprints or any other "trace evidence," as Mom would say.

The cops had sent Lark's bottle of Calming Essence to a

testing lab, but the results were inconclusive. They decided to send it to another lab in Miami for analysis. Guru Sanjay's cause of death was also inconclusive. Did he die of a head injury? Or did he die from ingesting something?

A lot of uncertainties, but one thing was sure. The bottom line was that Lark was still the key suspect. The only suspect.

The afternoon went rolling along. Vera Mae had announced a last-minute schedule change. At Cyrus's insistence, we were doing a surprise show: "It's a Jungle Out There: Hanging Tough in a Dangerous World." It was obvious Cyrus wanted to capitalize on the break-in in any way he could. As Cyrus says, "It's all about the numbers, baby."

So Vera Mae had run promos throughout the morning, inviting my listeners to call in with safety tips and home security products. It turned out to be a popular topic, and a lot of women asked me why I didn't carry pepper spray or a Taser gun.

"You could have Tasered him, sistah!" the first caller told me.

"Um, right," I agreed weakly. Except I don't own a Taser gun and I doubt I'd have the guts to actually zap someone with one.

The next caller said I should have used something more lethal, like a Beretta. And someone else swore by a Glock.

I had the sneaky feeling that my listeners thought I'd been way too passive in the attack on my home and self. Maybe they've never been thwacked over the head in the dark, completely taken by surprise. At the end of the first hour, I was beginning to feel like a wuss.

"You should have gotten one of those cell-phone stun guns," Wanda from Boca said.

"Never heard of them," I admitted.

"Honey, you just whip out your cell phone, pretend you're making a call, and zap the guy like a bug. Nine hundred thousand volts and wham! He'll be crying like a baby."

"It has a built-in flashlight, and it comes in pink," Vera Mae offered helpfully. "It fits nicely in a fanny pack."

"You have a cell-phone stun gun?" I asked her at the break.

"I saw one in *Soldier of Fortune*." There was a touch of defensiveness in her tone. "Not that I would hesitate to buy one. I'm a sucker for gadgets."

I sipped my coffee as we went live again. It was obvious I was way behind the curve on the hottest trends in weapons.

Marlene from north Hollywood explained the concept of "pistol purses" to me. Pistol purses are leather shoulder bags with compartments for sunglasses, cell phone, and oh, yeah, your trusty nine-millimeter Glock. It's the latest in don't-leave-home-without-it personal safety devices.

The hour was winding down when Gina, who refused to give her city, described a Stinger twenty-two one-shot handgun that folds in the middle to create a revolver. It's practically the size of a pocket comb when it's folded. Yowsers.

Who knew? Even Vera Mae's eyes widened at that one.

"They've all been watching too many Bronson movies," I said, slipping off my headphones at the end of my shift. "It sounds like half of Cypress Grove is packing heat. And the other half would like to."

"Well, I really enjoyed the show, except I have my doubts about that one-shot gun," Vera Mae said idly. "What if you don't get him on the first try? Then you'd have created a real problem for yourself." She scooped up the afternoon logs and headed for the billing department, where the logs would be recorded and the sponsors would be billed for their spots. "When the chips are down, give me a .38 anytime," she added over her shoulder.

"A .38?"

She nodded. "You bet. No mess, no fuss. Two in the head and you know he's dead."

I spent the rest of the afternoon finishing up some paperwork at the station, and it was nearly six thirty when I decided to call it a day. The sun was low in the sky, but the warm air was still rising off the blacktop, and the whole scene seemed to shimmer in the summer heat.

I opened the door to my red Honda Civic, wincing as my fingers touched the white-hot metal handle. I tossed my briefcase on the front seat and hesitated as a blast of hot air rushed out. It was like a broiler oven in there.

I waited a couple of minutes, then groped around under the seats to see whether the day planner had ended up there. No luck. It had to be back at the apartment or the office; those were the only two possibilities. Finally, I gave up the search and drove to Johnny Chen's for takeout with the AC cranked up as far as it would go.

I had just placed my order for three veggie lo meins when someone walked up quietly behind me. I must have been more strung out than I realized, because I felt my pulse jump. I sensed a warm body standing just a little too close to me, and my heart somersaulted.

I told myself to cool it. I was showing classic symptoms of post-traumatic stress disorder: racing pulse, exaggerated startle reflex, shortness of breath. A textbook case. All the beginnings of a full-fledged panic attack were there, which shouldn't have come as a surprise to me.

My neurons were firing for no reason at all, and I was as jumpy as if a saber-toothed tiger were sprinting after me. A primitive fear response, but a dangerous one. I had to act fast and nip this glitch in my brain or it would take over my life.

Then the mystery person moved in even closer. I could practically feel his breath on my back. Was it the intruder back for another whack at me? The skin on the back of my neck tingled, and I whirled around, holding my straw tote bag in front of me like a shield.

I moved so fast, I nearly fell on top of him. My reptilian brain parts were in control, and all rational thought had vanished. My heart pounded as I connected with a powerful male body.

"Hey, easy, there. A little jumpy, are we?"

Rafe Martino.

Chapter 18

I felt the breath go out of me in a single whoosh, and he reached out his hands to steady me. He was looking terrific as usual, tanned and handsome in a pale blue golf shirt and khaki pants. His grip was light but firm, and I could feel the heat of his body.

"Sorry, but you startled me." I felt like an idiot. My heartbeat kicked up a notch, and I wished I'd taken a few seconds to put on some lip gloss and drag a brush through my hair. "Ever since last night, I'm just not myself, you know?" I was talking too fast, babbling. Pressured speech, as the shrinks would say. A sure sign that I was rattled.

He nodded, keeping his gaze cool and level. "How are you feeling? You were really out of it in the ER last night. I wanted to ask you a few questions but we had another call on the west side of town. I have Officer Brown's report on my desk."

Officer Brown. It took me a beat to realize he was talking about Opie. "My head's still throbbing," I admitted. "They say I had a mild concussion and there's not really any treatment. So I guess I'll just have to wait it out. I may take a few days off from work."

Rafe smiled. "I noticed they're playing it up on WYME. Hourly bulletins."

"I know," I said, feeling a wash of embarrassment. "They're laying it on pretty heavy. That's not my doing, believe me. That's all the fault of the news department. I guess it's a slow day for serial killers so they're going to concentrate on petty theft."

Rafe raised an eyebrow. "If that's what it was. Petty theft."

Some other customers were crowding in behind us and we moved to a red leather banquette to wait for our orders. Had there really been something else behind the break-in last night? As always, Rafe was holding his cards close to his vest, as Vera Mae would say, and I tried to draw him out. "The only things missing are two candlesticks I picked up at an estate sale. What else could it be?"

"You tell me."

"I don't know." I tried to read his expression, but it was neutral, revealing nothing. We were sitting so close, I could see flecks of gold in his dark eyes and could sense the coiled readiness in his body. He always seemed watchful, alert, and I couldn't decide whether it was part of being a cop or just his personality style.

"Why would anyone go to the trouble of breaking in just to grab a couple of candlesticks that were worth what, a hundred bucks?" His voice was low, reasonable. He spread his hands in front of him. "That doesn't make sense to me."

I shrugged. "It doesn't make sense to me, either, but I don't have an answer. The criminal mind is a mystery," I said lightly.

"Even to you? I thought you handled a lot of forensic cases before you moved here."

"How did you—," I began, and then stopped abruptly. I was living with someone the Cypress Grove PD considered a prime suspect in Guru Sanjay's murder. So naturally he'd done a background check on me, and, knowing Rafe, it was a thorough one. "Yes, you're right. I did some forensic work as part of my practice back in Manhattan."

Rafe nodded as if this was old news to him. "I've dealt with a few forensic psychologists before." I waited. There was something dismissive in his tone, and I reminded myself not to show my annoyance. Maybe he was baiting me, maybe he was serious, but I wasn't going to fall into the trap of playing games with him. I had the feeling that Rafe Martino could outmaneuver me at every turn, and I was on my guard.

"As consultants on your cases?" I kept my voice deliberately neutral.

"The state brought them in. Sometimes the prosecutors like to bolster their cases by including some psychological twists about the criminal mind. So the shrinks get on the stand and try to tell the jury why it's plausible that this particular suspect could have committed this crime. Or if they're working for the other side, they tell you why the suspect couldn't possibly have committed the crime. You hear both opinions in the same courtroom about the same case. It's mind-boggling."

I could feel my blood pressure inch up a tic when he gave a dry laugh. "Is that so?"

Rafe went on, clearly on a roll—or a rant. "Since they're hired guns, they say whatever they're paid to say. They do a lot of tests and some mumbo jumbo and make a few hundred bucks an hour. And then they file a thirty-page report that no one ever reads. It's a racket."

"The reports are called psych evals," I said mildly. "Psychological evaluations."

"Yeah, that's it," he agreed, "psych evals. Our file cabinets are full of them. After a while, they all start to sound alike. And some of the profiles I've seen are really over the top. You find out that a serial killer likes peanut butter and drives a Subaru. Some meaningless facts that could apply to millions of people. It's just useless information that any wing nut could dream up."

Wing nut? If Martino was trying to bait me, he was getting nowhere. I knew I had to stay focused so I could work the conversation around to Lark and see whether he had any new evidence. "It doesn't sound like you have much respect for my profession." I tried to match his low, calm voice and kept my face expressionless.

"Psychology is no match for police work." His tone was blunt. "Psychobabble theories can't match hard evidence. And most of these forensic types have never had to get their hands dirty at a crime scene."

He was right on that one.

Compared to CSI investigators, who have to deal with grisly sights like bodies floating in the Everglades and people riddled with bullet holes, forensic psychologists have a cushy life. We can sit in an air-conditioned office doing personality tests and clinical interviews while they're out sweating in the field. We can charge a hefty fee for our services, whether we're doing our evaluations, writing our reports, or testifying in court. And Rafe was right. We get paid up front and we never get our hands dirty.

There's a lot of mental stress involved, especially in the court, where we're grilled by the opposing attorney, but at least nobody shoots at us.

The server at the counter called my lo mein order then, and I turned to Rafe. I decided to take a chance and blurt out what was really on my mind: Was Lark just a person of interest or a prime suspect? I took a deep breath and plunged in. Nothing ventured, nothing gained, right?

"Is there anything new on the investigation into Guru Sanjay's death?" As soon as the words were out, I had the sinking feeling he wasn't going to give me anything. A long beat passed between us while I locked eyes with him.

The restaurant suddenly seemed hot and noisy, and I had the mother of all headaches. They called my order a second time, and I stared at him. Who would blink first? I had the feeling that Rafe could outwait a jungle cat.

"We're still moving along and looking at all the evidence," he said finally. "I hope you're planning on filling me in if there are any new developments."

"Of course I will." Any new developments? Did he expect me to get hit over the head again? Or did he expect me to magically solve the crime? He'd told me over and over to stay out of police business. Plus, he equated forensic psychology with mumbo jumbo. Hardly likely he'd want me as a consultant on the case.

"You *and* your roommate. We'll be talking to her again soon. You be sure to tell her that, okay?" He gave me a long look, his dark eyes cool and shuttered. We both stood up then, and the veiled threat in his husky voice was unmistakable, running like a dark undercurrent just beneath the smooth surface.

I knew it. He had set his sights on Lark, like a hungry tiger stalking a gazelle at a watering hole. I gave a tight nod and walked to the counter, his words sending prickles up my spine. I could feel his eyes drilling into the back of my head, and I willed myself not to turn around. As far as Rafe Martino was concerned, the Cypress Grove PD already had their man.

Or in this case, woman.

Pugsley raced to the door to meet me when I arrived home ten minutes later. He was so excited to see the aromatic bag from Johnny Chen's that he jumped straight up in the air, all four feet off the ground, just like a Hollywood stunt dog.

"Very impressive, Pugsley," I told him, "but you have to wait your turn. There's a steamed pot sticker for you, if you behave yourself." He gave an aggrieved yip but followed me into the dining area, his chunky body quivering with excitement. Pugsley is a foodie with eclectic tastes, but anything from Johnny Chen's sends him into canine nirvana.

I glanced at Mom, who looked flushed with excitement and was humming a little tune under her breath. She had a cat-that-swallowed-the-canary look on her face, and I knew something was up. But what? The three of us were crowded around the IKEA table, and Pugsley was sitting at Mom's feet, glancing up at her adoringly. Mom waited until Lark had dished out the lo mein and egg rolls before she dropped the bombshell.

"You'll never guess what I did today!" she said, clasping her hands together dramatically. She was wearing enough thin gold bracelets to outfit a gypsy, and they clanked together when she raised her arms. Lark sent me a sympathetic look. It was obvious that Mom was up to something, and Lark knew where the conversation was headed.

"Okay, I'll bite. You called Donald Trump and asked him out to lunch?" I said innocently.

"Oh, don't be silly. He's got that sweet young wife, Melania. He wouldn't be interested in an old broad like me." She paused, thinking. "Well, he might be tempted, maybe, but not seriously interested. There's a difference, you know. At this stage of my life, I need a man who's ready to make a commitment." She gave Pugsley a tiny corner of her egg roll. "Use your imagination, dear. I'll give you a hint. It fulfills my craving for something exciting and adventurous." *Exciting and adventurous?* She gave Lark a saucy wink.

I was stumped. "Stephen Spielberg called and he's offering you the lead in his next movie? Woody Allen invited you
to Michael's for an evening of jazz? You're replacing Mary
Hart on *ET*?"

"No, no, and no." Mom flashed me a sly smile. "You're
on the wrong track. Think hidden talent. Think of something
I've never done before."

"I give up," I said, helping myself to a hefty serving of
brown rice. My mother has always had a rich fantasy life
along with an obsessive interest in show business. I had no
clue what she had gotten herself into this time, but I had the
prickly feeling that whatever it was, it didn't bode well.

Mom leaned across the table and lowered her voice as if
she was about to impart a military secret. "I did some sleuthing today."

"Sleuthing?"

She nodded in my roommate's direction. "We all have to
step up to the plate to help Lark, honey. I know you've been
doing your best, but let's face it, Maggie, this investigation
is going nowhere. Lark is still the key suspect in Guru Sanjay's death, so I figured it was time for me to get into the act.
I did some snooping around." She paused. "And I seem to
have a real talent for it," she said with a note of surprise. "I'm
a natural."

"A natural," Lark piped up. The corner of her mouth
quirked in a smile.

Mom turned to Lark. "Did I ever tell you I played a private investigator once? It was on a Lifetime movie, just a
small part. But you know what they say—there are no small
parts, just small actors."

"Oh, no," I groaned. "Mom, what did you do?"

"Well, it all happened by accident. Serendipity, you know?"
Her eyes were bright with excitement, and I had to steel

myself for what I feared was coming. "That nice young man next door, Ted Rollins? I saw him out on the porch, and I just had to go over and introduce myself and admire his garden. I asked him how he managed to grow those beautiful pink hibiscus he has in the front of the inn."

"And then?"

"And as luck would have it, a rather stern-looking woman came rushing down the front steps. It seems she'd been part of Guru Sanjay's entourage and she'd left some papers in the lobby."

"Stern looking?"

Mom nodded. "She looked like a female version of Boris Yeltsin. And with no fashion sense at all, I regret to say. She was stuffed into an absolutely dreadful navy blue suit that made her look like a weiner schnitzel. With a matching pillbox hat, can you imagine?"

"Miriam Dobosh." I was surprised. *Why is Miriam back in town?*

"Yes, how did you know?"

"She was Guru Sanjay's right-hand man. Or woman," I amended quickly. "You spoke to her?"

"Oh, yes. We had quite a nice little chat." Mom toyed with her egg roll. "She remembered me from one of my early films, *Santa Cruz Love Song*. It's always nice to run into a fan, even after all these years. I was practically a schoolgirl when I played the part of Rosalita," she said wistfully. "I was a mere child. They were afraid it might be too sophisticated a role for me, but eventually they decided I had the right look for the part. The dewy-eyed innocence of youth. A Lolita type."

"Mom, you were forty-five years old."

"Pffft." Mom gave a dismissive wave of her hand. "Age is

just a number." She dropped another morsel of egg roll into Pugsley's open mouth. He was standing motionless by her chair, mouth open like a baby bird. "And anyway, Miriam remembered my work in the film. That's the important thing."

"She did?" Lark and I exchanged a look. As far as I knew, no one ever saw Mom's films, much less remembered them.

"Well, I had to prompt her a little. She had a Santa Cruz sticker on her notebook, and I mentioned I had once done a film that was set there. She told me Guru Sanjay had held a conference in Santa Cruz last month and that she was very fond of the city. Well, the next thing you know, we were talking away like best buds. Ted brought some iced tea, and we simply bonded. We have a lot in common, you know."

"You and Miriam?" I blinked. Surely she was kidding.

"Oh, yes. You know, Maggie, now that Guru Sanjay has 'transitioned,' as they say, poor Miriam is out of a job. And it seems like her whole life revolved around him and the organization. It's not going to be easy for her to find another job at her age, you know. Especially not with the same salary and perks she was getting from Guru Sanjay's organization."

I nodded. "That's probably true, but I still can't figure out why she told you all this." The crazy thing is, I actually could imagine it. People are always confiding in Mom, and perfect strangers tell her their innermost thoughts and secrets. Mom has a certain knack—maybe it's a trick all actors know—but when she talks to you, she makes you feel that you're the most fascinating person on the planet.

"I think she felt she could relate to me on some level." Mom shrugged. "We talked about how hard it is for women of a certain age to find employment. It's the same for actors, you know. I mean, how many Meryl Streeps or Diane Keatons do you see? Once you're over forty, they send you off to the La Brea Tar Pits."

"The La Brea Tar Pits?" Lark asked. "Isn't that in Los Angeles?"

"It's where the dinosaurs went to die," Mom said dryly.

Chapter 19

It wasn't until after dinner that Mom revealed the most interesting fact about her conversation with the ever-loyal Miriam. We were lingering over cappuccino and chocolate biscotti while Lark was flipping through the real estate section of the *Cypress Grove Gazette*. Lark has always dreamed of owning beachfront property—a nice fantasy, but not possible on a paralegal's salary.

"Real estate," Mom said, tapping the paper with one of her bloodred enameled nails. "That's what I should have invested in when I had the chance. The same thing happened to Miriam, you know," she said vaguely. "She told me could have made a killing, if only she'd listened to Guru Sanjay. It's so sad. She'd be financially secure if she'd just taken the plunge. Of course, she's kicking herself now, but it's all a moot point. It's too late, and now she's hustling for another job to support herself."

Now she had my full attention. "Do you mean Sanjay encouraged her to buy real estate?" This was the first I'd heard of this, but I wondered how a real estate deal could have related to his murder. "I didn't even know he invested in real estate."

"Oh, yes, he bought up properties all over south Florida. Condos, duplexes, some nice houses on the intracoastal. Really fabulous places. She said he had a good eye for real estate. Say what you want about him; he knew a smart deal when he saw one, and he wasn't afraid to take risks."

"How does Miriam fit into all this?"

"She found out he was buying properties and flipping them. You know, picking them up when they were about to foreclose, doing some quick renovations, and selling them for double what he'd paid for them."

"Interesting."

"He told her if she put up some cash, he'd cut her in on the deal, but she was afraid. She's at that age when a woman has to think about financial security, and the real estate market seemed too volatile." I wondered whether Mom was talking about herself or Miriam. Mom isn't the thriftiest person I know, and her erratic employment history didn't lend itself to fat IRAs or 401(k)s. As far as I knew, she hadn't even worked steadily enough to collect unemployment benefits.

"So she didn't lose any money, right?"

"No, she just lost a great opportunity." Mom gave a brittle laugh. "I told her I could certainly relate to that. When I think of the directors I could have worked with, the parts I should have had. Did I ever tell you about the time I had the chance to study at RADA? That's the Royal Academy of Dramatic Art. Just think, I would have trod the boards at the Old Vic with people like Gielgud, Richard Burton, Alec Guinness . . ."

Would've, should've, could've. Lark and I locked eyes over the table. She was too kind to tell Lola that she'd heard the story before. While Mom was regaling Lark with one of her many trips down memory lane, I decided to clear the table and take Pugsley out for a quick stroll. I'd walked only a couple of blocks when my phone chirped.

"Hey, there," Nick said when I picked up. "How's your head doing?"

"I still have a lump the size of a goose egg," I told him, "but I think I'll survive."

Pugsley stopped to inspect the base of his favorite banyan tree, and I stopped, too. "Mom just told me something interesting about Guru Sanjay. She ran into Miriam Dobosh, who gave her an earful about life with the guru." I quickly related the details of his lucrative real estate deals. "It turns out that Miriam didn't take the plunge, so she didn't lose any money. I was thinking that if she had, it would have been a motive for murder."

Nick's laugh, low and husky, eased over the line. "Maybe she didn't lose any money, but a lot of people did. Sanjay had a nice cash cow going down in Fort Lauderdale and Miami by buying properties and flipping them."

"That's perfectly legal," I pointed out. I never doubted that Guru Sanjay was a shrewd businessman, just a lousy excuse for a human being. Plus, he was an ex-con.

Flipping houses was the thing in south Florida. When the real estate market was flourishing, I'd heard of quite a few people making easy money by buying and selling houses. A new coat of paint, some new cabinets and flooring, and the houses were instantly rehabbed and put up for sale. A lot of them sold within a couple of weeks. If you were lucky and knew what you were doing, you could make twenty or thirty thousand over the price you had paid, in a very short space of time. As they say, "nice work if you can get it."

"Yes, but the plot thickens," Nick said.

"Do tell."

"Sanjay had an inside source with the Florida government. He knew which properties were going to be seized by the state, so he snapped them up first. Then he gussied them up, sold them for a whopping profit, and the new buyer was left holding the bag when the state came in."

"Wait a minute. Doesn't the state have to pay the market value of the property?"

"Yeah, but they decide what it is. And it might be a hell of a lot less than the buyer paid Sanjay for it."

"How can the state just come in and grab someone's property?"

"It's called the principle of eminent domain," Nick said patiently. "If the state can show that the property is needed for new development, that it will benefit the citizens, maybe bring in some added revenue, then they can force the owner to sell it to them. It's being tested in the courts, but so far the state is winning."

I'd heard about eminent domain but never really understood it until now. "And Sanjay knew which properties to buy? How could he do that?"

"He had an inside track. Maybe he just had good connections, or maybe he paid someone, but he was right every time. He made a killing."

"No pun intended."

"Sorry, that just slipped out." There was a beat of silence. "But you can be sure that Sanjay had to contend with some disgruntled buyers. They paid top dollar for these properties and then had them whisked right out from under them. They may have been forced to sell for a fraction of what they were worth, and it was all perfectly legal. I just started going through the real estate records, and it's only the tip of the iceberg. I think there's a big story here, waiting to be uncovered."

"Can you follow up on some of these people? Interview them?"

"I'd like to. But right now, I'm in the middle of that investigation into the high jinks at the mayor's office." Nick was following a paper trail of phony expense accounts in his investigation of corrupt government officials, from the mayor down to the councilmen. He was writing a hard-hitting series of articles that were making a lot of local officials run for cover, and I knew he'd made a few encmies along the way.

It was top-rate investigative reporting. With any luck, Nick would be nominated for a journalism award for his series and might be able to move to a bigger market. I'd miss him, but I knew this could be his chance to go to the big leagues, where he belonged.

"I've been following your stories. They're really good."

"Thanks. We've gotten a lot of letters to the editor and op-ed pieces on them. So I think the paper will make me go full steam ahead with the government corruption issue. I don't think I'll be able to spend too much time on Sanjay's death; it's already considered a cold case."

"A cold case? He was just murdered!" I said, feeling more than a little outraged.

"Maybe so, but don't forget, if murders aren't solved within the first forty-eight hours, they're likely to go unsolved. Plus, there don't seem to be any new developments. The police have Lark as a person of interest, and that's all. I don't think they have any other suspects. She was the last person to see him alive, and they're going to milk that for all it's worth. And preliminary results show that he cracked his head on the corner of the dresser. So did he fall or was he pushed? That seems to be the question. Of course, they're not even sure that was the cause of death." He paused. "How's she doing, by the way?"

"All right. You know Lark; she has this Zen acceptance thing going. It drives me crazy. She thinks everything happens for a reason and the universe will just magically tilt back in her favor."

"Not everyone tilts at windmills like you do, Maggie."

I snickered. My mother calls me the Patron Saint of Lost Causes. "You might be right." Lark's laid-back attitude was a perfect match for Nick's easygoing nature and I hoped the two of them would get together someday. "At the moment, I'm trying to persuade her to hire a lawyer, but she doesn't think she needs one, because she's innocent."

Nick let out a low whistle. "Bad thinking. She needs one if Rafe Martino thinks of her as a viable suspect. You should try to explain that to her. Even people who are innocent need lawyers; it's just an annoying fact of life."

"I know you're right," I said, letting out a breath. "She's like a babe in the woods. I'll talk to her again and see what I can do. In the meantime, how can I track down the people who bought property from Guru Sanjay? I've got a few days' sick leave coming and I was thinking of taking a trip down to Miami. I could check some things out, if you can part with the names."

"I'll fax you the names and addresses," Nick offered. "I'll make you a deal. Tell me what you come up with and I'll try to keep the story alive in the paper. Maybe a new angle will spark some extra coverage in the paper and get my boss interested again."

"Deal."

So early the next morning, Mom and I prepared to set off on a road trip. We were headed to Fort Lauderdale and Miami, and, if we had enough time, I was even thinking of adding a quick trip down to the Keys. Judging from the list Nick had faxed me, Guru Sanjay had conned people all over south Florida. Was one of them angry enough to kill him? Somehow I had to ferret out the truth, with Mom as my trusty sidekick.

She was in a tizzy of excitement at the thought of playing detective.

"I love it! We'll be just like Cagney and Lacey." She'd already tossed some clothes into a duffel bag and now was assembling her Avon-lady-size cosmetics case. She had enough makeup to cover the entire cast of *Aida*, if you didn't include the elephants.

"Cagney and who?" Lark asked. She was nursing a cup of peppermint tea and looked like she hadn't slept well. I hated to leave her alone in the condo, but she had Pugsley for company and she knew that finding Guru Sanjay's murderer had to be my focus right now.

Miriam Dobosh and Lenore Cooper, Guru Sanjay's ex-wife, were still high on my list of suspects, but I wanted to see whether I picked up any murderous vibes from people he'd conned in south Florida real estate deals. And of course, there was always Kathryn Sinclair, who said Sanjay had ruined her daughter's life. Wouldn't that be enough motive to kill someone?

"Cagney and Lacey were before your time, dear," Mom said breezily to Lark. "They were two gutsy female cops on television. How I would have loved to have been on that show." Her tone was wistful. "I even took lethal-weapons training so I'd look believable packing heat. I'd hoped for a part in *Charlie's Angels*, but sadly, that little minx Farrah Fawcett beat me out of the part." She leaned across the table. "All the blond hair, you know; that's what turned the tables."

"Wait. Back up a little. You said something about packing heat?" Lark raised her eyebrows, a hint of a smile touching her lips.

"It's all about realism," Mom told her. "Viewers are very knowledgeable, and I learned my way around a gun and how to squeeze off some shots." She turned to me. "Maggie, dear, do you think we'll need lethal weapons? I still have my permit someplace. I renew it every two years to keep it current. I have a license to carry a concealed weapon in the state of Florida," she added proudly.

Mom and a concealed weapon. A scary thought. In any state.

We drove into Fort Lauderdale around lunchtime and stopped for a quick lunch at an outdoor café on A1A to fortify ourselves. It was a perfect day. The sky was a paint-box blue with just a few wispy clouds to add interest, and across the street, the flat green ocean glittered in the sunlight. Everywhere, beautiful girls in bikinis were strutting their stuff along Ocean Drive, checking out the shops, leaving a trail of coconut Hawaiian Tropic in their wake.

"Don't they worry about their skin?" Mom whispered across the table. "They'll be leathery old hags by the time they're forty. Nothing ages you quicker than the sun, you know." Mom instinctively touched her own face, still taut and unblemished.

I smiled. "Forty seems like a long way off to them. A whole lifetime away." I looked at them and envied their carefree grins, long swingy hair, and perfect bodies. Life would catch up with them soon enough.

"Who's first on the list?" Mom asked when our pizza marinara and iced tea arrived.

"Ray Hicks. He's actually south of here, near a town called Briny Breezes."

Mom frowned. "Briny Breezes. That sounds familiar somehow. Isn't that the place where a couple of guys from New

Jersey made a killing? They each bought a trailer and a tiny spot of oceanfront property. It was minuscule, the size of a postage stamp, but they bought it anyway. And then a developer came in and offered them half a mil or something like that?"

"That's the place. It was written up in all the papers. But Ray Hicks wasn't involved in any of that. He's just someone who's living in a double-wide because he got screwed over in one of Sanjay's business deals."

"Does he know we're going to pay him a visit?"

I tossed her an innocent grin. "I thought it would be more fun to surprise him."

Chapter 20

Nearly an hour later, we spotted Brentwood Bay Village, a "manufactured home community" that offered "resort living at an affordable price." In case you're wondering, a "manufactured home community" is code for trailer park.

According to the signs dotting the highway, Brentwood Bay was nirvana for boaters and anglers, including fishing for large-mouth bass, bream, speckled perch, red-finned pike, bluegill, and sunshine bass.

"Are you sure this is the right place?" Mom had her head hanging out the window like a cocker spaniel, checking out the sad little development. A WELCOME TO BRENTWOOD BAY sign was riddled with bullet holes and hanging off its hinges. It seemed more humid here than it had at the ocean, and heat was rising off the black tarmac as we edged slowly past a row of dilapidated trailers.

"I'm positive. Nick got the address from the Florida courthouse records. Ray Hicks lost everything because of Sanjay, and he's reduced to living in this place."

Mom was frowning, reading the travel guide as we crept along, her eyebrows locked in concentration. "But there's been some mistake. There's no water here. What are they talking about? There's not even a bay! How could anyone go fishing?"

"Maybe the bay is somewhere around the back," I said, checking out the depressing lanes of rusting mobile homes lined up side by side. "Or maybe they shoot fish in a barrel here, who knows?" The whole place had a distinctly *Grapes of Wrath* feel to it.

"And what about the dolphins and manatees at play? It's a dust bowl!" Mom craned her neck to get a 360-degree view of the place. "And where are the state-of-the-art exercise facilities and spa? I don't see a trace of anything like that." She gave a delicate snort. "False advertising, that's what I say. It should be illegal to get people's hopes up."

"I don't think people like Ray Hicks have too many hopes."

I pulled up to number forty-six, a pale blue mobile home that looked so ancient, I figured a good wind could topple it. Weeds had taken over the tiny area in front of the trailer, along with a collection of old tires and hubcaps. A bouquet of pink plastic flowers made a valiant stand in a battered terra-cotta pot, and a tabby cat sat cleaning himself in the sunshine.

A scrawny man in his early fifties was standing outside, fiddling with something on a smoking grill. He had dark greasy hair and was wearing a wife-beater with a pair of dirty jeans. He looked up suspiciously when I pulled up and scowled by way of greeting. The trailer had two grimy windows and a battered screen door. The metal door to the trailer was open, which made me think he didn't have air-conditioning and was hoping to catch a breeze.

"Whaddaya want?" he yelled, not moving from the grill.

I flashed him my brightest smile and got out of the car

gingerly, keeping a tight hold on the door handle. I heard a wild barking coming from close by. For all I knew, a pair of pit bulls would come racing around the battered trailer any second and tear us to shreds. I wished I'd thought to tuck a can of Mace in my purse.

"Mr. Hicks? Can we speak to you for a moment?"

"Whatever you're sellin', I don't want any. And if you're a damn bill collector, I cut up my credit cards. You can go look in the garbage if you want."

What a charmer.

"What a beautiful area, Mr. Hicks," Mom said, suddenly appearing at my side.

She always did like a challenge. Mom likes to pick the most boring person at a party and engage him in conversation. She wants to see whether she still "has it," as she says, whether she can still work her fabled charm on men.

I bit my lip to keep from laughing. She had her work cut out for her with Ray Hicks.

"I've just been reading about your lovely development. It's such a pleasure to see it for myself. It is absolutely charming." She clasped her hands together dramatically. *Charming?* You would think she was talking about a thirty-room mansion in Boca, not a double-wide in the middle of nowhere.

"Well, it ain't for sale."

"No?" She gave a little moue of disappointment. "I can see why. Who would want to sell a such a lovely slice of paradise?" I noticed her spike heel was slipping into a brownish pile of what I hoped was mulch. She reached out for my arm to steady herself, but her smile never faded. A faint smell rose up from the pile.

It wasn't mulch.

"Exquisite!"

Ray Hicks merely grunted at her extravagant praise, but

Mom was undaunted. Maybe it's because she's dealt with rejection as an actress ("there were two hundred girls there, auditioning for a three-line part!"), maybe it's her strong personality, but she's persistent to the core. I grinned, wondering what was coming next.

She waved the *Florida Travel Guide* at him, giving him her best Hollywood smile.

"Homosassa," she said enthusiastically.

"What's that?"

"Homosassa." She gestured to his rusted-out trailer and sandy yard.

"Who you callin' a homo, lady?" He waggled a grilling fork at her as if he'd like to skewer her, and she backed up swiftly, stepping on my peep-toe shoes.

"Homosassa. It's an Indian word; it means 'land of many fish.'" She gasped her indignation.

"Yeah? Well, you ain't gonna see too many fish here," he said grudgingly. "Unless you count these catfish my fishing buddy gave me. They were so little, he was going to throw them back, but I told him I'd fry them up with some hush puppies."

"They look tasty," Mom said politely.

"If we could just have a few moments of your time," I began. "We need to ask you about Sanjay Gingii."

Ray Hicks turned a violent shade of purple. "That con man!" he said, jabbing the air with his giant fork. "Give me five minutes alone with him. That's all I want: five minutes alone." He grinned menacingly, showing a mouthful of missing teeth. "There won't be enough of him left to bury, I promise you."

Mom and I exchanged a look. "You mean you haven't heard the news?"

"What news is that?"

"Guru Sanjay is dead." I watched him closely, eager to see his reaction.

"Dead? Dead!" He paused to flip the fish, shaking his head, a satisfied expression on his sweaty face. "That's the first good news I've heard all week. I've been up in Panama City doing some fishing. Haven't read the paper or listened to the radio." He paused. "Doesn't change my situation any, but I'm glad he got what was coming to him. So what happened to the dude? He have a heart attack or something like that? He was carrying a lot of weight under those bedsheets he always wore."

"Someone killed him," Mom blurted out. I raised my eyebrows and gave her a warning nudge.

"For real?" Either Ray Hicks had taken some acting lessons, or he was genuinely surprised to hear the news. Since I couldn't imagine him studying the Stanislavski method through a home-study course, I decided to give him the benefit of the doubt.

"He died under mysterious circumstances," I said. "The police are investigating, but at the moment, they're really not sure what happened to him. He was giving a seminar up in Cypress Grove and was found dead in his hotel room." I carefully omitted the fact that my own roommate was considered a person of interest by the local police.

"Well, it couldn't have happened to a nicer guy," he said with grim satisfaction. "I hope his death was long and slow."

Mom gave a delicate shudder. "How well did you know him?"

"Too well," Ray said with a snicker. "That sumabitch ruined my life." He deftly transferred the cooked fish to a plate. "You ladies want to come inside? I can offer you a cold one."

"Yes, we'd love to," Mom said graciously.

"Not sure there's enough of this catfish to go around, though," he said, peering at the plate.

"Oh, we've already eaten," Mom reassured him. "We stopped at a delightful little seaside place up in Fort Lauderdale. But thank you, kind sir," she added. "Your hospitality to two visitors is certainly appreciated."

Now Mom was channeling Blanche DuBois in *Streetcar Named Desire*. I waited for her to say her favorite line: "I have always depended on the kindness of strangers," but she managed to restrain herself.

So far.

"Well, come in and take a load off," Ray Hicks said, holding the battered screen door open for us. The orange tabby whizzed past us and jumped on the kitchen counter. "Don't mind Oscar," he said. "He came with the trailer." The cat immediately jumped into the sink and began drinking water from a leaky tap.

"Delightful," Mom said, looking at the cluttered mess. There wasn't a touch of irony in her voice. All those years of acting training at the American Academy had finally paid off.

It was stifling in the trailer, like being entombed in a tin box. The ceiling was low, contributing to the claustrophobic feel, and layers of clothes and newspapers covered every available surface. The kitchen, living area, and bedroom all melded into one unsightly mess, and an open lavatory door gave us a view of a yellowing porcelain toilet. Mom's hand involuntarily went to her throat as if she couldn't get enough oxygen.

"How sweet. I see you have little dishes of food scattered around for Oscar," Mom said. She pointed to some chipped bowls filled with brown pellets that were lined up on the greasy linoleum floor. "I never trust a man who doesn't like cats. They always seem to be lacking in sensitivity some-how."

Ray chortled. "That ain't cat food. That there's rat poison. We got rats the size of possums in this danged place. I think they come up from the swamp."

"Oh, my." Mom blanched and for once in her life couldn't think of anything else to say.

Ray peered inside an ice-encrusted dorm-size refrigerator. "I have Coors and Rolling Rock," he said, ever the gentleman.

"Just water, please." Then I spotted a row of cloudy glasses lined up on the counter. A bluish substance that looked like mold was growing in several of them. It would be like drinking out of a petri dish. *Ewwww.* "Actually, I forgot, I have my own water bottle right here with me," I said, digging into my purse.

I triumphantly held up two water bottles and passed one to Mom. She practically grabbed it out of my hands. Pretending to be a Tennessee Williams character is one thing; coming down with Ebola is another.

"So how come you pretty ladies are interested in Sanjay?" Ray asked, a sly look crossing his face. "Don't tell me he did you out of some money, too?"

"Oh, no, not at all," I said swiftly. "Nothing like that. I happened to interview him on my radio show up in Cypress Grove. He was in town promoting his latest book. Maybe you've heard of my show? *On the Couch with Maggie Walsh*?"

A sudden light came into his eyes and he leaned forward eagerly, treating us to a blast of particularly rancid breath. "I knew it! You're that gal on WYME! Dr. Maggie. I should have recognized your voice. I listen to your show all the time."

"Well, I'm glad you're a fan," I said warmly.

"Never had the nerve to call in, though. Man, you've got some sick puppies on the show. I don't know how you stand it, listenin' to them whinin' and bitchin' all the time. I bet sometimes you feel like taking a rusty razor to the lot of them."

I decided to let that last comment slide. "Did you happen to hear the show I did with Sanjay?"

Ray suddenly busied himself with his plate of charred catfish. "No, I can't say that I did. Must have been busy that day." He knew enough to look me directly in the eye when he said it, but he hesitated just a fraction of a second too long. I figured he might be lying. Had he tuned in that day? But how could I ever prove it? And did it even matter?

"Sanjay's conference was held at the Seabreeze Inn right in the heart of Cypress Grove. We ran ads for it all week. We even ran a contest offering a free registration for one lucky listener."

"Really? Must have missed the show that day. Never heard of the Seabreeze. I don't think I've even driven through Cypress Grove. Is it a nice place?"

I ignored Ray's clumsy attempt to change the subject.

"So you didn't attempt to see Sanjay when he was in town?" I figured I might as well go for the direct approach.

Ray's face hardened. "I just told you, girlie, I never even been to your neck of the woods. And why would I be going to one of those silly-ass conferences or whatever he called them? I had a bellyful of Sanjay, and I sure wouldn't pay good money to listen to him."

A bellyful of Sanjay. Interesting.

"What happened between you and Sanjay? Was it some sort of a business deal that went awry?" Mom's voice was warm with empathy. Ray stared at her for several seconds, and his belligerence seemed to melt before my eyes like frost on a windowpane. It's true. Mom really can charm anyone once she sets her mind to it.

He swallowed hard before answering. "I guess it was old-fashioned greed that got me involved with Sanjay," he finally admitted. "I had some cash lying around and I never did have much faith in stocks and all that financial stuff. Never liked banks, either. As far as I'm concerned, a fool and his money are soon parted, you know what I mean?"

"I do, exactly," Mom said, touching him lightly on the arm. "So you had some extra cash and you met Sanjay. What happened next?"

"Well, I was looking to buy a nice little piece of property, and I especially wanted something on the ocean, you know, maybe on the intracoastal. Of course, there's hardly any waterfront property left in Florida these days. So I figured I'd settle for the bay. I didn't feel like buying anything inland."

Mom nodded. "I know; it's a shame." Her eyes never left his face. "And I always say, what's the point of living in Florida if you're not going to live on the water?"

"Exactly!" His weathered face creased in a grin. "I finally found a woman who understands me." He glanced over at me for affirmation, and I nodded. Mom was clearly on a roll, and I wasn't going to interrupt the flow of conversation.

"And that's when Sanjay entered the picture?" Mom lowered her voice as if signaling the arrival of Satan himself. "That's when the problems started?"

"You said it," Ray said and smacked his lips unhappily. "You know how they say if somethin's too good to be true, it probably isn't? Well, I fell for his line. And I admit, I was a mite foolish. You know, I'm the kind of guy who never can pass up a bargain. And Sanjay offered me somethin' beyond my wildest dreams." He paused for effect. "He offered me a nice little two-bedroom bungalow on Sunset Bay for six hundred thousand dollars."

"Wow!" I said in spite of myself. "That's an excellent price. Right on the water?"

Ray nodded. "You bet. It was the bay, not the ocean, but it had a boat dock and everything. Some of the neighbors had sailboats, but I just had me a little outboard. It was enough to cruise up and down the bay. I planned on living out my golden years on that little boat," he said morosely. "It was gonna be my own little piece of paradise."

I suddenly remembered reading a piece about Sunset Bay. A towering condo with underground parking had recently been constructed there. Uh-oh.

"And you bought the house," Mom said, trying to hurry him along.

"That I did; that I did." He took a long swallow of Coors and burped delicately. "And lived to regret it, let me tell you. Look at me now," he said, waving his hand at the dreadful trailer. "Stuck here for the rest of my days. Unless a miracle happens, and I believe they're in short supply. All I have to look forward to is going out to the tavern Friday nights. That's the highlight of my week, sad to say."

"But what happened to the house?" Mom asked. We exchanged a look. It seems that Ray Hicks had his own way of telling a story and couldn't be rushed.

He gave a harsh cackle. "Taken by the revenooers."

"Revenoors?" It was like Beverly Hillbilly–speak.

"I think he means revenuers," Mom said gently. "Are you saying the state came in and took over your house?"

"That's exactly what I mean. Imminent domain they call it. Well, it was imminent all right. One day I had me a nice little house and the next day I didn't. If that ain't imminent, I don't know what is."

"Eminent domain," Mom corrected him, but he was too caught up in his story to notice.

"The state sold it to some developer to put up a high-rise. All he really wanted was the land; he figured my nice little house should be a teardown. A teardown—can you believe it? Take a lookee and you tell me—does this look like a teardown to you?"

He opened a kitchen drawer and pulled out a picture of a modest ranch house on a barren stretch of beach leading down to the water. It looked like something out of the seventies, white brick and white wrought-iron trim and a scruffy lawn dotted with a couple of date palms. "This was it," he said sadly. "My dream home."

"Very nice," I said politely. "And you think that Sanjay knew all this was going to happen?"

"I'm more than sure. I know he did," he said savagely. "That bloodsucker knew exactly what was going on. Somehow he had some inside information. He sold the house to me, and then the state came right in and ripped it out from under me. They paid me some money, but nothing like what I paid for it. And there wasn't a thing I could do about it. Not a gosh-darn thing."

Except murder, I thought.

Chapter 21

"I think Ray Hicks got a raw deal from Sanjay, but I don't think he has what it takes to be a killer."

"Is that so?" Mom slung her long legs gracefully into the Honda Civic and took a deep breath. I immediately cranked up the AC. I'd deliberately left the car windows up, and now it was steaming like a sweatbox inside. A curtain fluttered at the trailer window and I suspected that Ray Hicks was watching us as we left.

"Did I miss something back there? What do you think?" I could tell from her offhand tone that she didn't agree with me. Mom has an uncanny way of ferreting out half-truths, evasions, and outright lies. I always tell her she missed her true calling and should have been a prosecutor.

"Let's get out of this dreadful place and I'll tell you," she promised. She fanned herself with a south Florida map. "How about a trip to Miami? That always raises my spirits."

"Mine, too. You're on. And I have a couple more people we need to see."

We drove south along A1A, admiring the glittering ocean on our left and the string of luxury hotels on the right. All the famous places I'd read about, the Eden Roc, the Fontainebleau, the fabled hangouts of Sinatra and the Rat Pack. Maybe the legends were gone, but Miami is still one of the most fabulous places on the planet.

And South Beach, playground of the hip and famous, is as exciting as ever. I pulled into a public parking garage on Sixteenth Street and we walked past Loews toward the beach and the News Cafe.

After ordering cappuccinos, we sat at a green umbrella table and checked out the scene for a few minutes. Across the street, girls whizzed by on roller blades. A vintage cream-colored Bentley with tinted windows purred by.

It was four thirty, but the sidewalks were already crowded. It was time for predinner cocktails or *cafés con leche*. Everyone looked tanned and beautiful, and a young couple at the next table was having an animated conversation in Spanish. The late afternoon sun splashed the Art Deco hotels with a golden glow, lighting up their Easter-egg pastel exteriors.

It was fun, hip, cosmopolitan.

Mom must have read the expression on my face. "Why don't you move down to Miami?" she asked softly. "You know you love it here."

I waited until our server placed steaming cups of coffee in front of us before answering. "Mom, you know my job is in Cypress Grove. I was lucky to get any job at all in radio; it's a tough field. How many talk radio shows does one city really need?"

"But you're exceptional. You're not just a talk show host. You're a licensed psychologist and you do a terrific job."

"And I think you might be a tiny bit biased." I grinned and blew on my coffee to cool it. "I'm not exactly a household name, you know. That's what it would take to get hired in a major media market like Miami. Big-time visibility. Name recognition. I'm under the radar screen, believe me. There are a zillion people who'd like a job as a radio host. I wish you could see how many audition tapes the station received, just from one tiny ad."

It's true. The station had placed a small ad in Media Bistro and had been deluged with applicants. I didn't even have an audition tape, so I cobbled together a few local radio interviews I'd done. The topics had all been psychological, women's health, stress management, relationships.

I'd been interviewed once on NPR, which must have caught someone's attention, because WYME listened to my tape and immediately invited me down to discuss the job. I did a sample audition (with Cyrus Stills playing the part of a call-in guest), and they decided I'd be a good match. Big Jim Wilcox came up with *On the Couch with Maggie Walsh* as the name of the show. I resisted the idea at first but finally realized it was catchy and gave in.

"Well, you should be a household name." She sniffed. "I think you moved too fast when you accepted that job at WYME. You should have held out a little longer and aimed for the top when you moved down here," she said. "You're loaded with talent. I think it's a confidence issue, really."

"Now you sound like the shrink." I grinned and held back a sigh. This was old territory, ground we'd covered many times before. I'd grabbed the WYME position because I didn't think I could take one more New York winter, and who knew when another opportunity would come along? Mom, however, was convinced that I had "settled."

"Let's get back to Ray Hicks," I said, pulling out a tiny notebook. "I know you're suspicious of him and I'd like to know why." I was really asking, *What did you pick up on that I didn't?*

"Oh, the hand to the nose. That was the tell," she said softly. "An easy one, actually."

"It was?" I stopped with my ballpoint hovering over my notes.

"Didn't you notice the way he swiped his nose with one hand when he pretended he'd never been to Cypress Grove?"

"No, I hadn't, actually." I shivered a little in the warm sunlight. Ever since we'd been to Ray Hicks's trailer, I'd had the irrational fear that bugs—maybe fleas—were crawling on me. "And then he went on and on talking. That's what people do when they're lying, you know—they add a wealth of unimportant details. They make the story even bigger than it has to be, and of course that's a sure giveaway."

"You could tell all that from his scratching his nose? What if he has allergies? Or a cold?"

"I don't think so." Mom shook her head. "It was classic."

"He looked me right in the eye when he said he'd never been to Cypress Grove."

"Easy. Con artists are good at making eye contact when they tell a bold-faced lie."

She was right. As always.

"What else?" I knew she was holding back and there were probably more things she'd picked up on. Sometimes I forgot that I was supposed to be the expert on human behavior and Mom was just a very observant actress. She picked up on dozens of things that I missed.

"Well, did you notice the way he covered his face when he talked about Sanjay? He pretended to be rubbing his eye with the back of his hand, but it was like he was covering his eyes, almost as if he was shielding them. He was concealing something. It reminded me of someone being blindfolded." She paused, toying with her spoon. "Or someone who deliberately was pulling down shutters. He didn't want us to see what his eyes might reveal. All on the unconscious level, of course."

"I didn't spot that."

My cell phone rang and I glanced at the readout. My reporter pal, Nick Harrison.

"What's up?" I said, after punching the TALK button.

"Just checking in." I could hear a low buzz of conversation behind him and I knew he was calling from the *Gazette*. I guessed they had just put the paper to bed and Nick was tying up some loose ends before heading out for dinner.

"Any good news?" After our meeting with Ray Hicks, I was ready to hear some.

"I did a little more background checking, and I came up with an R. Hicks who signed the register at the Seabreeze. The car license plate number he gave doesn't check out. There's something suspicious about him."

R. Hicks. Ray Hicks.

"Ray Hicks was at the Seabreeze?" My hand jolted involuntarily, and I splashed coffee on the white linen cloth. I glanced across the table, and Mom flashed me an "I told you so" look. "What night?"

"R. Hicks was there the night Sanjay died. Or went to his celestial resting place," Nick added with a low laugh. "It's either Ray or a heck of a big coincidence." I could picture Nick holding up his hand, palm out. "And don't remind me that Freud said there are no coincidences. What's your take on it?"

"I just talked to Ray Hicks." My mind was racing. Had Ray

Hicks been lying to me the whole time? This changed everything, and I wished I could rewind the tape in my head and
play the whole trailer-park scene again.

"You're kidding. What did he say?"

"He admitted that he got screwed over in a business deal
with Sanjay. He told me a complicated story about a real
estate buy and eminent domain. It was pretty much the way
you described it to me."

Nick grunted. "He got screwed over all right. I'd say to
the tune of a million bucks."

"Close enough. First I told him Sanjay was dead; then I
had to listen to his rant."

"What was his reaction to the news?"

"He was certainly glad to hear he was dead." I glanced at
Mom across the table; she was watching me with a laser-
beam intensity. She nodded emphatically.

"I bet he was." Nick gave a mirthless laugh.

"But he insisted he had nothing to do with it, and that
he'd never attended the conference. In fact, he even said he'd
never been in Cypress Grove."

"Where did you talk to him?"

"At his home in some awful mobile home park. He actually invited us inside." I shuddered, remembering the dismal
trailer with its smell of decaying cheese and onions.

"Was there a car parked out front?"

I nodded. "A beat-up Ford pickup truck. Black."

"Did you happen to get the license number?"

My heart sank like a stone. "I didn't think of it." *So much
for my investigative skills.*

"That's okay. I can get someone to run a background
check." I could hear Nick tapping away at his computer.

"Miriam Dobosh almost did." I suddenly remembered
Mom's conversation with her. "She said she wanted to, but

she didn't have the cash available. Sanjay acted like it was the deal of a lifetime."

"Interesting. So he wouldn't hesitate to cheat one of his own employees."

"And Miriam wasn't just an employee. She practically ran the whole show." *But maybe he wasn't planning on cheating her*, I thought. Maybe he was going to offer her a cut of his ill-gotten gains. It might be good to chat with her again to see whether she was willing to talk about Sanjay. "The part about Ray being at the Seabreeze is sort of a stretch, you know." Nick had stopped typing, and his voice broke into my musings. "I can't imagine him being the sort of guy who's into New Age conferences."

I tried to picture Ray Hicks walking into the Seabreeze in his filthy jeans. Wouldn't anyone have noticed? He hardly looked like one of Sanjay's well-heeled, if misguided, followers. He would have stood out like the proverbial sore thumb.

Mom scribbled a note on a paper napkin and passed it to me. "Did this R. Hicks use a credit card to pay for the room?" I relayed the question to Nick and gave her a thumbs-up sign. Good question. Ray Hicks had told us he'd cut up his credit cards.

"He paid cash. Hardly anyone uses cash, and that's why we missed it. The writing on the register is barely legible. It's practically a scrawl, like he used his left hand or deliberately was trying to conceal his name. The night clerk asked him for identification but he said he'd left his driver's license at a gas station a hundred miles back. So they took the cash and told him to write down his license plate number. No one checked, so he could have written down anything he wanted."

Something nagged at me. "Why would he sign the register with his real name if he didn't want to be discovered?"

Nick had an answer. "Sometimes criminals, especially the dumb ones, write their real name without thinking. If he'd been a little quicker on the uptake, he would have signed with an alias." There was a beat while he spoke to the assignment editor. "Did he seem smart to you?"

"I don't think he was the sharpest knife in the drawer. I'd say he was cunning rather than smart. Sort of a sly type."

There was silence on the line for a moment while I tried to think of my next move. I had to admit it: I was stumped. "Shall we go back to the trailer park?" I could see Mom wincing at the suggestion.

"Not yet," Nick said. "There's no sense in showing your hand. You can always do a follow-up visit when we have more information."

"What's going on in Cypress Grove? Anything new with the cops?"

Cops. I could feel my face flushing a little at the thought of Rafe Martino.

"They're keeping very quiet. I may pay them a visit tomorrow just to see if they throw me a bone. As far as I know, Lark is still the number-one suspect." He drew in a breath, and I knew there was more.

And then it came.

"I hate to be the one to tell you this, Maggie, but the DA is thinking of convening a grand jury next week. They're going to put everything they have on the line and see if there's enough to indict her for Sanjay's murder."

"Indict her? That's ridiculous."

"They have motive, means, and opportunity. She was obsessed with him, he tried to attack her, and she killed him."

"All they have is circumstantial evidence."

"People have gone to jail on less," Nick reminded me.

The sad thing is, I knew he was right. People have gotten the death penalty for less. Nick promised to stay in touch, and I told him I'd touch base in a day or two when I'd followed up on some more leads. It was a disappointing end to an unsettling conversation.

Chapter 22

Hearing the news about Lark cast a sudden pall over the beautiful day.

Mom, as usual, had the best take on the situation. "They're thinking of indicting Lark?" She raised a perfectly plucked eyebrow. "That is the most ridiculous thing I've ever heard. There's only one thing to do, Maggie. We just have to redouble our efforts," she said firmly. "What else did you find out?"

I filled her in on the mysterious R. Hicks who had signed the guest register at the Seabreeze, and she thought for a moment. "He could have been there, but why didn't anyone see him? Surely someone would have noticed. He's not the sort of man you can overlook, is he?" She gave a delicate shudder. "We can always talk to him again, but I think we should have a plan this time."

"We need an excuse to get back into the trailer," I said. But what? My mind had stalled.

Sleuthing was far more difficult than I'd realized. How come those TV cops always manage to wind everything up in a neat hour-long package? Actually, it's only forty-four minutes, if you subtract the commercials. A nice lineup of suspects, some clever detective work, and bingo, problem solved, suspect neatly placed in handcuffs and whisked away. If only real life could be so simple.

"Oh, there's a camera crew!" Mom said, immediately arranging her features in a practiced smile. She crossed her legs and tilted her chin up a tad, a trick she said she'd learned from Zsa Zsa Gabor—an instant way to tighten a sagging chin line before facing the cameras. "I think it's *ET* or *Access Hollywood*," she whispered excitedly. "Wonder what that's all about?"

"I heard they're shooting a new reality show here. Something about the beautiful young people of South Beach. I saw a promo for it earlier on *The Today Show*. They're probably in town to interview some of the stars."

"Not another reality show," Mom groaned. "Why does everyone in the cast look like they're under seventeen?"

"Probably because they are." I bit back a sigh. Nothing like a teen reality show to make a girl feel ancient at thirty-two.

We spotted a Lindsay Lohan look-alike, poured into a pair of skintight Cavalli jeans and a Pokémon baby T, doing a stand-up interview with Maria Menounos. A group of middle-aged tourists stood gawking nearby, looking like refuges from a Parrothead tour with their matching Margaritaville shirts. They were elbowing one another, holding up camera cell phones, trying to get a clear shot of the attractive entertainment reporter.

South Beach is the place to see and be seen, and it's not unusual to come across a camera crew setting up to shoot in the historic district. It's a cosmopolitan venue, with an interesting mix of cultures and styles. The trendy Art Deco hotels, with their signature pastel colors, are known all over the world. At night their dazzling neon facades attract a young, hip crowd.

Today they were setting up lights and sound equipment in front of the Art Deco hotels down the street. A sound truck was double-parked at the corner, a production assistant gabbing on her cell. "Look, there's Michael Aller," Mom said. She waggled her fingers at the man they called Mr. Miami, who flashed her a megawatt smile. "I think he recognizes me," she said happily. She beamed back at him. "He probably caught one of my recent movies. A few of them are still available on video, you know."

Maybe in Bosnia.

She gave me a wistful smile. As far as I knew, the last of her videos had gone out of circulation ten years ago. Mom was still waiting for the brass ring, even though the carousel had stopped running a couple of decades earlier.

"It's nice to be remembered," she said.

Who was I to burst her bubble? I didn't have the heart to tell Mom that Michael Aller, the tourism director and chief of protocol for Miami Beach, is a local celebrity himself. Did he actually recognize Mom from a dusty movie of times gone by? Whether he did or not didn't matter; she was thrilled at the attention.

I was planning our next move when I got a surprise call from Miriam Dobosh. Maybe there was such a thing as karma. How had she gotten my cell-phone number? Then I remembered I'd scribbled it on my business card and pressed it into her hand at the conference. She was all sweetness and light, different from the brusque woman I'd met at the Seabreeze Inn.

"I was wondering how the investigation was going," she said smoothly.

Funny, but she didn't sound at all broken up over Sanjay's death. No sign of desperation or anger, either. Had she come to terms with the fact that she'd been left jobless and penniless by Sanjay's sudden demise? Or had she discovered some new source of income that she was keeping a secret?

"The police are working on it," I said. A half-truth. They were just going through the motions because as far as they were concerned, they already had the killer. I had no intention of sharing that information with Miriam, though.

Mom gave me a questioning look, and I shrugged.

I still couldn't figure out what Miriam's game was, or what she wanted from me. "I'm sure the case will be resolved soon," I said carefully. A bland statement if ever there was one. Would the case really be solved?

You bet. Unless Mom and I did something fast to divert attention away from Lark.

"I had a nice chat with your mother over at the Seabreeze. . . ." She let the sentence trail off. I wasn't sure how I was supposed to respond to that, so I said nothing. "Did she tell you I hoped we could all get together for drinks if you ever come down to Miami?"

Now I was thoroughly confused. "No, she didn't mention that, Miriam. But I'd love to talk with you anytime."

Mom tapped me on the arm. "Miriam?" She mouthed the name at me across the table, and I nodded.

"Actually, Mom and I are in Miami right now. We're having coffee in South Beach at the News Cafe."

"Perfect!" Miriam gushed. "I came to town to meet with my accountant, and we're just wrapping things up. Meet me at the Delano in twenty minutes and I'll buy you the best dirty martini in town." I flipped the phone shut and stared at Mom. "You're not going to believe this. We're being summoned to the Delano to meet with Miriam Dobosh."

She raised her eyebrows. "Really? What does she want?"

"To buy us the best dirty martini in town."

"Make it a chocolate martini and I'm up for it," Mom said gamely. "Dirty martinis are awful, you know." She wrinkled her nose. "They put olive juice in them."

Olive juice? Blech. "But what does she really want?" Mom persisted.

"Good question. And I have absolutely no idea." I quickly paid our bill and we hurried back along Collins Avenue, which was quickly filling up with hungry tourists. Restaurant hostesses, all chic young women, tried to hand us menus as we rushed along the street, but I shook my head and barreled along, lost in thought.

I wondered how to play the meeting with Miriam. The investigation was taking a strange turn, but I had the feeling this might be my one chance to find out more about Sanjay. Who would know him better than the woman who had run his empire so successfully for all those years?

Miriam was waiting for us in the lobby. She was wearing a sleeveless sheath dress that revealed toned arms and an athletic build. My previous impression was mistaken—she was powerful rather than dumpy. "How lovely that we're both in Miami on the same day," she said warmly. "I have a table waiting for us in the Florida Room." She walked ahead of us while we oohed and aahed over the magnificent lobby. The elegant Florida Room was decorated like an old speakeasy, and I couldn't help but stare at the Lucite piano that dominated the room. The room was attractive, with a Bogey and Bacall feel to it.

Once we sat down and ordered (Mom and I wisely stuck to Evian and lime), Miriam leaned across the table, her voice oozing sincerity. "I hope you're going ahead with your plans for a Sanjay retrospective. There's been a lot of press about his death, and I hope we don't forget what he accomplished in his life. I want to help any way I can," she said, laying her hands on the table. "I'd like to be part of the effort, if I may."

I noticed that her hands were large, and her nails were blunt cut, almost like a man's. They looked powerful. Hands that could harm or even kill?

"You know I'd appreciate any information you can give us, Miriam. Was there something in particular that you recalled about the conference? Or about the guests?"

"Well," she said slowly, "I've noticed a few things, but I'm not sure how significant they are." There was something vague about her tone, and I realized that she was on a fishing expedition.

I thought of mentioning our meeting with Ray Hicks and decided not to. I was a little wary of telling Miriam all our secrets. Why did she want to be in the loop, anyway? Was it because she really wanted Sanjay's murderer brought to justice?

Or was it something more sinister? Nick always told me that the best way to deflect attention from yourself as a possible suspect is to get involved in the investigation itself. Be part of the inner circle, and you have a better chance of knowing what leads the police have, what the evidence is.

"Go on," I urged her. "Even the tiniest detail might be helpful."

"I saw you talking to Kathryn Sinclair at the transition service."

The transition service? I gave myself a mental kick and realized she meant Guru Sanjay's memorial. "Yes, she told me quite a shocking story." I locked eyes with Miriam, wondering how much she knew about the incident with Sarah Sinclair.

"It seems shocking at first," she said smoothly, "but really, Maggie, if you knew a little more about Sarah's background, you would see the girl was simply a train wreck. An accident waiting to happen. She was desperate for attention, you know."

"Really?" I tried to sound noncommittal.

Miriam tapped her head. "Sarah had a long history of psychological problems, I'm afraid. Deep-rooted personality problems." She smiled, her eyes gleaming with an inner light. Her devotion to Sanjay was beginning to seem almost pathological. There was definitely something off about the woman, and my antennae were twitching.

"But surely you screen for those sorts of problems before you let someone participate in the encounter-group weekend, don't you?"

Touché. Miriam looked flushed and toyed with her dirty martini. "Well, yes, we make every effort to, but I'm afraid there are always a few people who slip under the radar screen. It happens very rarely, and I'm probably to blame. My mother was sick that week, and I was out of the office. I would have vetted her more carefully if I'd been the one reviewing the application." She paused. "That girl has certainly caused a lot of trouble for all of us. I never want to go through anything like that again."

"No, I imagine you don't," Mom said sympathetically.

"She was one sick puppy," Miriam said, staring morosely into her drink.

I had the feeling that Miriam would do or say anything to preserve Sanjay's reputation, and I was baffled. Why the blind loyalty? I could see it as a Lifetime movie: *Obsession: The Miriam Dobosh Story.*

And hadn't Sanjay betrayed her? Wasn't he going to hand

over the reins to Olivia Riggs, the young woman who'd been crying in the ladies' room that day? Miriam had insisted at the time that Olivia was distraught and delusional. I was beginning to see a pattern here. Anyone who Miriam didn't like was labeled a head case.

"That's not the impression I got from her mother," I said mildly. There was no sense in antagonizing Miriam if I hoped to squeeze any information out of her. "I pictured Sarah as a sensitive, depressed young woman who probably was too emotionally fragile for an encounter group."

"Fragile, my ass," Miriam said bluntly. "She was a borderline, as manipulative as they come."

"Borderline?" Mom asked.

"Borderline personality disorder. Borderlines do tend to manipulate people; they sort of suck you into their world," I said slowly. I was surprised that Miriam even knew the term. It's not commonly used outside of psychological circles. "They tend to be very emotional, very needy, and form instant attachments to people."

I mulled this over. Could it be true? Hadn't Kathryn Sinclair said that Sarah had idealized Sanjay at first, thinking he would be her savior, and then she completely turned against him? Idealizing someone and then devaluing him was classic borderline behavior.

"I think you might have been taken in by Kathryn Sinclair," Miriam said, echoing my own thoughts. I could feel myself flushing. "She can be quite convincing." I waited, toying with my Evian and nibbling on a cracker. "It could be a case of erotomania, you know."

Erotomania?

Miriam's eyes were bright with enthusiasm as she tossed around psychological terms. "That's when someone is madly in love with someone else and is so delusional, she thinks he loves her back." She said this for Mom's benefit; Mom looked like her head was reeling with Miriam's psychological mumbo jumbo.

"You think Sarah Sinclair was in love with Sanjay?" I was beginning to wish I had ordered that martini. Now my head was swimming, too.

"It's very possible," Miriam said darkly. "Maybe she decided that if she couldn't have him, no one could. He had a devastating effect on women. Look at Lenore Cooper." She went off on a five-minute rant on Sanjay's ex-wife, while Mom and I sat silently. Interesting how she jumped from one suspect to the next, I decided.

"You really think Lenore Cooper might be involved in his death?" I asked.

"Lenore had it in for Sanjay because she stupidly thought he'd ruined her career. He had nothing to do with it. Her book sales went down and people didn't flock to her seminars anymore, but it wasn't Sanjay's fault. He was the one with the charisma; all she had were some dusty degrees. Audiences loved him; that's all that really matters."

"I suppose that's one way of looking at it," I offered, keeping my tone neutral.

"I just want to make sure you're looking at the right people in the investigation," she said finally, wrapping up her animated attack on Lenore Cooper. "Kathryn and Lenore: It's really a toss-up, isn't it? Mark my words, it's one or the other." She paused. "Or Sarah Sinclair."

I nodded and finished my drink. Miriam looked satisfied with herself, and it was clear that she had no idea that I was more suspicious of her than ever. After her annoying tirade, I was ready to move her to the head of the suspect list. My only hang-up was motive. What did she have to gain by San-jay's death? As far as I could see, absolutely nothing. Was I missing something?

As we said our good-byes and left the Delano, I turned to Mom. "What did you think of all that?" I asked as soon as we had blended back into the crowd on Collins Avenue. "She certainly was going out of her way to prove her inno-cence." I shook my head in bewilderment. "And she wants us to believe she's looking for Sanjay's killer. I don't know what to make of her."

Mom gave me an arch smile and repeated one of her fa-vorite Shakespearean quotes. " 'Methinks the lady doth pro-test too much.' " Mom has a quote from the Bard for every occasion. Sometimes they fit, and sometimes they're a stretch. This one was right on target.

"Methinks the same thing."

"So what's next?" she asked as we headed back to the parking garage. An enticing smell of garlic and tomatoes was wafting out of an Italian restaurant, but I ignored it, fo-cusing on the task at hand. I was a woman on a mission.

"I think we should go back to Cypress Grove," I said. "But we need to make a stop along the way. A very impor-tant stop."

"Okay," Mom said, as agreeable as ever. She gave me a tentative smile, as if she knew something was up.

I felt it was only fair to warn her we were heading into treacherous waters. "Mom, I want you to know that we're going to do something that's illegal, foolhardy, and probably dangerous. We could end up with a criminal record. I could lose my license and we could both go to jail. If you want out now, just say the word. I can drop you back at your condo and go on by myself."

Her blue eyes widened. "Illegal, foolhardy, and dangerous. Mmm, it sounds delicious. Let me guess. Are we going
to kidnap Ricky Martin?"

"Worse than that," I said dryly. "We're going to pay another visit to Ray Hicks." I paused, watching for her reaction. "And this time we're going to break into his trailer. It
might not be pretty. So, are you in or out?"

Mom blinked twice and giggled. Her face was lit with
excitement, but her laughter had a nervous edge to it. "I love
an adventure. Count me in."

Chapter 23

Dusk was settling in as we left Miami and tooled along the two-lane highway toward Brentwood Bay Village. Mom was unusually quiet, and I had the sneaking suspicion she was feeling some twinges of doubt about my plan. Or maybe she doubted my sanity.

I had no idea what I might come across in the trailer, and I wasn't even sure what I was looking for. I just knew that Ray Hicks was hiding something and that I had a better chance of finding it if he wasn't there.

Mom gave a nervous cough and took a deep breath. "A thought just occurred to me, dear. What if Ray Hicks is outside, grilling another platter of that foul-smelling fish? And he might have a gun, you know. He looks like the type who wouldn't hesitate to shoot us. I think Florida has some fairly liberal laws about what a homeowner can do to protect his property." She toyed with the clasp on her knockoff Fendi bag. "A lot could go wrong tonight. You know what the Greeks say: 'There's many a slip twixt the cup and the lip.'"

I didn't think she really expected an answer to that little gem, so I nodded and kept driving, my mind churning.

Mom's face was a sickly shade of white, and I knew she

dreaded another encounter with the delightful Mr. Hicks. She—and the Greeks—were right. It's one thing to talk about breaking into his trailer and another to be faced with actually doing it.

I tried not to think about the penalties the Florida justice system would levy for the crime of breaking and entering. In spite of what Ray Hicks had said about eminent domain, I had the feeling Floridians are pretty big on property rights. A man's home is his castle, even if it's a double-wide in the middle of nowhere.

Breaking and entering, or B and E, is considered a major crime in the Sunshine State. I could just see Big Jim Hicks running the story on WYME. "Radio Shrink Charged with B and E in Trailer Park Heist!" Not that there would be anything in Ray's trailer worth stealing, but Big Jim would play the story to the hilt. He'd love to see me handcuffed again, doing the perp walk, for his amusement.

Handcuffs. My thoughts veered toward Rafe Martino, and I wondered whether he would let me plea-bargain the charge down to malicious mischief. I realized my thoughts were bordering on the hysterical and I ordered myself to calm down and concentrate. Mom was already having her doubts about our excellent adventure, and I knew it was time to rein in my own fears and reassure her.

"Look, Mom, I'm counting on the fact that he won't be there. Remember when he said he always goes out for a few beers on Friday night? He's probably at some hole-in-the-wall tavern right this minute. We'll have the place all to ourselves." I forced a fake chuckle, even though I was quaking inside.

We turned down the road that led to number forty-six, and I felt Mom stiffen in the seat next to me, her hands trembling in her lap. "I wish I shared your optimism," she said, and then suddenly one hand flew to her mouth. "Oh, god, oh, no!" she cried.

"What? What is it?" My nerves were jumping, and I nearly slammed on the brakes.

"The dogs." She lowered her voice as if they could hear us. "Even if Ray Hicks is out for the evening, won't the hounds from hell be there? They'll tear us limb from limb." She shivered, and I felt a fine line of goose bumps sprout up along my upper arm.

The dogs! I had forgotten about the dogs. We'd heard their fierce barking earlier that day, but I'd never caught a glimpse of them. I remembered that their barking had a big-dog sound to it. I went through some big-dog images in my mind, and I didn't like the visual my brain pulled up.

Rottweilers, German shepherds, maybe even a pair of pit bulls. I pictured Cujo. Or maybe the Hound of the Baskervilles.

There was no way those barks came from cuddly little schnauzers or Pomeranians with cutesy pink bows in their fur. These dogs would be straight out of a Stephen King novel; I just knew it.

I took a deep breath and scanned the property. Where were they lurking? I pulled up in front of the trailer. I didn't see any evidence of a fenced-in yard; did he keep the dogs tied up in the back? We'd soon find out. It looked like we were in luck. No sign of the truck, and the lights in the trailer either were out or were turned down very low. The cheap brown curtains were tightly shut, so it was hard to tell.

"What do you think?" Mom said, her voice an octave higher than usual. "Is he out?"

"It looks that way. His truck is gone, and the trailer is dark."

"But the dogs. What about the dogs?"

"I think they would have come tearing around the trailer by now. Or at least there'd be some barking. They must have heard the car by now." I turned off the engine, and we sat quietly for a moment, while I explored my options. One option (the sensible one) was to admit that I was on a fool's errand and to make tracks back to Cypress Grove. A nice dinner at an oceanfront restaurant, and then back home in time for a glass of wine with Lark. Let the Cypress Grove PD sort out Sanjay's death. That's what they were paid to do, wasn't it?

Since this was the sensible option, I immediately discarded it. In for a dime, in for a dollar. "Okay, listen up. Here's the plan," I said, sounding like an actress in a B spy film.

Mom leaned forward eagerly. "Yes?"

"I'm going inside the trailer." I took a deep breath. "You're going to stay out here."

"Why do I have to stay out here?" I couldn't tell whether she was annoyed or relieved.

I thought for moment. "Because I need you as a lookout. You can let me know if Ray suddenly comes barreling along in his pickup. You can talk to him and stall him while I sneak out of the trailer." This was going to be a difficult feat. As far as I could tell, the trailer had only one door.

"But what will I say if he does show up?" she asked wildly. "How in the world will I explain that you're inside his home? And how will you get in there, anyway? I'm sure he keeps it locked up tight. He seems like a suspicious sort."

Good point. Actually, two good points. I licked my lips. "I haven't figured that out yet."

I opened the car door as quietly as I could and listened carefully. So far, so good. No canine attack team was headed my way. I took a deep breath and was about to slide out of the car when Mom put her hand on my arm.

"Wait a minute. You mean you haven't figured out what I'm supposed to say, or you haven't figured out how you're going to get inside?"

"Both. I haven't figured anything out yet."

She looked crestfallen, but then she brightened, easing back into the seat. "Oh. Well, I'm sure something will come to you, dear," she said warmly. "You've always been quite creative. Here, take this; you might need it." She passed me a tiny flashlight, the one she keeps on the key ring, and then she leaned over and silently closed the car door.

Then she pushed the button down to lock all four doors.

My mom. Always thinking ahead.

I approached the trailer. Dead silence. I tensed, waiting for Ray Hicks to come tearing out of his trailer or for the hounds from hell to come bounding over the dusty yard. No curtains fluttering at the grimy windows, no sound inside. It was as if a neutron bomb had struck, killing every living thing but leaving all the double-wides intact.

I swallowed hard and walked up the two concrete steps. I held my breath, tapped on the wooden frame around the screen door, and silently counted. When twenty seconds had passed and nothing had happened, I glanced back at Mom and gave her a cheery thumbs-up.

The battered screen door was closed, but it was warped and there was a good three-inch gap showing at the bottom. All I had to do was nudge it open quietly and then tackle the main door.

This was the tricky part. I gingerly tried the handle on the metal front door, and the skin on the back of my neck prickled. The door didn't budge.

Surprise, surprise. The trailer door was locked, but a quick swipe of my Visa card and it creaked open. I was amazed. I've seen that trick on a million cop shows but never really believed it worked until now.

My heart was hammering as I stepped inside the darkened interior. It smelled even worse than earlier in the day, and I realized that all the windows were closed. No sign of Ray Hicks, but I noticed an open can of beans on the counter and an old-fashioned black frying pan on the burner.

Now that I was inside the trailer, I had no idea where to start looking. I flipped on the tiny flashlight, feeling like Nancy Drew in *The Mystery at the Moss-Covered Mansion*.

The place was a mess, and I wondered where Hicks kept his papers and bills. I spotted a shoe box filled to overflowing with documents on the top shelf of a built-in fiberboard bookcase over the stove. I pulled it down and riffled quickly through the contents: coupons and past-due electric bills, a notice from the Brentwood Bay Village Association reminding him to keep lids on his trash cans. Nothing interesting.

A quick look through the cabinets under the four-burner stove. Nothing again. Dirty glassware and cheap crockery piled on the shelves above the stove. A pan lid clattered down to the floor, and I nearly jumped out of my skin.

Where to look next? I hated to tackle the bedroom, but it was my only option. The door was wide-open, and I could see piles of clothes scattered on the unmade bed, like a suitcase had exploded. The louvered closet door was tilting half off its hinges, and I spotted a couple of windbreakers hanging inside.

I quickly went through the pockets. A couple of matchbooks and loose change. I stood on my tiptoes to run my hand over the closet shelf and came up empty. I looked around with a sense of despair. There had to be something tying Ray Hicks to Guru Sanjay, but what?

And then I spotted it.

A well-thumbed copy of *Heal the Cosmos* on the bedside table.

I remembered Sanjay saying it was his latest release. Why would Ray Hicks be reading it? More important, where had he gotten it? It had one of those little gold foil "Signed by Author" stickers on the cover, and I opened the book gingerly. There, on the very first page, was a florid inscription to Ray Hicks from Sanjay Gingii.

It was dated the day Sanjay died.

Bingo. I felt a happy little surge of triumph. This placed Ray Hicks at the conference after all, on the very day that Sanjay went to that big ashram in the sky. Motive, means, and opportunity. I'd nailed him!

I picked up the book, turned off the flashlight, and prepared to make my way out of the trailer. I could hardly wait to see what Rafe Martino and the entire Cypress Grove PD would make of this new evidence.

Guru Sanjay always said that good karma is instantly followed by bad karma. It is the "way of the universe." Here is the CliffsNotes version of his philosophy: For every good thing that happens to you, you are immediately zapped with a disaster. Every smile is followed by tears. A burst of sunlight will inevitably give way to a torrential downpour. I've never really understood that philosophy.

Until now. Suddenly it all made sense.

I think having a gun jammed in my back really cleared my head.

Chapter 24

"Drop it, girlie." I felt something cold and hard nudging my spine, and my breath caught in my throat.

Ray Hicks. I'd recognize that hayseed accent and fishy breath anywhere.

"Turn around real slow, and don't try to pull a fast one."

"I won't," I warbled. "I promise. No fast ones. Not even a slow one." So much for my sleuthing technique. I hadn't even heard him slip into the trailer. How had I missed this one? I never saw it coming. I slowly raised my hands in a surrender pose.

My thoughts flew to Mom. What had he done to her? Had he knocked her unconscious, or something much worse? My mind was scrambling with dark thoughts, and fear began to explode like fireworks in my chest.

Ray Hicks had killed her, and I was responsible. I felt an overwhelming wave of sadness sweep over me, and my eyes blurred with tears. It didn't matter what happened to me now. Mom was gone forever.

And then I heard a familiar voice calling to me from the living room.

"You better do what he says, Maggie," Mom piped up.

Out of the corner of my eye, I spotted Mom standing in the living room shadows. She must have gotten out of the car and followed Ray inside. "He's armed with a bottle of Rolling Rock."

Rolling Rock? I spun around to see a sheepish grin on Ray Hicks's face and a beer bottle in his hand.

"I've always wanted to do that," he said, lowering the bottle. "Saw it on a crime show once. The killer poked someone in the back with a beer bottle, and they figured he had a snub-nosed revolver." He chortled with glee, which set off a phlegmy coughing fit. "Guess I had you goin' there for a minute or two," he said. He looked inordinately pleased with himself.

"Yes, you did," I said, nearly choking on the words. I swallowed hard. A lump the size of a walnut had appeared in my esophagus, and my knees had turned to Jell-O.

Ray Hicks reached over and flipped on a light switch. The trailer was filled with a yellowish glow.

"What's going on here?" I took a step toward Ray Hicks, tilting my chin. "You have no business intimidating me like that. I nearly had a heart attack. You could be charged with making a terroristic threat."

Ray laughed and motioned for me to follow him into the living room. "Girlie, listen to yourself. You broke into my trailer, I caught you going through my stuff, and now you're accusing me of terroristic whatever? You got some gall; that's all I can say."

"I'm afraid he's right, Maggie," Mom said. "We should have waited for Mr. Hicks to return and invite us inside." I stared at her. "You were terribly rude, I'm afraid, just barging in like this." A touch of a Boston accent had crept into her voice, and she was sounding oh-so-upper-class, chomping down on her vowels as if they were raw oysters.

I moaned softly and sank down next to her on the sofa. I was terribly rude? What was Mom doing now—channeling Emily Post? I felt the beginnings of a killer headache flare up behind my eyes, and I pinched the bridge of my nose, willing it away.

I turned to Mom. "What happened outside?" I hissed. "You were supposed to be the lookout for me."

"It didn't quite work out that way."

I'll say.

Mom's lips twitched, and I realized she was enjoying my predicament. "Ray pulled in next to me and asked me what we were doing here." She gave a helpless little shrug as if that explained everything.

"I didn't figure you were the Welcome Wagon lady," he said, snickering. "She's already come and gone and left me some jelly donuts. They were from the day-old store, but I ate them anyway."

Ray Hicks, master of the bon mot. I ignored him and focused on Mom. "And you told him . . . ," I prompted.

"And I told him that your roommate was accused of killing Sanjay and we really had to do everything possible to prove her innocence. That we'd launched our own investigation since we didn't trust the Cypress Grove PD to do it properly. We knew it was very naughty to come back to the trailer uninvited"—she giggled girlishly—"but we just couldn't help ourselves. We would do anything to help Lark."

Leave it to Mom to show our hand. I shook my head in dismay. If Ray was the killer, now he would certainly cover his tracks and send us off in the wrong direction. Time for some expert damage control, Dr. Maggie style.

"I thought you were gone for the evening," I said briskly to Ray. "I apologize for letting myself into your trailer." I figured it was better to say nothing about the Visa card and just let him think that the door had magically opened by itself, or that he'd left it unlocked.

I made a conscious effort to keep my body language open, my tone pleasant. I even arranged my features into a smile. I found it very hard to smile at Ray Hicks, but desperate times call for desperate measures. He nodded, as if he accepted this explanation.

"No harm, no foul," he said gruffly. "I'd probably do the same for a friend." He opened the miniature fridge, popped open another beer, and offered me one. I waved it away with my hand, my mind still mulling over the new turn of events. One question was nibbling at the edge of my thoughts. "What happened to the dogs? Where are they?"

"The dogs? Oh, they belong to my brother. I was just keepin' 'em for a few days while he went down to Orlando with his family. He came back this afternoon and picked them up."

"You told us you always spent Friday nights at a tavern," Mom said.

"So I did. But when I got down to the Crab Shack, I saw that my favorite bartender wasn't workin' tonight, so I came home after a couple of beers. Figured I'd watch a little television and relax." He grinned. "Never thought I'd see Thelma and Louise campin' out here, though." He laughed and slapped his thigh. "Man, you two are one for the books."

"Look," I said firmly, determined to end this silly charade. "You've got to explain how you got this book. You told us earlier you'd never been to Cypress Grove and you never attended the conference." I tapped the cover decisively. "Yet I find an autographed book and it's signed and dated on the day Sanjay died."

"Well, here's the thing, missy," Ray said, sitting down on a stained armchair. "I wasn't completely honest with you." I started to interrupt, but he held up his hand. "Yes, I was in Cypress Grove. I lied about that. I figured it would be my last chance to see Sanjay and figure out if I was going to get any of my money back. I was so fed up, I would have taken twenty cents on the dollar at that point. It was better than nothing."

"You were there," I said softly. I was surprised he admitted it.

"Yep. So I did lie to you, but I didn't lie about the important part of the story. I didn't kill him. What would be the point? The money was gone and the money was all I ever cared about. Knocking him off wouldn't get me back a penny of my investment. Why bother?"

"I believe you," Mom said feelingly, and I shot her a look. Why were we having a lovefest with this guy? He was still a suspect—maybe our best suspect.

"Not so fast, Mom." I looked at Ray. "So you're telling me you did talk to Sanjay and he signed this book for you."

"Not exactly." Ray wiped his hands on his grubby jeans. "I never stuck around to see Sanjay. He was doing those crazy workshops, and he had goons surrounding him every minute. You couldn't get past them, you know?" I nodded. I remembered the guy in the black T-shirt who stopped me at the back of the conference room. And the two gorillas who'd accompanied Sanjay to the WYME interview. "So I figured I'd have a drink at the bar and hit the road. It wasn't worth my time to spend the whole day listening to him spouting off, and I knew he probably would brush me off. I decided to have a quick beer at the bar, and that's when I met Travis."

"Travis?" The name sounded vaguely familiar, and I remembered seeing it on an organizational chart of Team Sanjay in a seminar brochure.

"Travis Carter. He's a nice guy, but he got screwed over by Sanjay, too." He snorted. "Looks like we both got taken in by him. His situation was different from mine, but Sanjay stole from him just the same. It wasn't a real estate deal, though. It had to do with work."

"Travis was an assistant to Sanjay, or an associate or something, wasn't he?" I suddenly remembered that Travis Carter was the one who had sent me a press kit about Sanjay's latest book so I'd be prepared for the interview.

Ray leaned back in the armchair. "Well, that's what Sanjay wanted everyone to think. But the truth is, Travis was the brains behind Sanjay's next book."

I raised my eyebrows. "His next book? You don't mean *Heal the Cosmos*?"

"Nah. The next book was the one that was gonna make a fortune for Sanjay. It was going to be bigger than all his other books put together. Travis told me there was a lot of—what's the word . . . noise? I think that's what he called it. He said there was a lot of noise about the book already."

"Noise? Do you mean buzz?"

Ray nodded. "Yeah, that's it. He used the word 'buzz.' He said there was gonna be a lot of buzz about this particular book. And that didn't sit well with Travis, let me tell you. He could see that Sanjay was going to make a ton of money and he was gonna be left looking like a schmuck."

"Why's that?" Mom said, leaning forward. "Why would he be concerned about Sanjay making a lot of money on the book?"

"Because Travis is the feller who wrote it."

"Travis Carter wrote it?" I was stunned.

"He sure did. He did all the research and spent about five years of his life puttin' it all together. But he made a big mistake. Yessiree." Ray wagged his index finger for emphasis and put his beer down on the scratched coffee table.

"And what was that?" I was so caught up in the story, I almost forgot that Ray could be fabricating the whole tale, making it up as he went along.

"Well, here's the thing. He gave Sanjay all his research notes. Every lick of paper connected to the book." Ray raised his eyebrows. "And ole Sanjay just ran with it. He decided to peddle it as his own book. Not a word about Travis or the work he'd done."

"Wow," Mom said softly. "I can't believe Sanjay would do that."

Ray took another swig of beer. "It makes sense if you think on it a little. Sanjay was the one with the big connections and a New York agent. He just added a few lines here and there, and he was gonna pass it off as his own. Pretty smart, huh?"

"This is amazing." I shook my head. "When Sanjay was a guest on my show, he didn't say a word about another book coming out. All he wanted to do was promote *Heal the Cosmos*. He never let on there was anything else in the pipeline."

"Sanjay was a pretty shrewd guy, you know. He knew how to play his cards close to his vest. He figured no one would be the wiser, and he was right. I don't even know if his agent was in on it. Travis was going to be left holding the bag once the new book came out."

"But what evidence did Sanjay have that he actually wrote it?" I wondered what Nick, my investigative reporter pal, would make of all this. I tried to remember other plagiarism cases I'd heard of. Hadn't there been lawsuits? "What was he going to do if anyone challenged him on it?"

"Oh, Sanjay doctored up some e-mails to prove it was his idea all along and that Travis was just a jealous employee. You know, a wannabe. Some nobody who was tryin' to ride the coattails of a big star. He said it happens all the time and the public would believe him, not some nobody even if he did have a bunch of fancy degrees."

I suddenly thought of Lenore Cooper. She had a "bunch of fancy degrees" and had been left out in the cold by Sanjay, too. His career had soared, while her star had fallen. Was this a case of history repeating itself? He'd stolen from Lenore in a way, too. Sanjay had learned the ropes from her, glommed on to her career, and figured out how to write books and give seminars. The minute he had what he needed from her, he'd dumped her.

For a moment, there was dead silence in the trailer as we pondered this new information. Mom shot me a questioning look, but I tried to keep my face completely neutral.

This put a completely different spin on things, but was Ray telling the truth? Or was he simply trying to divert suspicion away from himself and onto Travis Carter? A good offense is the best defense, and even a backwoods guy like Ray Hicks probably had a strong survival instinct.

"What happened then?"

"Well, Travis was hopping mad; that much I know. He was drinking and talking up a storm. He said he wasn't going to roll over and take it. I knew he was up to something, but I didn't know what."

"But why didn't Travis consider going to the police or a lawyer?" Mom asked. "How could he let Sanjay get away with this?"

"I guess he figured he had no choice. Sanjay had a whole

legal team on retainer. He said he'd hammer Travis into the ground and drain his bank account dry if he ever tried to sue him. I guess Travis was scared of him."

"It certainly sounds that way," I offered.

"Sanjay isn't the kind of guy you want to mess with." Ray gave me a meaningful look. "If you dig into his background a little, you'll see what I mean."

Chapter 25

"What did you think about all that?" I was driving a little too fast, speeding south on A1A. "I still can't figure out Ray Hicks. The whole story about Travis Carter was puzzling, wasn't it?"

"I'll say. Puzzling isn't the word for it." Mom leaned forward and braced her hand on the dashboard, her signal to me that she didn't like my driving.

I eased up on the gas a little, my thoughts swirling. I was rattled by this sudden turn of events and decided I needed a good night's sleep to deal with it. Mom had suggested we spend the night in her condo and visit South Beach again the next day.

I quickly agreed. We'd have a shot at meeting Travis Carter, or at least visiting Sanjay's headquarters. I decided it was best to visit the corporate offices unannounced. I was sure Travis would blow me off with some flimsy excuse if I tried to make an appointment to see him. I wanted to have the element of surprise on my side.

As far as I knew, all the employees were still on duty, and someone must be doing strategic planning for the company. Sanjay the guru was gone, but Sanjay the brand was still going strong. His name and photo were splashed all over the tabloids, and I heard *People* magazine was doing a cover story on him later in the week. I wondered what it would say about how he died.

"You know, there was something convincing about the man," Mom said, cutting into my thoughts. "I hate to say it, but I think Ray Hicks was telling the truth."

Mom rolled down the window, and the balmy night air rushed in, tinged with the scent of the sea. If I hadn't been so preoccupied thinking about Sanjay, I would have enjoyed the drive along the ocean.

"I know. It means we're back to square one. I was sure Ray Hicks was our number-one suspect."

"And now everything is up for grabs," she pointed out. "Funny, it goes along with Sanjay's theory. Just when you think you've figured something out, the universe tilts and you're right back where you started."

"Exactly."

We rolled into the parking lot of Mom's condo around nine o'clock and had a late supper of grilled cheese sandwiches and sangria at the kitchen table. Mom drifted off to watch an old Marilyn Monroe movie on Turner Classic Movies, and I decided to go over my suspect list. I poured myself another glass of wine, grabbed a legal pad, and scribbled some notes.

Travis Carter's name was now at the head of the list, but realistically, I wouldn't know anything more until we met up with him tomorrow morning. Still, he was a strong suspect, if Ray Hicks's story was credible. Money, jealousy, and revenge are proven motivators for murder.

What did Travis have to gain by Sanjay's death?

He must have been angry and resentful at Sanjay's plan to highjack his book, and maybe he really felt he had no legal recourse. I decided to see what Nick's take was on all this when I got back home.

As an investigative reporter, Nick might be able to tell me whether Travis really had no legal recourse, or Ray Hicks was just blowing smoke with the story. And without a manuscript, how would I know if a book even existed—or that Travis really wrote it? Would Travis just wait a decent interval and then peddle the book to a New York publisher or agent himself?

I made a note to ask Miriam Dobosh about Travis. She'd offered to help out with the investigation, but I remembered Nick's warning that sometimes the person who offers to help you solve the crime is the guilty party.

An interesting thought.

Miriam was still number two on my list. She didn't appear to be angry or resentful when we met at the Delano Hotel. In fact, she seemed to be protective of Sanjay's name and reputation. I was drawing a blank on her, and I couldn't quite get a handle on her motive. Unless she had killed him in a fit of rage.

Maybe she'd confronted him about Olivia Riggs and he'd blown her off? But how could I ever determine what had really happened between the two of them? Sanjay was dead and Miriam wasn't talking.

She must have been furious to think she was going to be replaced by a younger, prettier woman. She would have to be a saint not to be resentful, and I didn't pick up any celestial vibes from Miriam. Whatever she was feeling, she covered it well.

I mulled over her situation. Being cast out of Team Sanjay would like being thrown off the island on *Survivor*.

And that was exactly what had happened to Lenore Cooper, I reminded myself. Was there a pattern here? Sanjay used women and then discarded them. First Lenore and then Miriam, but how did this all tie together? And were there other women, ones I hadn't even met yet?

I didn't see how Miriam would have anything to gain from Sanjay's death, at least from a financial point of view. As far as I knew, she was losing her job. But was she really going to be replaced by Olivia Riggs, the blonde I found crying in the ladies' room at the Seabreeze Inn?

Miriam had been dismissive of Olivia and claimed she was delusional. Who was telling the truth? I wished I'd thought to get Olivia's address. It would be good to catch up with her again, and I regretted the missed opportunity. She might have been able to tell me what Miriam had really thought about Sanjay.

I found myself drawing a circle around Miriam's name. Then I put little stars around it. I was really just doodling, the way I used to do when I was talking with a particularly difficult patient. The patient thought I was writing down every word that came out of his or her mouth, but really, I was just drawing as a way to center myself. I found it calming to make some sketches and turned my chair at an angle so the patient couldn't see my scribbles.

Miriam was still a possibility. Revenge would be the motive. Though who would want to face a murder charge just to settle a score?

I put an asterisk next to Miriam's name and drew a line on the page, connecting her with Lenore Cooper, who was number three on my list. Lenore had every reason to be furious with Sanjay, but still, what would she gain from his death? Her books weren't selling well while he was alive, and unless she wrote a juicy tell-all, she probably wouldn't gain a penny from his death.

My thoughts drifted to Kathryn Sinclair. She flatly believed that Sanjay had almost killed her daughter. She had every reason to be angry with him, and she'd told me at the memorial service that she was glad he was dead. You can't get more specific than that. She was number four on the list. The problem was, I didn't really have any new information on her.

All I knew was that she was very angry.

Still, did she have what it took to be a killer? I thought of the perfectly coiffed hair, the designer clothes, and the professionally bleached teeth. Not to mention the thousand-dollar Ferragamo shoes. For some reason, I couldn't imagine anyone with expensive shoes and a French manicure murdering someone, which is probably a personal idiosyncrasy on my part.

I remembered a case in Houston, Texas. Clara Harris caught her husband cheating and confronted him with his mistress in the parking lot of a hotel. She ran him over three times with her Mercedes, killing him.

So even well-dressed women can be killers. And usually the motive is money or revenge. I put a big question mark near Kathryn Sinclair's name.

Of course, there was also her daughter, Sarah, whom I hadn't met yet. If anyone had the right to be angry, Sarah certainly did. She'd been hospitalized because of Team Sanjay's insensitivity to her medical condition. She might have died because of their carelessness.

But somehow I pictured her as a rather timid, powerless person, probably not able to murder anyone. Maybe it was time to track her down. I wondered whether Kathryn would give me her daughter's contact information, and I was afraid that she might not. I wondered how Sanjay's death had affected her. It sounded like she'd been traumatized by the dreadful encounter group, and maybe she'd be unwilling to talk about Sanjay. She might feel like she was being victimized all over again, forced to relive unhappy memories.

After a cup of peppermint tea and another half hour of musing, I decided to hit the sack. I still was no closer to solving Sanjay's murder, and I could only hope that Travis Carter would be the break I needed. He certainly had motive, but did he have means and opportunity? That remained to be seen.

Early the next morning, I checked in with Vera Mae, who insisted that she was holding down the fort at WYME and there was no need for me to hurry back. She told me that Cyrus was rerunning some of my most popular shows and that several listeners had sent me cards and flowers. I checked my voice mail. A few messages from Nick, but nothing that couldn't wait for another day. I caught myself thinking about Rafe Martino and was oddly disappointed that I hadn't heard from the hunky detective. No news is good news, right? What was wrong with me? Could it be that I actually missed seeing him? Just thinking about his sexy smile and smoldering eyes gave me a little buzz inside that warmed me clear down to my toes.

I gave myself a mental shake. The last thing I needed right now was Rafe Martino. He would only be a distraction, and for all I knew, the next time I saw him, he might be slipping handcuffs on Lark.

"Delete, delete," I muttered. That's a thought-stopping technique I used to teach to my obsessive clients. It's a way of banishing an intrusive thought or image, and unlike many psychological interventions, this one actually works. Bingo. In an instant, Rafe's face disappeared.

I left a quick message at the condo for Lark, and then threw on a vintage Lily Pulitzer and sandals. The clock was ticking and I needed to track down Travis before the DA decided to convene a grand jury to indict Lark. All they had to go on was circumstantial evidence, but from what Nick had told me, that might be enough.

The thought sent a chill through me.

After a light breakfast of coffee and croissants, Mom and I hit the road once more, headed south for Sanjay, Ltd. We zipped through the historical section of South Beach, past the big hotels and Calle Ocho, until we found ourselves on a wide avenue lined with stately palms. This was the *Robb Report* version of South Beach, a place filled with pricey real estate, fabulous yachts, and expensive cars. Old money, new money—it didn't matter. It took big bucks to live here.

I spotted a sprawling Spanish-style mansion just ahead of us, complete with a red tile roof, a creamy white stucco exterior, and masses of expensive landscaping. An underground sprinkling system kept the grass lush and green in the Florida heat. A couple of bored-looking flamingos were hanging out on a pond dotted with water lilies, and there was a tennis court planted next to the house. It was a blisteringly hot day, and the court was empty. I doubted Sanjay played much tennis, remembering that sizable gut lurking underneath those white robes.

Was this even the right place? There wasn't a corporate logo anywhere, but the GPS system confirmed it. This dazzling mansion, looking like something straight out of the set of *Miami Vice*, was the headquarters for Sanjay, Ltd.

But how to get inside? Those elaborate Graceland-style gates looked like they could withstand a horde of rampaging Visigoths. All I had going for me was Mom and my elderly Honda.

I was pondering my next move when a golden opportunity dropped into my lap. A FedEx truck pulled around and stopped at the black wrought-iron gates. After a moment, the driver leaned out the window and said something into a squawk box mounted on a wooden pole.

"Go!" Mom urged. The moment the gates swung open, the FedEx truck barreled through and I zipped in right after him, just inches away from his rear bumper. The gates swung closed slowly behind us. So far, so good.

I realized I was holding my breath and let it out in a soft whoosh. We were inside the Sanjay compound!

No alarm sounded, so I assumed no one had spotted us. We were safe for the moment. I pulled up behind a giant pink hibiscus bush on a little side path leading to the swimming pool on the left wing of the house. The mansion was still in sight, but I felt confident we were hidden from anyone peeking out the front windows.

I cut off the engine and watched silently, waiting.

Mom raised her eyebrows. "What's going on? What's the problem?" She was whispering, even though there was no one to hear us.

"Let's see if he gets inside or if he just leaves the package at the front door."

As if on cue, the heavy double doors swung open and a petite blonde accepted the FedEx package and signed for it. I watched while the driver got back in the van, gunned the engine, and spun down the driveway. I craned my neck to watch. The gigantic gates swung open for him, and he passed through.

"Well?" Mom asked.

"I'm thinking," I told her. Actually, I was stumped. How to get inside?

"Well, so am I," she said tartly. With that, she yanked open her car door and swung her legs outside. She reached behind her for her tote bag, which was lying on the seat.

"What do you think you're doing? Where are you going?" I hissed. She ignored me, so I jumped out of the car, too, hurrying to catch up with her. She was moving at a good clip along a narrow path made of oyster shells that led past a small pool cabana to the main house.

She turned around to smile at me. "Why, I'm going inside the mansion, dear. I would think that would be obvious."

Chapter 26

Before I knew what was happening, Mom had reached the mansion and was rapping smartly on the mission-style front door with the brass handle.

"Mom, what are you doing?"

She put her finger to her lips. "Shh. Let me handle this."

My heart was in my throat when the door suddenly swung open and one of Team Sanjay's goons was framed in the doorway, staring at us. He had a shaved head and some vine-leaf tats winding around his neck and was wearing a black Team Sanjay T-shirt that showed off his ripped biceps. The guy was buff and dangerous looking. His arms were too long for his body, giving him a vaguely simian appearance. If he recognized me from my attempt to butt into Sanjay's work-shop at the Seabreeze Inn, he gave no sign.

"Whaddaya want?" he growled.

Before he could react, Mom pushed past him into the enormous marble foyer. "FedEx!" Her tone was crisp. "We have a rush delivery."

"FedEx?" It took a few seconds for the synapses in his brain to connect, and then suspicion registered in his beady dark eyes. "They were just here."

"Yes, I know; we couldn't get back in past the gate, and we have an urgent delivery for a Mr. Travis Carter. Our colleague left it in the truck by mistake. Very sorry about this." To my amazement, she produced a FedEx envelope from behind her back and pretended to be scrutinizing the address on the front.

I peered over her shoulder to read the writing. The envelope was blank.

"Mr. Travis Carter, of Sanjay, Limited. And I'll need a signature."

"Okay, I'll take it up to him." The thug reached for the envelope, but Mom was too quick for him and clasped it to her chest.

"Oh, sorry, this has to be delivered personally. Company rules. It's a highly sensitive document, and our instructions are to deliver it only to Mr. Carter." She raised her eyebrows and stared him down. "If we can't deliver it to him directly, I'm ordered to take it back to the truck. And that means the addressee will have to drive all the way down to our main office in Miami to pick it up. Is Mr. Carter here?"

The goon glanced over his shoulder at the stairwell leading to the second floor. "Yeah, but, I just told you—"

"Then, no problem. We'll just find our way upstairs and give it to him. You can go back to whatever you were doing." Her tone was imperious, very Leona Helmsley. "We know the way. We've made deliveries here many times before. You must be new to the organization." A clever touch. Put goon guy on the defensive. A not-so-subtle put-down.

I was stunned, impressed as always by Mom's quick thinking. All her theatre training had paid off in ways I never could have predicted.

He looked puzzled but quickly went back on the offensive. "Hey, you're not wearing a FedEx uniform," he said, pointing accusingly to her. "And neither are you," he said, whirling around to confront me. I'm ashamed to admit it, but I'd been hiding behind Mom, hoping we could both make a quick getaway if things turned sour.

"Well, of course not. It's dress-down Friday," she said gaily, trotting up a wide, sweeping staircase that looked like it belonged in Tara, the mansion in *Gone with the Wind*. "We'll just be a sec."

"Today ain't Friday."

I thought for a moment, but as usual, Mom was quicker. "It's a leap year."

"Huh?"

And with that, we barreled up the stairs to the second floor, ready to confront the unsuspecting Travis Carter.

"Quite an operation," Mom muttered, hurrying past reception areas, media rooms, and what looked like a suite of offices. The place was a labyrinth, buzzing with people, and Mom's Ferragamos were tapping a brisk staccato on the pink marble floor. I was trotting along at her heels like a dutiful border collie, eyes front and center.

"Where are we going?" I looked around worriedly, expecting to be stopped at any moment.

"I have no idea," she hissed, "but just keep walking fast, and look confident." She stopped to nod and smile at a harried young blonde in a black suit who was carrying a giant file box. "Hellooo!" Mom said gaily. The girl gave her a quick nod and turned down a corridor to a door marked PUBLICITY AND PROMOTIONS.

"That was nice," I said admiringly. "She didn't try to stop us."

"Of course not. You just have to look confident, Maggie; that's the secret. Look like you belong here. You can pretend you're playing a part, if that helps."

"I'll try to," I muttered. I flashed a nod and a smile at three young men who were walking toward us, deep in a conversation about stock options. They barely glanced at me and certainly didn't challenge me, so maybe Mom was right after all.

"Where can Travis be?" Mom said, looking at the maze of corridors. "I'd like to meet with him alone. At least we have the element of surprise. But I'm not sure where to start."

"That goon downstairs will come looking for us any second, Mom. What if he calls upstairs to Travis and says we insisted on making the delivery ourselves? Travis will be on the lookout for us. He'll know we're up to something."

Mom smiled and patted my arm. "You worry too much, dear. Far too much. And you would think that in your line of work, you would know how to deal with stress—" Mom broke off suddenly and pulled me into an alcove. "Isn't that Travis?" she whispered. "Quick, get out the photo."

I caught a glimpse of tall young man in a tailored suit zipping into a room marked SANJAY GINGII. PRIVATE. NO ADMITTANCE. I pulled a wrinkled publicity photo of Travis Carter out of my purse. I had ripped it out of Sanjay's conference brochure. "I think so," I said. "But how can we go in there? It says no admittance."

"And you think that's going to stop us? Here's what we're going to do. We're going to wait thirty seconds and then storm the inner sanctum."

I took a deep breath. "Why thirty seconds?"

"To give him enough time to get into trouble. Who knows what he's he doing, poking around Sanjay's private office? Mark my words: He's up to no good." I had to smile. Mom seemed to forget that we were the intruders here and could be arrested for trespassing. She checked her watch, and then we remained absolutely still, huddling in the alcove. "Twenty-eight, twenty-nine, thirty. Okay, time to roll, Maggie!"

Mom pushed opened the door marked PRIVATE, and we found a very surprised-looking Travis Carter scowling at us.

"Hey, what are you two doing in here? This is a private office!" I saw him glance toward the phone on the gleaming rosewood desk and wondered whether he was going to call Security.

"Oh, I'm so sorry," Mom said, pretending to be a dotty Miss Marple. She kept one hand on the doorknob while taking a quick look around the room. "We're looking for Media Relations. We must have taken a wrong turn."

"Media Relations?" His tone softened, but his brows were still knotted with suspicion.

"Yes, that lovely girl with the blond hair told us to come up here. I forget her name, but she was wearing a black suit, quite stylish. She's pretty enough to be a fashion model."

"That would be Marissa." Travis relaxed a little and leaned against the desk. His eyes were watchful, though, and I knew he was still wary.

"Yes, Marissa," Mom said, brightening. "Such a helpful young woman. Quite an asset to your organization, I'd say."

"So you're here to do an interview? I didn't see anything scheduled on the calendar. I'm Travis Carter, by the way." He didn't offer to shake hands; instead he flipped open his BlackBerry. Again, his eyes darted to the phone. My heart was doing a quickstep and my palms felt sweaty. Before we knew it, we'd be deposited outside, next to the flamingos lounging in the lily pond. I just knew it.

"It looks like you're packing up to leave," Mom said sweetly. She pointed to some large cardboard boxes filled with Sanjay memorabilia, plaques, trophies, and giant-size photos of Sanjay with politicians and heads of state. There was even a photo of Sanjay with Mother Teresa, feeding small children in India. The man was shameless!

Mom picked up a framed photograph and glanced at it. "Very nice," she said politely before Travis yanked it out of her hands and stuffed it back in the box. He closed the lid on the box to discourage further snooping.

"I'm taking a position somewhere else." His tone was flat and his expression gave away nothing. He stood in front of the desk, arms crossed in front of him, eyes shuttered. Defensive body language, I noticed. The man was clearly hiding something, but what?

"So you're leaving the organization for good? That's very interesting." She looked at me and raised her eyebrows. "We won't quote you on that, if you don't want us to."

"Who are you exactly?" Travis eased himself into a leather swivel chair and motioned us to a couple of lavender upholstered armchairs. Mom settled herself in as if she was ready for a long chat. I perched on the edge of the chair, ready to bolt if Travis went for the phone.

"I'm with WYME," I said slowly. "I'm a radio talk show host. Sanjay visited my show the day he . . . uh . . . transitioned."

"The radio shrink! I knew you looked familiar." He turned to Mom. "And you are—"

"Her assistant," Mom said quickly. She flashed a bright smile. "I'm a little puzzled about something. You're leaving the organization, but you're taking Sanjay's personal belongings with you? Are you planning to sell them on eBay?" She shook her head in mock bewilderment and gave a little chuckle. Travis wasn't amused.

"Is it really any of your business what I do?"

"Oh, it's the journalist in me," she said, touching her hand to her heart. "We just love a good mystery. And of course, Maggie is a psychologist, and so naturally she's fascinated by human behavior."

"Well, you'll have to figure out another mystery, because there's nothing out of order going on here. I'm only taking what belongs to me." There was a granite edge in his voice, and he stood up. "Now, if you don't mind, I'll have to ask you to excuse me. The Media Relations office is the second corridor on the right. I can call Marissa to accompany you, if you like."

"Oh, that won't be necessary." I leapt of my seat like a performing otter at Sea World. "We can find it. So sorry for taking up your time. Good luck with your next move, whatever it is."

Travis gave me a curt nod and walked to the door. He opened it wide and stood there watching as we passed through. Mom couldn't resist giving him a flirty little wave, and we found ourselves alone in the corridor. I figured they might have video surveillance, so we headed for the media relations office, just as he had instructed.

"Now what?" I whispered.

Just then the goon from downstairs rounded the corner and spotted us.

"You're still here!" He hurried toward us, practically oozing testosterone from every pore in his beefy body. "I knew you two were up to something!"

I looked at Mom. "Now what?"

She shrugged her shoulders. "Uh-oh. Now we make tracks. Let's hit it, Maggie!"

With that, she slipped off her Ferragamos and we raced down the wide staircase all the way to the front door. We didn't even break stride as we galloped down the front steps and made a beeline to my car. Out of the corner of my eye, I spotted a vintage Phantom Rolls leaving the compound. It was nosing up to the front gate, the engine giving a satisfied purr, pale lemon paintwork dazzling in the bright sunlight.

I quickly unlocked my Honda with the remote and we threw ourselves inside.

Did we dare try our luck again? I slipped in right behind the fabulous car, admiring the gleaming chrome on the bumper. I gunned the motor just before the gate closed. Success!

I drove like a maniac for several minutes until I knew we were clear of Sanjay's goons. Finally, I stopped at a water-ice joint, ordered two lime slushies at the drive-through window, and turned to Mom.

"What in the world were you doing with a FedEx envelope? You must be a magician. It appeared like a rabbit out of a hat."

"Not exactly, dear," she said, patting her straw bag. "I had an extra mailing envelope with me. I needed to overnight a contract to Edgar, and I was going to mail it from one of those FedEx drop boxes."

"Amazing," I said.

A flash of a wry smile was followed by a happy sigh. "Yes, dear. I really am, aren't I?"

No one can accuse Lola of false modesty.

Chapter 27

Half an hour later we were heading back to Cypress Grove. I needed to check in with Lark to find out the latest on the case. And I wanted to call Nick and tell him Travis was getting ready to fly the coop and ask him to do a deep background check on him.

What else? I wanted to touch base with the ever-elusive Rafe Martino. I felt a little tingle of anticipation at the idea of picking up the phone and hearing that sexy voice. I gave myself a stern reminder that my interest in him was purely professional. It had to be.

But was it? The rational side of my brain, my prefrontal cortex, told me that it made perfect sense to check in with him. How else would I discover what leads he had and whether any new suspects had emerged during the course of the investigation? But the emotional center of my brain, the amygdala, was doing the happy dance at the thought of seeing him again. A dilemma.

I had no idea how to resolve it, but I knew I needed to get my emotions under control before calling Rafe.

Mom was silent for most of the ride, but she broke into my thoughts as we pulled up in front of my condo.

"That meeting with Travis Carter. It was all very interesting, you know." She was speaking in a stagey way that reminded me of Joan Hickson playing Miss Marple. I waited for her to say that it reminded her of another case, or maybe someone back in Saint Mary Mead. It was obvious that she wanted me to go along with the game, so I took the bait.

"Okay, I'll bite. What was interesting about it?"

"The fact that Sanjay and Travis went deep-sea fishing together."

That was interesting? Who cares? And anyway, how did she know that?

"I missed that."

"It was the photo, of course, that tipped me off to the fishing expedition. You know, the one that Travis slapped back into the box."

The photo? "I didn't get a look at it."

"It was a picture someone took of Travis deep-sea fishing with the guru. And you notice he tucked it away as fast as he could. Either he didn't want me prying through Sanjay's things or there was something significant about that photo. It has to be one or the other, doesn't it?"

"I don't know," I said honestly. The idea that Sanjay occasionally went deep-sea fishing with Travis Carter didn't surprise me. They worked closely together, and maybe Sanjay made it a habit to socialize with his employees. He was always harping on the idea that Team Sanjay was one big happy family. So what was the significance of a fishing trip? I didn't think Mom was going to give me any more hints, so I decided to call Nick as soon as we walked into the kitchen.

Lark was out, but Pugsley greeted me with doggie devotion, winding himself around my legs, begging to be picked up. I gave him a liver treat while he licked my face, delirious with joy at my return. I called Nick and he picked up on the first ring.

"Maggie? What have you got?" he said. I heard Rage Against the Machine blaring in the background. I briefly filled him in on our visit to Travis. "He's hiding something. I know he is. You can check him out for me, right?"

I heard keyboard noises in the background. Nick has an uncanny ability to find out people's secrets. If information exists anywhere on paper or online, he'll find it. The clicking stopped and I heard Nick muttering to himself. I could just see him hunched over the keyboard, chin jutting forward, as he pushed his glasses up on his nose. "Okay, nothing is coming up on him."

"Nothing?" I was dismayed.

"Nothing incriminating. He won an award for sports fishing." A pause. "Actually, he won a few awards for sports fishing. But that's not the kind of thing you're looking for, right?"

"Unfortunately not." I put Pugsley down on the sofa. "Anything new from the cops?"

Nick's tone thumped up a notch. "Yeah, I was gonna call you tonight. The tox screen came back."

"You're kidding! What's the verdict?

"Sanjay was poisoned. It's conclusive."

Mom glanced over at me, and I raised my eyebrows. Was this good news for Lark, or was this adding to the case against her? I didn't think it was good news.

"What kind of poison?" I pulled out a writing pad, ready to jot down notes.

"They're keeping quiet on that, at least for the moment. I couldn't even get them to tell me the name of the poison or what class it belonged to. Rafe told me off the record that

it was fast acting, but that's all he'd say." Nick hesitated.
"There's something else I need to tell you, Maggie."

Uh-oh. I steeled myself. This was bad news coming—I
felt it. "Go ahead."

"There are only two sets of fingerprints on the bottle of
Calming Essence. The fingerprints belong to Sanjay and to
Lark. I'm afraid it's not looking good for her."

"The Calming Essence bottle—is that what you're talking about?"

"You got it." I heard more clicking as Nick was checking
out something else.

"Nick, she's innocent!" I wailed. "What can we do?"

"Nothing for the moment." He sounded preoccupied, as
if he was hot on the trail of another investigation. "Maggie,
all you can do is hang in there with her and ride this out. Got
another call coming in. Talk to you later."

I sank onto the sofa next to Pugsley and flipped on the
local news. I blinked in surprise when I channel surfed for a
few minutes and spotted Lenore Cooper on a talk show. She
looked younger and more attractive than the last time I'd
seen her, and I wondered whether she'd had a makeover. I
suspected she'd had her teeth bleached, and her hair was cut
in a sleek bob, taking years off her face. She was looking
almost telegenic.

Mom wandered out into the kitchen and returned with a
dish of maple walnut ice cream, Pugsley's favorite. He immediately abandoned me and crawled into her lap, looking
up at her with adoring puppy eyes. She pointed to the TV.
"Isn't that Sanjay's wife?"

"Ex-wife. She's the one who got him started in his career,
and then he dumped her."

"Ouch."

I turned up the volume. Lenore Cooper was being interviewed about a new series of seminars and book-signing events she was doing. She'd just signed with a new agency, she said gushingly, and she was happy her career was back on track. Happy? That didn't surprise me. Success is the best revenge.

Ironic. Maybe Sanjay's death had given her the visibility she needed. Her book had made both the *USA Today* list and the *New York Times* list, and it looked like she was back in the game.

At one time, she'd been my number-one suspect, but now everything had changed. Sanjay's death may have revived her flagging career, but I didn't think that was enough of a motive for murder. It was just a lucky outcome for her.

Lark came in later that evening, looking pale and distracted. She slumped with exhaustion but brightened when she saw us in the living room. "You're back!" She enveloped each of us in a hug. I could tell she had dropped a few pounds from her already-thin frame.

"How are you?" I pulled back to look at her, taking in the gaunt expression and dark circles under her eyes. "You haven't been sleeping, have you?"

She shook her head. "Not really." She put on the kettle and reached for a canister of chamomile tea, which she claims has soothing properties. "I've been going over and over what happened that night."

"The night Sanjay—"

"Yes, that night," she said quickly. She gave a helpless little shrug. I had the feeling she couldn't even bring herself to say the word "murder." Or "death."

"Have the police contacted you again?"

"They've tried to. Nick put me in touch with a lawyer, Sebastian Martin. He won't let me talk to the cops unless

he's there with me." She carefully measured out the shred-
ded chamomile into a little silver tea ball. It looked like
catnip. "I'm a person of interest. But he said the cops are
putting together a mountain of evidence, and depending on
how they spin the facts, it could get a lot worse for me." Her
eyes filled with tears.

I nodded. "I know. What did he tell you to do? Did he
have any suggestions?"

"Just to try to remember everything I could about that
night. I told him I've gone over it a hundred times, but I
think I have a mental block."

"A mental block?" I immediately thought of suppressed
memories—one of Freud's classic defense mechanisms. Had
something happened that night, something so traumatic that
Lark had unconsciously pushed it deep into her psyche? Of
course, she had been blindsided by Sanjay's clumsy attempt
at seduction, but was there more to the story? Was there
some key detail we had all overlooked?

Apparently Mom's mind was running along the same track.
Mom loves pop psychology and buys every self-help book
on the market. "A mental block? I know how to fix that."
She arranged some Lorna Doones on a plate to go with the
tea.

I stared at her, trying not to smile. "You know how to fix
a mental block?"

"Yes, dear, I do. Perhaps you're forgetting that I played
Dr. Ivana Romanoff on *Whispers*. My character was an expert at hypnosis, and she used it quite successfully on her
patients."

I remembered *Whispers*, all right. It was an afternoon
soap that ran on a cable channel. It had overwritten dialogue
and improbable plots and lasted only fifteen episodes.

"Mom, that was a soap opera character. You're an actress,

not a shrink. You don't have any training in how to induce a trance."

"I think you're forgetting something. My character was a Russian psychoanalyst." She sat down at the kitchen table, her expression serious. "We had a psychologist as an adviser on the set. She told me how to play the character believably, and she even taught me the art of self-hypnosis." She looked aggrieved. "I know more about psychoanalysis than you think I do."

Lark and I exchanged a look. "We could give it a try." Her voice was tentative.

"You're kidding. Are you sure you really want to do this?"

"If it will help me remember some important detail about that night, why not?" She turned to Mom. "Where do you want me to sit? Or do I have to lie down?"

"No, sitting up is fine, but we have to get you in a comfortable chair." Mom was bustling around, pleased to be reprising her role as the intrepid Dr. Romanoff. "How about the Barcalounger? That looks comfy."

Lark nodded and, taking her mug of tea with her, sat down in the plush lounge chair. Mom pulled up a kitchen chair very close to her. "I want you to close your eyes," Mom said in a stagey monotone. "I want you to completely relax, and feel all the tension in your body drain away. Take three big breaths and let them out slowly."

"Okay," Lark murmured. She set her cup of tea on the end table and closed her eyes. She sank back into the cushion and wriggled until she was comfortable.

"Are you feeling relaxed? Or do we need to do a visualization exercise?"

"No, I'm relaxed," Lark assured her. I remembered that Lark was into mediation and relaxation techniques.

"Okay, Lark, I want you to tune out any distractions and just listen to the sound of my voice. Do you think you can do that?" Mom's voice was slow and languid, the words dropping softly, like cherry blossoms in the spring.

"I think so." Lark seemed to be matching Mom's slow cadence. I pulled up a chair and watched, impressed. I was surprised at Mom's hidden talent. Maybe she did know something about hypnosis and trance states after all.

"I want to take you back to the night that you visited Sanjay."

A frown flitted across Lark's face, and Mom hurried to reassure her. "Don't worry, Lark; nothing bad is going to happen. There's nothing to be afraid of, nothing to worry about. We're just going to drift back in time to the evening when you visited Sanjay in his hotel room. You are completely safe." She paused. "Can we go on?"

"Yes," Lark said softly. "I'm not afraid. I can go back there, if you want me to."

"Good girl. Now, I want you to see yourself in the Seabreeze, walking up the stairs—did you walk up the stairs or take the elevator?"

"I walked up the stairs. The carpeting is brown and burgundy with a diamond pattern on it, and it's a little frayed around the edges."

Mom looked over at me. Lark was getting into this. Some people are very good candidates for hypnosis, and some aren't. Usually people who are creative and have a vivid imagination can be hypnotized and go into a trance state quite easily.

"You are walking down the hall looking at the doorways until you come to number . . ."

"Sixteen."

"Sixteen. Now you are knocking on the door. Can you see yourself doing that?"

"Yes," Lark said, her voice dreamy and distant. It sounded as though she was drifting away.

I shot Mom a worried look, and she whispered to me, "It's okay; she's going into a deep trance state. Look at her hands; they're completely limp, with the palms up." I nodded, not wanting to interrupt the process.

"You're knocking on the door. What's happening?"

"I'm tapping very lightly. I feel shy. I don't want to disturb Sanjay. What if he's meditating or something?"

I roll my eyes and Mom ignores me. "But he's not meditating, is he? He answers the door."

"Yes." Lark's voice is so low and muffled, it sounds as though she's underwater. I notice she's slumped a little farther into the Barcalounger, her arms hanging limply at her sides.

"And then what happens?"

Dead silence.

"Lark, stay with the image," Mom said. "You are in the hallway, and Sanjay opens the door. He invites you in. You walk in the room . . ."

"I walk in the room." Lark's voice was robotic, as if she'd been drugged. "Sanjay shuts the door behind me."

"Good, good. Now look around the room. What do you see?"

Silence.

"What do you see, Lark?" Mom raised her voice slightly. Lark is slumped in the chair, very still, her breathing light and shallow. "Don't be afraid, Lark. Take a mental picture of the room and tell me what you see."

"I see . . . I see . . ."

"Yes? What do you see?" Mom's voice ratcheted up another notch. She looked at me and shrugged. Lark's reaction seemed to be unexpected, but since I had no experience in trance states, I decided not to butt in.

A low droning noise. "What's that?" I looked around the room anxiously.

"She's snoring," Mom said. "It seems that our subject has fallen asleep. This has never happened to me before."

"Well, wake her up, David Copperfield. We need to find out what she saw in that room."

"Lark," Mom said, leaning over and touching her lightly on the leg. "I am going to count backward from five, and when I reach one, I will snap my fingers and you will wake up. Okay?" There was no response from Lark, but Mom went on anyway. "Five, four, three, two, one."

She snapped her fingers in front of Lark's face, and Lark jerked awake, her body twitching. She immediately wrapped her arms around her chest as if she was cold and reached for her mug of tea.

"What just happened?" She looked dazed and disoriented.

"You were sleeping," Mom began.

"I know," Lark said irritably. She reached for a quilt draped over the back of the chair and pulled it over her, nestling in the soft folds. "Why did you wake me up? I was having this amazing dream."

"You were?" Mom grabbed a notepad and pencil. "An amazing dream? Tell me everything about it." She leaned close to me and whispered, "It wasn't a dream; she was in a deep trance state." I nodded. "Go on, Lark," she urged.

"Well, I was out in Hollywood . . ."

"Hollywood?" Mom frowned.

"Yeah, it was Hollywood all right," Lark said, nestling back under the quilt. She gave an enormous yawn. "I know it was Hollywood because I was on Rodeo Drive—"

"Rodeo Drive?" Now I was getting interested. Where was this leading? Three thousand miles away from the Seabreeze Inn, it seemed.

"I was shopping on Rodeo Drive and decided to stop for a coffee at Café Rodeo." She gave a happy smile and her eyelids fluttered as if she was about to doze off again. "So I bought a latte—you know, the nonfat, no-foam ones I like, with just a hint of vanilla."

"Yes, we know what you like," Mom said. There was a touch of irritation in her voice. This was clearly not part of the plan, and I wondered what had gone wrong with the "induction."

"What happened next?" I prodded.

"This is the best part." Lark reached out her arms in a languorous stretch. "I was sitting at one of those cute little patio tables outside the restaurant. This incredibly good-looking guy in aviator sunglasses came up to me. It was very bright out and he was sort of silhouetted against the sun. I couldn't figure out who it was. He said, 'May I join you?'"

I noticed Mom had stopped taking notes and was staring at Lark, spellbound.

"So I said, sure. And, here's the amazing part of the dream." Lark opened her eyes wide. "He sat down and took off his sunglasses, and guess who it was?"

"I give up." I shrugged and waited.

"It was Brad Pitt! I was having coffee in Hollywood with Brad Pitt! How incredible is that? And then he reached across the table and took my hand. He said, 'Lark Merriweather? I've always wanted to meet you. You're the woman of my dreams. I've waited my whole life for you.'"

"You were having coffee with Brad Pitt?" Mom looked stunned.

"But what about Angelina?" I said. Not the world's most intelligent comment, but I was caught up in the story.

"Oh, he said that Angie was just a phase. Can you imagine? Just a passing phase. I was the one he really wanted." Lark stood up, giving a secret little smile as she gathered the quilt around her. "If you don't mind, I'm going to take a little nap. Maybe I can find my way back to that incredible dream." She walked into the bedroom, leaving the door open a crack.

"What was all that about?" I said the moment she was out of earshot. "She didn't say a word about that night at the Seabreeze Inn. All she talked about was having a latte with Brad Pitt! Where did that come from, anyway?"

"Probably from the depths of her unconscious," Mom said. She was clearly embarrassed by the hypnosis fiasco. "Maggie, you know these trance inductions are unpredictable. They don't work every single time. As Dr. Romanoff said, 'Hypnosis is an art, not a science.' I'm afraid this hypnosis was a failure."

I watched as Pugsley jumped down from the sofa and waddled into Lark's room, all set for a nice long nap. He would be dreaming doggie dreams and Lark would be dreaming about Brad Pitt.

"I'll say."

As Irina would say, we were back to "square zero."

Chapter 28

It was nearly one a.m. when Lark staggered into the kitchen, eyes bleary with sleep. I was sitting at the table, eating a dish of maple walnut ice cream and going over my notes.

"Something just came to me about the case," she said, slipping into a chair across from me. "Something I had missed before. I don't know how I missed it, but I did."

"You remembered something about Sanjay and that night at the Seabreeze?"

She pulled her robe tightly around her and nodded. "I do. I guess Lola's hypnosis session really worked." She widened her eyes. "I woke up a few minutes ago, and it was amazing, but I could see his room at the Seabreeze. I could see every single detail, just like I was standing there or watching a movie."

My heart kicked into high gear. "What did you see?"

"The sushi dinner. It was sitting right on the bed."

"A sushi dinner?" I shot her a sideways glance. "You never mentioned this before."

"I know. It's silly, isn't it? I completely forgot about it. I think that hypnosis session must have nudged something in my brain. Now I realize that Sanjay must have ordered some takeout, because there was one of those white take-out containers sitting on the bed."

"How do you know it was sushi?" My detective instincts were on red alert.

Lark wrinkled her nose. "I'm a vegetarian, remember? I'm very sensitive to smells. If someone eats meat or poultry or fish, I pick up on it right away. I can't stand the smell of sushi. And there's another thing."

"Yes?" I pushed Pugsley away. He was trying to leap into my lap to get at the ice cream, and the vet had already said he was overweight.

"Sanjay was supposed to be a vegan. So what was he doing eating fish?"

"I have no idea." I thought for a moment. "Was the container marked in any way? Would you recognize it if you saw it again?"

Lark thought for a moment, and then shook her head. "I don't think so. There might have been something on it, but I really can't remember." She pushed her hair out of her eyes and ran her hand over her forehead. "It's funny, but the whole scene is fading right now. It was so clear a moment ago."

"That's okay," I said quickly. "You gave us something to go on."

"But what can we do with this? I don't think the police will believe me."

"I'll make sure they do. And you need to call that lawyer, Sebastian Martin, and tell him about the sushi. This could be a break in the case. We need to keep him in the loop."

"You really think this is significant?"

"I know it is."

The desk sergeant gave me a "not you again" look when I marched into the Cypress Grove PD the following morning

and demanded to see Rafe Martino. I didn't call ahead, de-
ciding it was better to just show up unannounced and take
my chances. I waited in the lobby, and a scruffy-looking guy
with bleached blond hair and a soul patch nodded to me.
A surfer dude. I hesitated, then nodded back, and then he
winked.

He's winking at me?

Not good. My eyes dropped, and then I noticed he was
handcuffed to a metal loop on the wall. Hmm. Was this a
lobby or a holding cell? Loverboy was still winking, but I
turned my back on him, opened my purse, and delved into
the latest Donald Bain mystery.

I always carry a paperback with me and read on the fly.
Reading even a few pages of a mystery relaxes me and trans-
ports me to another time and place. It's my escape hatch, my
stress buster.

After a few minutes, Rafe strolled down the hall, looking
like a million dollars in a white knit shirt and khakis. He
looked like he should be playing golf with Donald Trump in
West Palm Beach instead of working in a small-town police
department.

I ignored the little thrumming in my heart at the sight
of him and tried to focus on what I was going to say. I
was going to be concise, confident, and in control, just like I
encourage my patients to be in my assertiveness-training
classes.

Except when I saw Rafe I melted. He looked good, he
smelled good, and he stood a little too close when he greeted
me. Or maybe it felt that way to me. Maybe it was projec-
tion, as Freud would say. Maybe I was the one who wanted
to stand too close, so I projected that desire onto Rafe. I
could have pondered that theory in more depth, but how

could I think straight when Rafe was standing right next to me?

"Dr. Maggie," he said, flashing a sexy grin. "To what do I owe the pleasure?" He had a Mario Lopez dimple. I tried to ignore it. I also tried to ignore the "Dr. Maggie" jibe. Whenever anyone calls me that, I think I should be munching cookies with Oscar the Grouch on Sesame Street.

"I have new information about Sanjay's death. Information that will *break* the case." I tried to ignore my heart, which was doing a salsa rhythm in my chest. "Can we go somewhere to talk about it?" I felt strangely out of breath, as if I'd just delivered a long speech or run a marathon.

He pushed a lock of hair out of his eyes. "Is my office okay? I'll even get you a cup of coffee." Again, the trademark grin. One look from Rafe Martino and I was a goner.

A few moments later, I was sitting on a metal folding chair holding a cup of brown sludge that Rafe had produced from a battered pot. I stared at it suspiciously.

"It's not a grande latte with skim milk, two Splendas, and a light dusting of cinnamon," he said.

"How did you know?" That's my standard order at Starbucks.

"Just a lucky guess." He glanced at his chirping cell phone, scrolled through some messages, and then put his elbows on the desk and stared at me. Suddenly he was all business. "So what gives? What's the new evidence and where did you get it?"

I was a little startled by the abrupt transition, and it took a few seconds for my synapses to make the connection. "It's sushi," I said, stammering a little. Rafe was looking at me so intently with those fiery dark eyes that I was finding it hard to concentrate. "Sushi," I repeated in a thin little voice that

ended in a quaver. So much for sounding brisk and professional.

"Sushi." He said the word flatly, and there was a long beat
of silence between us.

"Sanjay's sushi."

"Sanjay's sushi," he repeated. It suddenly sounded like
"Peter Piper," and I had to resist the urge to laugh. This wasn't
a laughing matter. Lark's life was at stake.

I flushed. "That sounds silly when you say it that way,
but yes. Sanjay's sushi. I just learned from Lark that Sanjay
was eating sushi the night he died. Or if he wasn't eating it,
he certainly ordered some from a take-out place. So we have
to assume he ate it?"

"Do we?" It was clear from Rafe's tone that he didn't
think we had to assume anything at all. He reached for a file
and began to flip through it. "I don't recall anything about
sushi at the crime scene, either in the reports or in Ms. Merriweather's statement." He riffled through some papers. "It's
not in here."

"It wasn't in the original statement she gave you because
she just remembered it." I nearly added "Honest!" and then
stopped myself in time.

"Really." His tone was flat, and one eyebrow rose. It was
obvious he didn't believe me. "She just magically remembered it?"

"Something like that. It's a long story." I decided not to
tell him about Mom's failed attempt at hypnosis. But had it
really failed? Who knows, maybe the trance state—if there
was one—had jiggled Lark's memory and she really had
recalled the sushi because of Mom's intervention.

Rafe was drumming his fingers on the desk. "Don't you
think we would have found some evidence of the sushi at

the crime scene? Our investigators went over the room very carefully. They're all top-notch CSIs."

"Did they check the wastebasket?"

"Of course." I heard a hint of irritation in his voice, and he sneaked a look at his watch. "If there was a take-out box, we would have found it."

I thought about this for a moment. "Maybe so, but if Lark says she saw it, then it was there. Somewhere. Sanjay certainly didn't eat the box." I realized I didn't sound very convincing and my story had a million holes in it. Where was the white take-out box? How come it hadn't been discovered? Both were good questions, and I knew Rafe was going to demand answers. I noticed he wasn't taking notes, which made me think he didn't believe me at all.

"You're not going to write this down?" I demanded.

With a world-weary sigh, he reached for a legal pad. "Okay, I'll write it down. You realize this is all hearsay. Why doesn't Miss Merriweather come in herself if she has something to add to her statement?"

Good question. "I'm sure she will," I said with all the strength I could muster. I remembered that the best defense is a good offense. "And maybe you could start looking for that take-out box, since you must have missed it the first time around."

"I'll be sure to do that," Rafe said, standing up. His look said it all. I was just a radio talk show host; he was a skilled investigator who didn't have time for my silly insights.

I knew I was being dismissed.

What next? A quick call to Ted Rollins at the Seabreeze confirmed my worst fears. Ted told me he hadn't seen anyone make any deliveries that night, and that drivers always have to stop at the front desk. Not what I was hoping to hear.

"Can you think of a restaurant that serves sushi?" I asked. I felt like I was failing a major test and needed to use a lifeline.

A beat passed while he considered the question. "Here in Cypress Grove?" His tone was doubtful. "Maggie, you're not back in Manhattan. We don't really go in for sushi here. Maybe red snapper," he added playfully. "Or even catfish." *Catfish?* I flashed on Ray Hicks, standing over the grill, cooking up catfish. But there was no way anyone could mistake catfish for sushi, was there?

I thanked Ted and then dashed into WYME to do my afternoon show. Vera Mae greeted me with a big hug like I was a returning war hero.

"How's it going, girl?" She was bustling around, lining up the spots to be read live that day during my show.

"Fine. Can you do me a big favor?" I slapped my briefcase on the desk and checked my phone messages. Nothing urgent—a few calls from publicists hounding me to invite their clients on the show. Nothing from Nick; nothing from Rafe. Although why would there be?

"Just name it, sugar."

"Do a Google search for me. Find out if there are any restaurants around Cypress Grove that serve sushi. You'll have to check surrounding towns as well, but don't make it too far away. Close enough that they'd do a take-out delivery to the Seabreeze."

Vera Mae raised her eyebrows but didn't ask any questions. We both went into the studio, and she gave me the bio on the day's guest. Then she zipped into the control room to organize things before my two o'clock show and fielded some phone calls from Cyrus and Big Jim Wilcox.

The protocol for guests was always the same. Irina would

greet the guest (Dr. Samuel Nitterstein, author of *Keeping Sane in Crazy Times*) in the lobby and walk him back to the studio.

There'd be time for a quick bathroom break, or a cup of coffee in the green room, but once he was in the studio, he'd have to hit the ground running. I used to greet the guests myself and make small talk in the lobby, and then I realized that it was better to just meet them in the studio. That way our conversation sounded more spontaneous, less planned, and I came up with more interesting questions. It seemed to work better when I was meeting the guest at the same time the listener was.

I didn't think Dr. Nitterstein would say anything controversial. He'd sent me a tape he'd done for NPR, and he was well informed, if a little pedantic. No one could ever accuse him of being Mr. Charisma.

Ever since I'd had Sanjay on the show, I'd been deluged with calls from authors peddling their self-help books. It didn't seem to bother any of them that Sanjay had appeared on my show and been murdered that same night. They just wanted to be on the show and were giddy with excitement at the idea.

The show with Dr. Nitterstein (who insisted I call him "Dr. Sam") went by quickly, and the control board was lit up with calls the whole time. It was a topic everyone in Cypress Grove seemed to relate to—who knew so many people were questioning their sanity? Most of the callers were women, and my guest told me during the break that women seemed to fear losing their minds more than men did. Interesting. Was this scientifically proven or just anecdotal? Sometimes guests fudge the facts a little to make a better story.

Were women really more prone to worries about their men-

tal health than men were? Or were women just more willing
to admit to their fears? The show ended on a high note, and
Dr. Sam gave me an autographed copy of his book.

I thanked him and practically rushed him out of the studio because Vera Mae had slipped me an intriguing note during the last commercial break. "Looking for sushi? Try the
Golden Palace." She scribbled the address of a restaurant near
Stuart, Florida. Even with rush-hour traffic, I figured I could
drive there in twenty minutes. I called home to leave a message for Mom and Lark. "Bringing home Chinese takeout
for dinner; don't cook." My heart was leaping in my chest.
Was the Golden Palace the break I'd been looking for?

Chapter 29

"Three veggie lo meins, please. With three egg rolls and one order of steamed dumplings." It had taken me exactly seventeen minutes to reach the Golden Palace, a small restaurant in a strip mall near Stuart.

I hoped the girl behind the counter was in a chatty mood. "Nice place," I said idly, staring at the scratched Formica counter as though I'd never seen one before. She nodded and didn't comment. A full assortment of sushi was staring at me from a refrigerated display case.

"I'll have to come back and try the sushi the next time," I told her.

She gave a shy smile. "It's very good." She slipped on some gloves and reached into the case. "I just made these. Here, try a piece."

"Thanks," I muttered. I loathe sushi but managed to gulp it down in one bite, like an oyster. "Do you deliver to Cypress Grove?"

"Cypress Grove?" She shrugged and looked down, scooping up lo mein for my order. "I'm not sure. That's a little far away for us."

"Is there anyone here who would know? I'm giving a

party," I said, improvising madly. "I'd love to have the whole thing catered. Maybe thirty people."

"I could ask the manager, but he's not here." I knew from her closed expression that I wasn't going to get any information out of her. She'd already rung up the sale, but I tried one more time. "I don't suppose you remember if you delivered any sushi to the Seabreeze Inn last week, do you? That's in Cypress Grove, very close to where I live."

"No, I have no idea. I wasn't at work last week." She quickly completed the transaction and handed me my change.

"Well, thanks," I said, forcing a smile and heading for the exit. I jumped back in the car and headed home with a bag full of take-out containers on the seat next to me. The containers had a small red dragon emblazoned on the lid.

Mission accomplished.

"That could be it, but I'm not sure," Lark said half an hour later. She stared at the red dragon on the lid of the take-out box for a full five seconds, chewing on her lower lip. "I do remember seeing something like this on the box in Sanjay's room. It was some sort of a red logo, but I just can't bring it to mind. I'm not sure it was a dragon, but it could have been. This looks about the right size." She shook her head as if to clear it. "The maddening thing is, I can see the white container sitting right there on Sanjay's bed, and then the image on the lid just disappears. I wonder why that is."

"Don't force the memory. It will come eventually," Mom assured her. I wondered how Mom could be so optimistic after Lark's colorful description of her meeting with Brad Pitt at Café Rodeo. Hope springs eternal with Mom. Sometimes I think her level of optimism is almost pathological, but maybe it works in her profession. Mom always says she's optimistic because there is no other option. The vast majority of SAG members are unemployed at any given time.

If an actor didn't have a certain degree of optimism, it would be tempting to jump off a bridge.

Lark turned in early that night, and by ten p.m., Mom was sleeping soundly on the sofa, with *Hollywood Boulevard* playing on the TNT channel. I was sitting at the kitchen table going over my notes on the case when the phone rang. I grabbed it by the second ring so it wouldn't wake up Mom. Pugsley gave a soft yip of surprise, emerging from some doggie dream, and jumped into my lap.

"Back off," a gravelly voice said.

"What?" The voice was low and indistinct, and there was some static in the background. It sounded like someone was dragging a plastic comb over the receiver, maybe to disguise the voice?

"You heard me. Back off. You know what I'm talking about." This time the threat in the voice was unmistakable, and a chill passed through me. "Unless you want to lose your mother, your roommate, and oh, yeah, your stupid little dog."

I froze, every brain cell on red alert. "Who is this?" Pugsley must have sensed the urgency in my voice, because he nestled closer, looking up at me in alarm.

"You don't need to know that. And I'm not dumb enough to stay on the line long enough for you to trace the call, if that's what you're thinking." I nearly laughed out loud. I am the most low-tech person I know, and the idea of me tracing a call is about as likely as me piloting a space shuttle. "Stop butting into things that don't concern you, or you're a dead woman."

Click.

A dead woman? A line of goose bumps sprouted on my forearm, and the skin on the back of my neck prickled.

"Who was that?" Mom murmured from the sofa, her voice thick with sleep.

"Nothing," I said, muting the television. "Go back to sleep."

"Okay," she said agreeably, nestling back into the sofa pillows.

I grabbed my purse and my cell phone and went out onto the balcony. Rafe had given me his cell phone number for emergencies. I thought it was silly at the time, but now I wanted to hear his warm, reassuring voice. I punched in the number, and he answered on the first ring.

"Maggie," he said. "What's up?"

For a second I was taken aback, but then I recovered. Caller ID. What did I expect? He was a cop.

I quickly filled him in on the phone call, wondering whether I'd been silly to call him.

"Look at the readout," he instructed. "What does it say?"

"Private number."

"Probably a phone card, but we can try to trace it tomorrow." A pause. "Was it a man or a woman?"

"I'm not sure. It was sort of muffled, and there was a scratchy noise in the background."

"Is everything locked up tight? You need to check all the doors and windows and double-check that the security system's turned on."

"I don't have a security system."

A muffled curse. "Why doesn't that surprise me?"

"I thought this was some little backwater town, you know, like Mayberry. I figured the biggest crime you had to deal with was someone stealing newspapers off the front porch. Or maybe a kid snatching one of Aunt Bee's apple pies off the windowsill."

"Do we seem like hicks to you? Is that what you're saying?"

Oops. "No, that's not what I meant at all. Sorry. I just

meant Cypress Grove is a quaint little place, totally different from Manhattan. I didn't think people locked their doors here." Rafe didn't say anything, so I babbled on. "I guess I'm just a little shaken up, that's all."

"Do you want me to send someone over?" His tone had softened. I was forgiven.

I knew I had to be careful. I didn't want to come across like a ditzy heroine in some silly woman-in-jep movie. That wasn't the image I wanted to project. I wanted to be more of an Angelina Jolie, kick-ass heroine type. But the wobble in my voice probably gave me away.

"No, I'm fine," I said, trying to sound confident. "Let's just chalk it up to a prank call and leave it at that. It's not like I'm in any real danger."

"That's not true. You could be in very real danger," Rafe said evenly. "But I'm not going to let anything happen to you; you can count on that. Lock everything up, Maggie. Do it now. I'll catch up with you first thing in the morning, and I'll let you know if we manage to trace that call. And Maggie . . ."

"Yes?"

"Stop playing Nancy Drew. This isn't a game."

His voice was low and intense, as if he cared what happened to me. Or was he just doing his job? PROTECT AND SERVE was the motto emblazoned on every Cypress Grove patrol car.

Was he as attracted to me as I was to him?

It was impossible to tell.

I clicked the phone shut and stayed out on the balcony for a few minutes. The air was soft and balmy; a full golden moon hung in the black sky. The lyrics to "Moon over Miami" came rushing into my head, and I smiled at the incongruity of it all.

Here I was, the perfect target, standing on the balcony overlooking a darkened garden. And I was enjoying the night air, thinking about the lyrics to a syrupy song. What if someone was lurking out there, spying on me, waiting to hurt me? I quickly went inside, double-checked the lock on the glass door, and closed the drapes.

I debated whether or not to tell Lark and Mom about the late-night call and finally decided against it. The next day was bright and sunny, a typical Florida morning, and the threatening voice on the phone had faded from my thoughts. It could easily have been a prank call.

Couldn't it have? Rafe reminded me, small southern towns had their share of crime and random violence. I tried to push aside the nagging thought that the caller was serious. Drop-dead serious.

But I told myself the best thing to do was to ignore it. Mom had left to go shopping with Lark. It was nearly nine o'clock, and I was standing on the balcony, sipping a cup of bananas Foster–flavored coffee. I was idly looking over at the Seabreeze next door when something caught my eye.

A big ugly Dumpster. It looked like a gunmetal gray monster sitting there.

It was invisible at eye level if you were standing on the ground, shielded by a latticework privacy fence. Had anyone checked the Dumpster for a take-out container? It seemed like a no-brainer, but evidence has gone missing before in criminal cases. Nick told me that only 1 percent of collected evidence is actually used at trial, and things get lost all the time. I wondered how I could ask Rafe whether anyone had checked the Dumpster without sounding like I was telling him how to do his job.

I decided to do his job for him.

I shoved my feet into flip-flops and crossed the backyard into the garden behind the Seabreeze. There's a little place between the hedges that's easy to slip through. I did a quick check of the lawn. No unsightly debris, no signs of a take-out dinner. Holding my breath, I lifted the lid on the ugly Dumpster. Empty.

For a moment, I was stymied, and then I saw Francesca, one of the maids, coming toward me, lugging a wastebasket. She gave me a puzzled smile, probably wondering why I was fascinated by the Dumpster. She was in her mid-thirties, attractive and slightly plump, her black-and-white uniform stretched tightly over her hips.

"Señora," she said, lifting the lid and skillfully tossing a bag inside.

"Francesca, right? I live next door." I flashed my most reassuring smile and pointed to my condo.

"*Qué?*"

"*Me llamo Maggie,*" I said, using up my limited knowledge of Spanish.

"Oh, Maggie, *sí,*" she said politely. She nodded and headed back to the Seabreeze, but I blocked her way.

"I'm trying to get some information on Sanjay."

"Sanjay?"

"Guru Sanjay Gingii," I repeated. "I need to find out what happened to him. He stayed here at the Seabreeze, and then he died."

"Died?"

"Died. Dead. *Muerto.*"

A sudden recognition flickered in her eyes and I realized she knew something about Sanjay. About the room. About that night. Something.

She shook her head. "*No sé nada. Nada.*" She didn't know anything. Or so she said. I had the feeling her English was much better than she was letting on.

"Maybe you're frightened, Francesca," I said, leaning close. "Don't be. I just need to know if anything unusual happened the night Sanjay died." I had no idea how to translate that, so I just looked at her intently. "Anything would help, any little bit of information. Even *un poco. Un poco de información.*" I touched my thumb to my index finger to show that even a tiny bit would help.

Francesca looked at me, her dark eyes wide. For a moment, I thought she was going to tell me something, and then she shook her head. "*Por favor, señora.*" She angled her body so she could brush by me and return to the Seabreeze. "*No sé nada.*"

I decided it was time for the direct approach. "Francesca, Lark needs our help. She's in a lot of trouble with the police."

"Lark?" Her dark eyes looked troubled.

"You know Lark, my roommate, right? We live right next door." I pointed again to our condo. "You've seen Lark many times."

She nodded her head vigorously. "Lark, *sí*! Very nice lady. Blond." She smiled and touched her own dark hair. "Very *simpática.*"

"Yes, that's right; she's very *simpática.*" I paused, wondering how much to say. "Francesca, listen to me carefully. The police think that Lark killed Sanjay." I let that sink in for a moment before going on. "We both know that's not possible. Lark is not a killer." I shook my head from side to side, and Francesca became more animated.

"No!" she said firmly. "Not possible. Lark is not killer."

"Right. Lark would never hurt anyone." I blew out a sigh.

"But we need to find out what really happened that night in Guru Sanjay's room. You could help me. You could ask a few questions, maybe talk to the other maids? Do you understand?"

"*Sí.*" Her voice was somber.

"Maybe they saw something or heard something. You could ask them, right? Could you do that for me?" Francesca nodded, and I grabbed a pen out of my pocket. I scribbled my condo number and my phone number on a napkin that had fluttered out of the Dumpster. "*Por favor.*"

"*Sí.* I will help you." Francesca said softly. She nodded and hurried down the path away from me.

"Maggie?" Rafe's sexy voice raced over the line a few minutes later. I had just fed Pugsley and was finishing off the rest of the coffee while catching a few minutes of the *Today* show. "Just checking in about the phone call."

"Yes?" My heart was thudding with excitement. I told myself it was due to the case, but the truth is, I always felt a little buzz talking to Rafe.

"We didn't get anything on the call." A beat. "But I have some interesting news about the break-in at your apartment. We managed to get a match on a fingerprint one of our techs lifted from the scene."

"You did? But how is that possible? Whoever attacked me that night was wearing gloves. I'm sure of it."

"I know, but we got a print off the handrail leading up to the outside door to the building. And it matches a partial we got from the bedroom doorknob inside your condo. They always slip up somewhere."

"Clever." I was impressed. "I didn't know you dusted there."

"Our techs are good. Funny how perps can get careless about leaving prints around, especially outside the building,"

Rafe said. "They don't want to wear gloves in public; it would look suspicious. So they wait until they get inside to pull on them on. A big mistake."

"So this guy wasn't as smart as he thought."

"Except it wasn't a guy. It was a woman."

"It was a woman?" My mind was reeling, and I grabbed the TV remote and turned it to mute.

"That's right. And here's some more good news. I was going to get prints from you and your mother and your roommate to rule them out, and then I just took a chance and ran the crime-scene prints through the system. Bingo. There was a match. Her prints are already on file because she took out a license to carry a concealed weapon. So now we can place her at your building, and that's all we need to bring her in for questioning."

I could hardly process what he was saying. Rafe kept saying *her*. The person who broke into my apartment and slammed me against the wall was a *woman*?

"This woman," I began. "Is it . . . is it someone I know?"

"You do know her. At least you've met her. The prints belong to Miriam Dobosh."

"Miriam Dobosh? I can't believe it," I blurted out. And then I remembered sitting at the Delano with her and noticing those powerful hands resting on the table. She was a strong woman under that frumpy suit. A powerful woman. "Why would she do it?"

"Why do you think?"

"She must have killed Sanjay," I said doubtfully. "Or somehow she's involved in his death. But I was sure she didn't have anything to do with it. At least—"

"At least what?"

"Nothing." I didn't want to tell him about the Delano and her offer to help solve the crime. Then I'd have to admit to having done some Nancy Drew–type sleuthing. Exactly the kind of thing he'd ordered me not to do. "I just can't believe it. What would her motive be?"

"That's what we need to find out."

"She might be protecting someone else, the real killer, I guess."

"Any idea who that might be?"

"No." I felt like I was grasping at straws. "You're sure you can place her in my apartment? Not just outside?"

"We have a couple of footprints we lifted from the kitchen floor. If we put those with the fingerprints on the outside handrail, we've got a strong case. She certainly has some explaining to do."

"That she does."

I clicked the phone shut and sat for a few moments thinking. Miriam Dobosh had been inside my apartment looking for something, but what? I needed to move her up a few notches on my suspect list. This changed everything.

I had just finished showering and was going to call Vera Mae to go over the day's show when someone knocked at the door. *Was it Miriam Dobosh?* I peered out the peephole, feeling a little silly, and saw a young girl, probably still in her teens, wearing a maid's uniform. I relaxed and pulled the door open.

"*Hola*," she said shyly. Her name tag said NINA and she worked at the Seabreeze.

"*Hola*," I stood back. "Please come in."

"I am Francesca's niece, Nina." She looked nervous and was twisting her hands together in front of her. "Francesca told me that Lark is accused of killing Sanjay. I have something you need to see." She reached into her pocket and pulled out a fortune cookie.

"Where did you get this?" I turned it over in my hand.

"Sanjay. He gave it to me. That night he was killed."

"He gave it to you?" I motioned her to the couch, and she sat down. "Did it come as part of a take-out dinner?"

"*Sí.* I saw it myself. The dinner was on the bed. It was in one of those—how do you say—" She frowned, her eyebrows knitted together.

"A container? Like this?" I jumped up and grabbed the Golden Palace container off the kitchen counter and showed it to her.

"*Sí, sí!*" Nina nodded her head vigorously. "That's it. That's what I saw in his room." She tapped the red logo in the center. "I remember this very well."

"How did Sanjay happen to give it to you?"

Nina shook her head in disgust. "He called down to the front desk. He wanted more towels. I brought them in, and when I arranged them on the towel rack, he tried to pinch me. You know, here. On the butt." She made a face. "He was a disgusting old man."

"And what happened then?"

"I got out of there as fast as I could. He caught up with me at the door and said take this cookie for good luck."

"So you took it?"

Nina's mouth twisted. "I put it in my pocket and forgot about it. I was too busy getting out of there as fast as I could."

"Nina, I'm so glad you told me this." I took both her hands in mine.

"I had to," she said shyly. "I know Lark would never hurt anyone. I should have said something before. I didn't think of the importance."

"That's okay, Nina. Now the police will know what to do. With your testimony, we can prove that there really was a sushi dinner in Sanjay's room that night. It's a good thing you brought this—better late than never."

"Más vale tarde que nunca." She grinned. "We say the same thing in Spanish."

She was about to leave when suddenly we heard a voice that turned my blood to ice.

Chapter 30

"What a touching moment. Don't let me interrupt."

A chill passed through me when I heard the low voice, the sarcastic laugh. It was one of those moments when you're pretty sure you're dreaming, but you don't want to count on it.

I whirled around to the sliding glass door that opened onto the balcony. It was wide-open. Travis Carter was framed in the doorway, and we locked eyes for a long moment. I stood frozen to the spot, raw terror clawing its way up my throat. My mind scrambled to make sense of what I was seeing.

Then he walked into the living area and pointed a gun at Nina's chest.

"Don't make a sound," he said. He moved closer and stared at us. He had beads of sweat popping up on his forehead, and I could feel the tension rolling off him.

"Travis, you're making a terrible mistake." Nina was trembling beside me, making a little choking sound in her throat. I rested my hand lightly on her arm.

Travis put a finger to his lips in an eerie gesture. His eyes were glazed, from either psychosis or drugs, and I felt a stab of terror go through me. How could I ever reason with someone like this? He appeared to be deranged. Completely unhinged.

Nina's hand flew to her mouth, and she gulped back a sob. She rattled off a barrage of Spanish, and I couldn't understand a word except "*Dios mío, Dios mío,*" which she repeated over and over.

I felt like sobbing myself. If ever there was a time for divine intervention, this was it. I flattened myself against the wall as Travis came closer, the gun still pointed at Nina. "Tell Chiquita Banana here to shut up. Or I'll silence her myself."

"Nina, it's okay," I said softly, putting my arm around her. "Take deep breaths. You're going to be fine." She was shaking with sobs and buried her face in my shoulder. I was still reeling from shock and trying to unscramble my thoughts. So it had been Travis Carter all along? Mom had been suspicious of him that day we'd met up with him at Sanjay, Ltd., but I'd never come up with a motive. What did he have to gain from Sanjay's death?

"Let her go, Travis," I said coldly. "It's obvious I'm the one you're after. She doesn't know anything."

"Really? Then what's this?" He spied the fortune cookie on the counter and waved it in my face. "I saw you out at the Dumpster, Maggie. Snooping around, sticking your nose where it doesn't belong. And I followed you to the Golden Palace last night. You just don't learn, do you? Funny, I thought that's what psychology was all about. Helping people learn from experience. But then, you're not much of a psychologist, are you? More of a talk show jock. What are your ratings like? I bet they can't be very good." He gave a wild, maniacal laugh. "I knew it wouldn't take long before you connected the dots."

I bit my lip, trying to slow my racing pulse. I was supposed to be a professional, calm and in control, but my heart was slamming against my rib cage like a battering ram. I started to edge slowly toward the door, but Travis was too quick for me.

"Sit down," he ordered. "Both of you, on the sofa." He looked around the room and then backed up slowly and closed the sliding glass door. He never took his eyes off us.

I glanced at my cell phone, which was tucked away in my purse hanging over the back of the chair. Was there any way I could reach it? Did I dare risk it?

"Travis, don't make a bad situation worse. We can talk about this, straighten it out."

Travis gave a short bark of laughter. "Straighten it out? Don't try your psychobabble on me, Maggie. I'm not some yahoo caller on your radio show. So don't think you can try any shrink games on me. It's too late for that. I wouldn't do well in prison, not well at all." He gave another crazy laugh. "And orange really isn't my color."

Nina was whimpering beside me, and Travis shot her an annoyed look. "It's too bad about the girl, but collateral damage, you know. Innocent people get hurt; that's all part of the game."

"Why hurt her? Why hurt either one of us?"

"You really don't know? You must be more stupid than I thought." He paced a little, crossing to the glass door and peering out. There was a faint scratching noise coming from the bedroom. I was glad that Pugsley was closed safely out of sight. Travis was so absorbed in his own shattered mind, he didn't seem to hear it.

"Because somehow you figured out what really happened that night. You brought all this on yourself. Ironic, isn't it?"

"You killed Sanjay." I made it a statement, not a question.

"Score one for the shrink." He pulled over a kitchen chair and sat down a few feet away from us. He was holding the gun with two hands; it was still pointed directly at us. He waved it back and forth slightly from side to side as if he was drawing a bead, hoping to win a teddy bear in a carnival game.

"Why?"

"Because he was a thief. He robbed me. Didn't you know that? I thought you would have figured that out by now."

A harsh, grating laugh. "A book deal. My ticket out of his stinking organization. Money, fame, everything I've spent my whole life working for. He took it all away. You know what they say: Once a con man, always a con man. I knew what he was when I started working for him, but I didn't think he'd ever turn on me. There's loyalty among thieves, you know." His face twisted in a sneer. "Or at least there's supposed to be. I guess I underestimated him. "

"You had a book deal and Sanjay took it away from you?" So Ray Hicks had been telling the truth after all. I had no idea what he was planning for us, but it couldn't be good.

"I would have had a book deal. A big deal. I stupidly showed Sanjay a book I've been working on for years. He loved it and said he'd give it to his agent. Then he made some suggestions, a few things that should be added here and there to pump it up, he said. I figured he knew more than I did about marketing and the book business, so I went along with it."

"I understand." I was beginning to see where this was headed.

"Yeah, dumb on my part, I know. Big mistake. He made more and more suggestions, and then suddenly the book was taking off in a different direction. Sanjay's ideas were okay, but it wasn't the book I envisioned. And by now there was loads of evidence that Sanjay's philosophy was all over it. If the case went to a jury, I knew they'd side with Sanjay. He has a huge following. People trust him."

Travis's voice had a flat, "blunted affect" as the shrinks say. He was telling the story in a dull monotone, without any strong emotion, and his face was expressionless, nearly blank.

"What happened then?" I figured the longer I kept him talking, the better chance I had of coming up with a plan. But what?

"Sanjay was a genius. I have to hand it to him. He can be very persuasive, you know."

"I know." I thought of Lenore Cooper. She'd helped him jump-start his career, and as soon as it was going full throttle, he'd dumped her. His star had risen and hers had fallen.

"Sanjay took his book to his agent and told him this was something he'd been working on for the past few months. He told him he hadn't shown it to him before because he wasn't really sure he could pull it off. He wanted his agent to have the finished product, not just a partial manuscript."

"What was he going to do about you? He must have known you'd object."

"Yeah, but who'd believe me? He was going to fire me and then paint me as some disgruntled employee. Someone bitter about his success who was just out to make money on a frivolous lawsuit." He paused, looking idly at the barrel of the gun. "You know what they say: If a lawyer says you have a case, you have a case."

I raised my eyebrows. I could see that Sanjay might have had a good chance of getting away with this. If Travis hadn't shown the manuscript to anyone, and Sanjay had made loads of notes and kept a record of them, who could say who the book really belonged to?

I glanced at Nina, who looked almost catatonic. Her eyes

were dull, and she was staring fixedly at the carpet. "What happens now?" I said softly. "To us."

Travis grinned, an ugly rictus spreading across his face. "Oh, didn't you know? You're going to have some new carpet delivered today." He glanced down at the Danish throw rugs on the polished wood floors. "These are getting sort of threadbare, don't you think?" He glanced at his watch. "So in less than five minutes, a delivery guy is going to show up with a big van. He's going to carry the new rugs inside . . . and take the old ones out." He paused. "Do you get the picture, Maggie?"

I swallowed hard. "I think I do." I stole another quick look at Nina, but she seemed to be in a world of her own. I don't think she even heard our conversation. "This delivery guy is a friend of yours."

"Very good. And what do you think will be different about the rugs when he takes them back out to the van?"

I shook my head. I couldn't bring myself to say the words. Not in front of Nina.

"Think, Maggie. What will be different?" He cupped his chin in his hand like that statue *The Thinker*. Then he snapped his fingers. "Oh, I know. They'll be heavier." He let go a burst of harsh laughter that made Nina look up in alarm. "And why will they be heavier? Because you and Nina will be wrapped up in them."

"You're sick. You need help," I told him.

Travis laughed, pleased with his performance. "You'll be cozy as two bugs in a rug, get it?" His laughter rang through the condo. "I hope you're not claustrophobic. It will be pretty cramped in there. Except—oh, wait, I forgot. You won't mind at all because you'll be dead."

"People will hear the gunshots," I said quickly. "These walls are thin."

"That's why I'll use a pillow. One of those nice sofa pillows with the pug on it. It looks like someone embroidered a picture of your dog. How touching."

"Yes, that's Pugsley," I said.

And then two things happened at once.

The front door opened and Mom and Lark walked in, loaded with shopping bags.

"Dear, what is that van doing parked outside? I asked the young man if he needed directions and he seemed very edgy." She suddenly spied Travis and said, "Good heavens, is that a gun? Please tell me it's a fake." She gave a nervous laugh, her eyes bulging a little as though she couldn't quite believe what she was seeing. I'm not even sure she recognized Travis. I think all she saw was the gun.

And the second thing? Pugsley, always excited by visitors, somehow managed to escape from the bedroom. He exploded through the door and headed straight toward Travis, an idiotic doggy grin on his face. Whoever says dogs are good judges of character has never met Pugsley.

"What the—," Travis began, throwing his hands up to shield himself from Pugsley's slobbering kisses. He couldn't decide whether he should keep the gun trained on me, Nina, or the new arrivals. With Pugsley in his lap yelping with joy, Travis lost control of the situation.

His arm jerked up and the gun went off, blasting a football-size hole in the ceiling. All of us watched, stunned, as flakes of plasterboard drifted down on us like snowflakes. Pugsley gave a startled yelp and hid under a chair. Lark was the only one who was smart enough and fast enough to seize the moment. While the rest of us were staring blankly at the ceiling, she picked up a giant copper meditation gong and walloped Travis over the head with it.

The impact made a comical sound, and for an insane

moment, I expected a butler to appear and say, "Dinner is served, madam."

For a long moment, Travis sat frozen in his chair, staring at Lark with wide, Homer Simpson eyes. And then the gun dropped out of his hand, his eyes rolled back in his head, and he went down for the count.

"Ohmigod, call 911!" I finally came to life and scrambled for my cell, but Lark was way ahead of me, already punching in the numbers on the wall phone. "Hurry," I pleaded. "He may suddenly come to."

"Not to worry," Mom said, springing to life. She yanked the cord off the living room drapes and bent over Travis, locking his wrists together in an intricate set of knots. Then she tied his feet together.

"You were a Girl Scout?" Lark asked. She had already given the dispatch operator our address.

"No, these are nautical knots," Mom said proudly. "A reef knot and a round turn with two half hitches. Tight enough to withstand a forty-mile-an-hour wind." She glanced down at Travis. "He's moored here, believe me. This guy's not going anywhere."

I raised my eyebrows. "You're full of surprises."

"I learned how to tie knots for my part in *Romance on the High Seas*. That was a few years ago, dear, but once a sailor, always a sailor." She stood up and smoothed her skirt, her face flushed.

Chapter 31

The Cypress Grove PD, headed by Rafe and Opie, were the first on the scene. Rafe and Opie came in crashing in with guns drawn, shouting for everyone to stay still. Not a problem, as no one was moving and Travis was still trussed up like a Thanksgiving turkey. Opie checked out the rest of the apartment, yelled "Clear!" just like they do on *CSI*, and returned to the living room.

"Is everyone all right?" Rafe meant all of us, but his eyes were focused on me. A few more of Cypress Grove's finest crowded into the room. I wanted to throw myself into Rafe's arms but realized that would be ridiculously unprofessional. Tempting, but unprofessional.

"We're fine." I glanced down at Nina, who was still clinging to me. "Maybe I can get her some water, though. She's pretty shaken up."

"Sergeant Ramirez will get it," Rafe said. He nodded to a pretty Hispanic officer who smiled at Nina and went into the kitchen.

"Do you know this guy?"

"Travis Carter," I told him. "Sanjay's right-hand man."

"How did he get in?"

I pointed to the sliding glass door. "Through the balcony. He confessed to killing Sanjay. And he planned on killing us." I felt myself shiver. "It's a long story."

Rafe nodded and resumed talking to his captain on his cell, while Opie replaced Mom's nautical knots with handcuffs.

"Get him out of here," Rafe said to Opie, who was pulling Travis to his feet and reading him his Miranda rights. Travis had come to but looked bleary-eyed and dazed as he was led out to a waiting squad car.

"What happens now?" I ventured.

"I need to get back to the station to get a statement from Carter, and the other officers will take statements from all of you. Are you sure you're okay? Does anyone need any medical attention?" He moved closer, his eyes dark and intent, and touched me lightly on the upper arm.

"All of us are okay," Mom piped up.

"Are you sure?" Rafe asked me, his voice serious. "You look a little pale."

"I'm fine. I really am." I managed a grin. "I'm glad to be alive."

He leaned close and brushed the back of his hand lightly against my cheek. "I'm glad you're alive, too."

The rest of the day was a blur. After giving a statement to Opie, who looked properly somber, I decided to go in to WYME, even though Cyrus had told me to take the day off. I knew he would be secretly pleased if I showed up for work, because the ratings for my show would be off the roof. Naturally, I wouldn't say anything about the case because it was an ongoing investigation. But I could say that I'd been held at gunpoint by an intruder, and that would be enough to give me fifteen minutes of fame.

The news about Travis had already hit the media when I

arrived at the station. Big Jim Wilcox had already prepared a promo to air every fifteen minutes, "WYME Shrink Cheats Death from Crazed Killer. Don't miss an exclusive interview with Jim Wilcox, exclusive at six this evening!" He recorded it himself and picked a particularly cheesy piece of music to be played under it.

Vera Mae rolled her eyes, but Jim was adamant that the promo run exactly as he'd written it. I shrugged. If Big Jim was determined to get some publicity out of the Travis Carter arrest, so be it. I still was puzzling over how Travis had managed to kill Sanjay with the poisoned take-out, but just then Nick called to give me some breaking news.

He called me just when I was getting ready to go on the air. "Here's a news flash, Maggie. They identified the poison that killed Sanjay."

"They did? Rafe didn't say anything about it." I felt a warm little glow inside remembering how Rafe had touched my cheek, his eyes dark with worry. "Of course, a lot was going on at the time. So, what was the poison?"

"Tetrodotoxin. It's found in the puffer fish."

"The sushi. That's got to be it."

"The sushi?" I'd forgotten. Nick didn't know anything about my trip to the Golden Palace. "Someone brought San-jay a sushi dinner from a Chinese restaurant the night he died. It had to be Travis. He confessed to killing Sanjay, you know."

"You're very lucky, Maggie," Nick said softly. "He would have killed you, too."

The two-hour show flew by. All the callers wanted to wish me well and find out how I'd "cheated death," but I told them they had to wait until Big Jim's six o'clock exclusive. It was a call-in show that day, no guest, so I tried to steer the conversation to other topics—relationships, family disputes, and parenting issues. The board was lit up the entire time. Everyone wanted to chat with Maggie Walsh, Cypress Grove's latest It girl.

I went to the police department late that afternoon. Rafe was talking to the desk sergeant when I walked in, and he looked tired and happy to see me.

"Hi," he said softly, walking up to me. "So you managed to do the show?"

I nodded. "I kept it on safe topics. You know, just psychological mumbo jumbo. And don't worry about the Jim Wilcox piece. I've already taped it. It's just a teaser. I don't say anything at all. It's just a little promo to boost ratings."

We walked back to his office and sat down. Rafe reached for the coffeepot, looked at the thin layer of brown sludge inside, and frowned.

"Don't worry," I said quickly. "I've had enough of an adrenaline rush for one day."

"Me, too." He played with some papers on his desk.

"Well—" we both said at the same time and laughed. "You go first," he told me.

"I was just going to say that I gave my report to Opie. I mean Officer Brown. Have you had a chance to look it over?"

Rafe smiled. "Yes, I have. I've been trying to read between the lines. You've been a busy girl, haven't you?"

"If you mean did I do some investigating, even after you told me not to, then guilty as charged." I grinned to show there were no hard feelings. After all, I had cracked the case, hadn't I?

"You know we identified the poison?"

"Tetrodotoxin. A little bird told me."

"Were you surprised?"

"Yes and no. Travis and Sanjay used to go deep-sea fishing together."

Rafe reached for a yellow legal pad and started making notes. "How did you know that?"

I sighed. "It's a long story."

"We've got all night."

"Okay, here goes." I told him about visiting Sanjay, Ltd., and Mom noticing the photo of Travis and Sanjay on a fishing boat. It was funny, because she knew there was something significant about that photo, but I hadn't picked up on it. Her Miss Marple musings had been right on target.

"You took a chance going there," Rafe admonished me. "Travis said he made that late-night phone call and tried to scare you, but you didn't give up on the case. So he made up his mind to kill you."

I shrugged and leaned back in the chair. In spite of what I'd said earlier, I was dying for a cup of coffee. Or even better, a mojito.

"Yeah, well, I had to get inside the mansion to get information. I had the feeling that Travis might be involved in Sanjay's death, but didn't think he had a strong enough motive." I paused. "Until he broke into my condo and explained about the book deal. Then I realized why Sanjay had to go. If Sanjay were dead, Travis could destroy any notes Sanjay had made and go ahead with plans for his own book. Sanjay's death would probably boost sales. It would make the book topical. Publishers love that."

"Like Lenore Cooper's book."

"You saw the infomercial, too. Funny, I didn't think you were the type to watch those."

"I'm an insomniac."

"Really? We should get together sometime at three a.m." I flushed. Where did that come from? Time for a quick save. "I didn't mean that the way it sounded."

Rafe looked at me, his mouth quirked. "Sorry to hear that." He riffled through some papers. "We'll do another interview tomorrow, but I think I have enough for now. The DA will have a really strong case unless Travis tries to go for an insanity plea."

"I thought that the insanity defense was used in only one percent of cases."

Rafe looked impressed. "Less than one percent. I see you've done your homework."

"I try." My stomach growled and I quickly jammed my hand in my lap. "Sorry. I missed lunch."

"We can remedy that," Rafe told me. "There's the best Tex-Mex restaurant just a few blocks away. Tico's." He seemed to be waiting for me to say something. My heart was thudding at the thought of going to dinner with him. "Your roommate isn't a suspect anymore, so there's no reason we can't have dinner together."

"I'm glad." The understatement of the year. Rafe was still staring at me, an expectant look on his face.

"Isn't there something you want to ask me?" he said finally.

"Oh!" I snapped my fingers. *How could I be such an idiot?* "Tell me about Miriam Dobosh. Was she really the one who hit me over the head? Why did she do it?"

"Yes, we brought her in and she confessed. She did it because of this." Rafe reached into the desk drawer and pulled out the audience evaluation form, the one that had slammed Sanjay's seminar. "She wrote it herself. She wanted Sanjay to realize he had some enemies out there—enemies that only she could deal with. Miriam hoped to convince him that she should stay at the helm of the organization."

"He was thinking of dumping her for a newer, younger assistant."

Rafe nodded. "That's what she told us. So she wrote this really negative eval and tossed it in the pile with the favorable ones. Of course she had no idea Sanjay would be murdered that very night and the note would point right to her as a suspect. It could be a key piece of evidence."

"If anyone ever discovered it."

"Exactly. She had to make sure that didn't happen. So she went back to the Seabreeze to rescue it and saw you sitting on the front porch going through the audience evals with the innkeeper."

"Ted Rollins." I remembered the creepy feeling that someone was watching me that night.

"She figured you'd lifted the eval, which was evidence, by the way." He tried to look stern, but something about those flashing dark eyes and chiseled features made it hard to pull off. "So she decided to break into your apartment and find it. She'll be charged with B and E and aggravated assault." He looked at me. "At least you didn't take the original."

"Of course not," I said. "I would never do that. I made a copy."

Rafe grinned. "I'd hate to have to arrest you for evidence tampering. Of course, you shouldn't have touched the note at all, once you suspected it might be evidence. "

"So maybe I did a little tampering," I confessed. I thought

for a minute. "And the sushi container? What really happened to it? It wasn't in the Dumpster, was it?"

"Nope. Travis admitted that he slipped back into Sanjay's room that night to retrieve it. Apparently Sanjay didn't eat much of it, but it was enough to kill him. Travis grabbed the container and the leftovers and flushed them."

"Pretty clever."

"Diabolical." Rafe grinned.

"What happens now?"

Rafe picked up his cell and pager and locked his gun in the desk drawer. "We go out to dinner. Unless you'd like to hang around here shooting the breeze with me."

"I'd rather go to dinner." I stood up, suddenly feeling a little shy and wondering why. "I still have some questions, but we can talk over dinner, right?"

"Of course," he said guiding me out the door. "I have some questions for you, too."

"You do?" We were walking down the hall, heading for the double glass doors that opened onto State Street. It was a beautiful evening, the sun setting in a blaze of gold and orange. The air was soft and balmy, and was filled with the dizzying scent of magnolia blossoms. I could hardly believe Travis was in jail, Lark was off the hook, and I was having dinner with Rafe Martino.

"I guess I have only one question," Rafe said, glancing at me.

"Ask me anything." He surprised me by taking my hand as we headed toward the restaurant. His grip was warm and firm, and it felt right. Very right.

"Tell me about Ted Rollins. You two live next door to each other, but you don't have something going on with him, do you?"

"With Ted Rollins? Good lord, no. He's just a friend. Like a brother."

Rafe gave my hand a squeeze and edged a little closer to me on the sidewalk. "Just a friend? Oh, Maggie," he said feelingly, "that's exactly what I was hoping to hear."

ACKNOWLEDGMENTS

To Kristen Weber, for her wonderful editorial guidance and killer sense of humor. And to the whole terrific team at Obsidian—you're the best.

To Stephen Viscusi, author, friend, and rainmaker. Stephen, you're an inspiration to millions of people.

To my Florida friends who helped me research settings and attractions in their beautiful state, Michael Aller, tourism and convention director for the city of Miami, and author Brian Antoni.

To Alan, who is not only my fabulous British husband but also my computer guru.

To Nancy Martin and Kate Collins, my longtime writer pals, and to new friends Carolyn Hart, Hallie Ephron, and Jan Brogan from Sisters in Crime.

To Jerry Lee, for his generous help with Spanish phrases and dialogue. Any mistakes are mine, not his.

To James V. Tsoutsouris, Esq., for sharing his legal expertise with me.

And of course to Sally and Eric Ernsberger, guardians of the delightful Pugsley, who is the model for Maggie's pug in this series. Pugsley, sweetie, I owe you a gallon of maple walnut ice cream.

Read on for a sneak peek at
Mary Kennedy's next Talk Radio Mystery,

REEL MURDER

Coming from Obsidian in June 2010

Something was horribly wrong.

I knew it before I opened my eyes, before I saw the faint pinkish orange light seeping between the faux-teak blinds that shutter my bedroom windows. It was barely dawn, yet I could hear someone rattling around my condo, moving from the hall into the kitchen.

I instantly slammed into DEFCON 1. I sat up straight in bed, pulse racing, nerve endings tingling, skin prickling at the back of my neck. An icy finger traced a trail down my spine and I crept out of bed, yanking my arms into my favorite terry bathrobe.

I was gripped by a fear so intense, I could hardly breathe.

A home invasion? *Call 911!* I reached for my cell phone, then realized with a stab of despair that I'd left it in the kitchen. How annoying. Not only was I going to die, I was going to die because of my own stupidity, just like the heroine in a Kevin Williamson flick—never an ideal way to go.

I could only hope there would be enough of my body left for the police to make a positive ID. Maybe the pale blue bathrobe decorated with goofy yellow ducks would give them a clue. My roommate, Lark Merriweather, always says that no one older than twelve years old would be caught dead in it.

Or alive, for that matter.

I tiptoed to the bedroom door, my heart lodged in my throat. I felt the beginning of flop sweat sprouting under my arms as I cautiously turned the doorknob. At least Lark would be spared. She was away for the weekend, visiting friends in Key West. But where was my dog, Pugsley? He'd been dozing at the foot of my bed when I'd drifted to sleep watching Letterman. Had he been abducted? The victim of foul play? I couldn't face life without Pugsley. My hysteria was rising.

And then I heard a familiar voice.

A breathy, smoke-filled voice, early Kathleen Turner. My shoulders slumped with relief and I shuffled out of the bedroom, my pulse stuttering back to normal.

In the kitchen, I found both good news and bad news awaiting me.

The good news was that there was no sign of a crazed serial killer, no ax murderer.

The bad news was that my mother, Lola Walsh, was back in town.

In my condo, to be precise. She must have let herself in with her key sometime during the night, and now she was padding around my living room, talking on her cell.

"That would be just fabulous, darling, fabulous! How can I ever thank you?" A pause, and then, "Oh, you naughty boy. I'll have to think of something, won't I? But will your wife approve? You know what they say: 'What the mind doesn't know, the heart doesn't feel.'" Her tone was lascivious, bordering on high camp, and I had to stifle a grin. She turned around and flashed me a broad wink.

Lola was on full throttle, charming someone with her Marilyn Monroe "Happy birthday, Mr. President" voice. Lola's an actress, although she's having trouble finding parts these days because she's "of a certain age," as she likes to say.

According to Lola, the Hollywood establishment has been highjacked by the Lindsay Lohans, the Hannah Montanas, and the Lauren Conrads, long-legged ingenues who edge out classically trained actresses such as herself. Although god knows, she tries her best to stay in the game.

Sometimes she tries too hard.

Today, for example, she was wearing a spaghetti-strap tank top with a pair of skintight, red and white Hawaiian-print capris. Her considerable assets were spilling out of the tank top, making her look like a geriatric version of a Hooters girl.

Age is "just a number" to Lola. A flexible number. I'm thirty-two, and ten years ago Lola listed her age on her résumé as thirty-eight. As far as I know, she's still thirty-eight. Don't try to do the math; it will make your teeth hurt. And her head shot is a sort of reverse Dorian Gray, since it makes her look younger than I do. She often introduces me as her sister, which would probably have me in analysis for years, if I didn't happen to be a shrink by profession.

"You're awake!" she said, flipping the phone shut and enveloping me in a hug. Her voice was as warm and breezy as a summer's day. "Maggie, you'll never guess who that was," she added playfully.

"Nicolas Sarkozy?"

"Oh, don't be silly. He's married to that supermodel Carla Bruni." She glanced at the clock. "Besides, it's two a.m. in Paris. C'mon, try again."

I gently untangled myself from her embrace and made tracks for the coffeepot. I always set everything up the night before so all it takes is a quick push of the ON button. That's all my sleep-fogged brain can handle first thing in the morning. A nice mug of steaming *dolce de leche* to start the day. I was still feeling shaky with adrenaline and took a couple of deep calming breaths.

"Mom, you know I hate to guess." She made a little moue of disappointment and I sighed. I knew I had to play the game, or I'd never be able to drink my coffee in peace. "Okay, Daniel Craig called. He wants you to fly to London and have drinks with him at Claridge's tonight."

"Nope." She giggled and clapped her hands together. "Although that certainly sounds like fun. I love his movies and he's a major hunk."

I smelled the coffee brewing, my own extracaffeinated type, and greeted Pugsley, who heard my voice and came racing in from the balcony. Pugsley is the furry love of my life, a three-year-old rescue dog who understands my most intimate thoughts and feelings. He's the next best thing to a soul mate and gives me what every woman craves— unconditional love and a ton of sloppy kisses.

Plus he's game for anything, if it makes me happy. I can't think of many guys who would curl up on the sofa with me on a Saturday night to watch *Marley & Me* for the third time.

Mom's voice pulled me back from my reverie.

"Guess again! Who called!" She held up my favorite WYME mug and dangled it just out of reach. WYME is the radio station that I left my Manhattan psychoanalytic practice for; I host a call-in show, *On the Couch with Maggie Walsh*. It's a small south Florida market, and strictly a bottom-rungs-of-show-biz operation, but I love my job and I don't miss those New York winters.

"Mom, I swear I don't know." I sank into a chair at the kitchen table and put my head in my hands. I said the first Hollywood name I could think of. "Aaron Spelling?"

"Don't be silly. He's already passed," Mom said crisply. "It would take James Van Praagh to reach him now."

"Then I give up."

Mom shook her head. "You give up way too easily." She paused dramatically. "Okay, that was Hank Watson on the phone." She waited for a reaction, her blue eyes flashing with excitement, her magenta nails beating a tattoo on the table. "*The* Hank Watson." She raised her perfectly plucked eyebrows for emphasis.

She released the mug and I immediately crossed to the counter and poured myself a hefty cup of coffee. Ah, sweet bliss.

"Hank Watson!! Director Hank Watson," she added, shaking her head in exasperation. "Don't you watch *Access Hollywood*? What in heaven's name *do* you watch? The History Channel? C-SPAN?"

"I take it he's a film director." I sipped my coffee, enjoying that first quick jolt of energy flooding my system.

"Not just any film director." Her voice was gently chiding. "He's a master of the horror genre. Didn't you ever see *Night Games*? Or *Highway to Hell*? And what about *A Night to Forget*? He won the Okaloosa County Film Festival Award for that one."

I frowned. These all sounded like B movies that probably played to three people in Kentucky before going straight to video. Only one name rang a bell. "*A Night to Forget*? Was that the old flick about the *Titanic*?"

"No, that was *A Night to Remember*," she said with heavy patience.

"Okay, tell me about Hank Watson. And the phone call." Pugsley jumped into my lap, hoping for a piece of croissant that didn't materialize. Unless Lark had picked up some "bakery" before she left town, Puglsey and I were both going to be stuck with a healthy breakfast. Kibble for him and high-fiber cereal for me. *Blech.*

"Well, brace yourself, darling. Hank made me an offer I couldn't refuse. Your mom's going to be a movie star—again." She sat down across from me, her cornflower blue eyes dazzling.

"A movie star?"

"It's a speaking part," she said, backpedaling swiftly. I raised my eyebrows. "No, it's not an under-five," she added quickly with a toss of her head. "It's a small role, but you know what they say . . ."

"There are no small roles, only small actors," I parroted.

She grinned. "I've taught you well." She smiled approvingly. Some of Mom's recent roles had been the dreaded "under-fives," meaning she had fewer than five lines of dialogue. As an "under-fiver," she's relegated to lousy pay and the tiniest of bit parts. Last month she was a waitress in a Georgia barbecue joint ("Do you want hush puppies with that, hon?"), and just last week she played an emergency room nurse ("Get the crash cart! He's flatlining!").

In an industry rife with rejection (98 percent of Screen Actors Guild members are unemployed at any given time) mom has learned not to turn down work. You never know when another part will come along, and the competition is fierce. Five hundred people can turn up to audition for a two-line role.

"Tell me about the movie."

I rummaged in the pantry, found a five-day-old Entenmann's crumb-topped coffee cake and zapped it in the microwave for exactly five seconds. Then I cut a hefty wedge for each of us. Fiber has its place, but you can never go wrong with Entenmann's. Breakfast of champions.

"Well, you know Hank and I go way back," she began.

"Years ago, when I was getting my feet wet in Hollywood, Hank was making a name for himself as a director."

"So the two of you started out together?" I broke off a corner of coffee cake for Pugsley, who was beating a staccato on the floor with his tiny feet. He wolfed it down and gave me one of those intent stares that pugs do so well, his dark eyes riveted on my face.

"In a way," Mom said cautiously. "I'm much younger than Hank, of course."

"Of course." I plastered a nonchalant look on my face. According to Mom, she's younger than everyone in Hollywood, with the possible exception of Dakota Fanning. "So he wants you to fly out to Hollywood to work on his latest flick?"

"No, something better! He's going to be filming part of the movie right here in south Florida, in Cypress Grove. How perfect is that? He got a really good deal from the Florida Film Commission, and he can't wait to start shooting here. You know, the sunlight, the ocean, the scenery—this place is paradise for a cinematographer." She was as giddy as if she'd taken a hit of ecstasy. "Just think, Hank and I will be together again, just like in the old days."

"I'm happy for you, Mom. What's the movie called?" I wanted to take a peek at the *Cypress Grove Gazette* that was spread out on the table, but I knew Mom was on a roll and I figured I'd better play along. I couldn't imagine anyone shooting a movie here, but I decided to take Mom's word for it.

Cypress Grove is a sleepy Florida town, north of Boca, not too far from Palm Beach, and a pleasant ride to Fort Lauderdale. As the Chamber of Commerce says on their welcome sign, "Cypress Grove. We're near everyplace else you'd rather be!" I never could figure out if that was said tongue-in-cheek. Maybe, maybe not.

"The film is called *Death Watch*, and it stars Adriana St. James. It will be wonderful to work with her again. I haven't seen her in years, you know."

I frowned. "Adriana St. James? Mom, I thought you loathed her. How can you stand to be in a movie with her?"

"Oh, that was nothing, a mere creative difference of opinion." Mom reached down to pat Pugsley, her face melting into a dreamy smile. "You know how it is with us theatre people. One minute we're discussing Larry Olivier and *Hamlet* and the next we're arguing over whether Jeremy Piven really had mercury poisoning when he bailed out of that David Mamet play." She gave a wry little laugh. "It doesn't mean a thing, darling. It's just the artistic temperament shining through. We're bound to clash from time to time. We always kiss and make up."

"Mom, you told me Adriana dumped a very large Caesar salad in your lap at Chased's one night. She claimed you were sleeping with her husband. The whole story was on Page Six."

"Oh, yes, the Caesar salad." Mom frowned. "You know, I never did get that stain out of my Chanel suit. I had to donate it to charity. Just think, some poor homeless person is probably wandering around Rodeo Drive wearing a vintage Chanel with a really big stain on the skirt."

"Mom, I don't think homeless people spend much time on Rodeo Drive—"

Lola cut me off with a curt laugh. "Well, darling, no one could seriously believe I would sleep with her husband. What a dreadful little man! The funny thing is, I was probably the only woman in Hollywood who *wasn't* sleeping with Marvin." Mom chortled. "He had so many girlfriends, he made Warren Beatty look like a celibate monk."

I took at peek at the *Gazette*. Nothing on the front page

about the film. I quickly riffled through the sections, local, business, arts and entertainment. Zilch. I'd have to call Nick, my reporter pal, the moment I got into work.

"The movie deal isn't a secret, is it, Mom? Because there's nothing in the local paper about it."

"Well, maybe not in *this* paper," she said. "Hank said the news is hitting the *Hollywood Reporter* today. And the *Los Angeles Times* and the *New York Times*." She reached over and tapped the *Gazette* with a manicured fingernail. "You're living in a time warp, sweetie, a time warp. I wonder when the news will make it to this burg."

ABOUT THE AUTHOR

Mary Kennedy is a former radio copywriter and the award-winning author of forty novels. She is a clinical psychologist in private practice and lives on the East Coast with her husband and eight eccentric cats. Both husband and cats have resisted all her attempts to psychoanalyze them, but she remains optimistic. Visit her Web site at www.marykennedy.net.